Cuffed By Candlelight:

An Erotic Romance Anthology

Prisoner
by Beverly Jenkins

Gunns and Roses
by Katherine D. Jones

Handcuffs Mean Never Having to Say You're Sorry
by Gwyneth Bolton

Noire
Passion

Parker Publishing, LLC

Noire Passion is an imprint of Parker Publishing, LLC.

Cuffed By Candlelight: An Erotic Romance Anthology
"Prisoner" copyright © 2007 by Beverly Jenkins
"Gunns and Roses" copyright © 2007 by Katherine D. Jones
"Handcuffs Mean Never Having to Say You're Sorry" copyright ©
2007 by Gwedolyn Pough

Published by Parker Publishing, LLC
P.O. Box 380-844
Brooklyn, NY 11238
www.parker-publishing.com

ISBN: 978-1-60043-007-7

First Edition

Manufactured in the United States of America

Cuffed By Candlelight:

An Erotic Romance Anthology

Prisoner

by

Beverly Jenkins

Acknowledgements

I'd like to thank the execs at Parker Publishing for allowing me this opportunity to stretch my wings a bit and to be a part of their opening act. Many thanks to Ms. King-Bey for her editing magic and endless patience. Good luck Parker Publishing! Much success.
B

Prologue

January 17, 1884

My dear Bess,

I hope this letter finds you well in both body and spirit. I have handled my late Uncle Bradford's affairs and seen to it that his last wishes were carried out as dictated by his last will and testament. Imagine my elation when his barrister informed me that I too had been left a bequest. It is a substantial amount of money, Bess, over seven hundred dollars! Never in my life did I dream of gaining such a fortune, but it is wholly and legally mine. I have enclosed a bank draft made out to you for two hundred of those dollars. I'm certain the sum will not erase the pain I am about to cause you, but it is all I can offer. I've fallen in love with the daughter of Uncle Bradford's barrister. Her name is Malinda. I am aware that this news will cause you great distress, but I can not and will not return to Kansas and pretend that she does not have my heart. I am asking that you release me from my vows, so that I may marry Malinda. I've had her father draw up the divorce papers for you to sign, so please do so and return them to me. With the money you can start a new life, and I hope that one day you may forgive me. Again, my apologies, and may God be with you.

Your husband,

William Franklin

Chapter One

July 1884

When she saw him for the first time, he was standing against the wall, and thoughts of backing out immediately filled her mind. It was his eyes mostly; dark, smoky, penetrating eyes filled with such raw male power that her hand moved unconsciously to the high collar of her blouse covering her throat. He was also larger in stature than she'd considered. Back East men were shorter and thinner like the traitorous William, but this dark-skinned mountain of a man with his manacled wrists represented the West. His frame filled Sheriff Cody's office.

Elizabeth forced her eyes back to the sheriff. "Is he the only candidate?"

Cody nodded.

Filled with misgivings, she hazarded a glance his way again and found his dark eyes watching her intently. It took all she had not to send her look scurrying off, but she held his gaze. He certainly appeared strong enough; the forearms visible beneath the hacked off sleeves of his blue prison shirt could have passed for chiseled oak, but would he work from sun up to sun down? The only reason she'd agreed to consider this outrageous proposal was to get the help she needed to keep the farm going. He on the other hand had no choice; he could either agree or face the gallows.

"Yes or no, Miss Elizabeth?" the sheriff enquired.

Cody's voice brought her back. In truth, she wanted to say, no. A woman would have to be insane to be party to such a plan; insane or desperate, and she was that. She took in the silver cuffs around his wrists, then sought his eyes again. In them lay something she couldn't name; something disturbing and elemental, but the memory of William's betrayal and the nights she'd cried as a result came back to her, as did her vow to make the farm profitable in spite of his perfidy, so she answered firmly, "Yes."

"You sure?"

"No," came her reply, "but what other choice have I?" In addition to the dangers faced by a woman alone on the plains from predators both human and animal, one of the conditions homesteaders like herself had to meet in order to get title to the land was to turn a profit by the third year. For her that meant next April.

She and the sheriff had talked about these things last evening at her kitchen table, so the gray haired Cody nodded his understanding, then spoke to the prisoner. "Over here, Yancy."

The prisoner complied, and even though he stopped a distance away from where Elizabeth stood, she could feel his heat.

The sheriff asked him, "You agreeable?"

"Like the lady said, got no choice." His eyes touched hers once more, and this time she had to look away, hoping to hide her nervous trembling.

"Then, let's get this over with," the sheriff declared.

In the end, the words were spoken and the legal documents signed. Once the shackles were removed, Elizabeth and the convicted felon Jordan Yancy left the sheriff's office as lawfully wedded man and wife.

The long ride back to her farm was silent but for the sound of the wheels on the buggy and the measured cadence of the mare's hooves on the hard ground of the narrow road. It was a hot, humid July day. The cloudless blue sky allowed the sun to beat down unmercifully, and as Elizabeth held the reins, perspiration pooled beneath the layers of her clothing and between her breasts, but she was more aware of the man on the seat beside her than she was of the sweltering heat.

"How big is your place?" he asked.

"Sixty acres."

"What do you grow?"

"Corn."

Elizabeth didn't volunteer any further conversation. She still considered herself mad for having agreed to this unconventional marriage, but there was no turning back now.

They reached the farm an hour later. She stopped the wagon in front of her small house, set the brake and after a few moments of wrestling with her misgivings and nerves, forced herself to turn his way. "I need a man to help me work the place. Nothing more." She wanted him to know up front that he'd not be sharing her bed.

"Got no problem with that. Where can I wash up?"

Her eyes grazed the sweat shining on his mahogany shoulders and arms. "The pump's behind the house."

"Soap?"

"I'll get it." Leaving him sitting, Elizabeth hastened inside.

In the small shadow-filled bedroom she'd once shared with William, she picked up the soap lying on the basin atop the dresser, then knelt to open the carved top of the cedar chest positioned against the wall. Retrieving a towel, she closed it, stood and jumped; startled to find him standing in the doorway. Her nerves fluttered in the thick silence.

He said quietly, "Since you didn't invite me in, thought I'd come in and see the place for myself. Didn't mean to spook you."

Her heart was pounding now, too, no longer from surprise, but from his overwhelming presence and nearness. "I wasn't meaning to be rude. I just…" She had no words to explain herself.

"I make you uncomfortable."

"Yes," she answered, her voice a whisper.

"That's understandable. It's not every day a good woman finds herself hitched to a man like me, but I swear to you, I've never hurt a woman in my life, and I'm not planning to start now."

The truth in his intense gaze calmed her, but only a bit. "Here's the soap. It's scented. It's all I have."

"That'll do fine."

She handed it to him, and as he took it, his hand brushed hers. The contact was like touching lightning. To hide her reaction, she said, "I'll fix us something to eat."

"Thanks." And he departed, leaving the deeply breathing Elizabeth alone in the shadows.

Elizabeth was a product of her times. She could do needle-point, play a passable piano and set a proper table. She knew never to venture out without the requisite undergarments, let a man see her ankles and had endured the marriage bed because it was a woman's duty to do so. However, in the two years she'd been married, she'd never seen William totally undressed, so when she entered the kitchen and heard Yancy boisterously singing a tune about a gal named Sal, she went to the window to see what he might be about and found herself staring wide-eyed at her first naked man. Blessedly, he had his back to her and any respectable woman worth her salt would have instantly looked away, but she found herself mesmerized by his God-given male beauty. The dark muscular back, legs and buttocks once again reminded her of a sculpture. He was a man in his prime, not a soft spot on him anywhere. She knew she was risking eternal damnation by viewing him this way, but she couldn't seem to move. As he lathered his hair and then his body, she took in the play of his muscles, studied the subtle ripples in his powerful legs and thighs. He bent down for the bucket. He poured the contents over himself, and she watched the water slowly and sinuously cascade down his back and thighs. She noticed that her breathing had increased and that there was a strange warmth infusing her veins. The inner heat had nothing to do with the temperature. Scandalized by her behavior, Elizabeth moved quickly away from the window and set her mind on preparing the evening meal.

He ate like a man who hadn't had food in a while. He wasn't without manners, but he quickly consumed the ham, beans and cornbread she set before him as if there might be no tomorrow. His appetite matched his size, and she sensed the small stipend the state

7

promised to send each month for the next year to help pay for his food and clothing would be a blessing, even to a woman with finances as sound as her own.

"Mighty good food, ma'am," he offered, once he was done. He wiped his mouth on one of her embroidered cotton napkins. "Mighty good."

Tearing her eyes away from his full lips, she said, "Thank you."

He was seated in the chair William had always used, and she was in the chair opposite him, still nervous as a long-tailed cat in a room of rockers. Rising, hoping to rid herself of the memories of Yancy at the pump, she collected their now-empty plates and utensils and placed everything in the iron tub for washing later. It was impossible not to feel his eyes on her as she moved around, and again she wondered where this might all lead.

"The sheriff said your husband left you."

Hot embarrassment washed over her for a moment, but she didn't lie. "Yes. He went back East to handle his late uncle's affairs and met someone else."

"Sorry to hear that."

"So was I."

Silence settled between them.

"He must have been a fool."

Elizabeth didn't know how to interpret such a remark, so she didn't reply. Instead, she said, "Let's go out to the barn. I'll show you where you'll sleep."

The heat outside was like walking into an oven. There was no breeze to lighten it, and the humidity was as heavy as a winter cloak. Elizabeth had gotten into the habit of taking a cooling bath at the height of the day, but decided there would be no more of that. Now that there was a man around, she'd just have to suffer.

The interior of the dim barn was noticeably cooler. The barn housed the mare at night and also the buggy. In anticipation of his arrival, she'd swept the place clean and prepared a place for him in one of the corners. There was a short nightstand that had been donated by one of the ladies at the church, and atop it stood an old but useable oil lamp. The cot he'd be sleeping on held a thin clean mattress that she realized now would be too small for his large frame. "When we go into town, I'll get some ticking to make you a bigger mattress."

"I'd be real appreciative, but until then, this is fine."

"I'm sorry I can't offer you anything better."

He looked around. "This is a palace compared to what I had at the penitentiary."

The subdued power in his eyes touched her again, silently increasing her awareness of him as a man, and of herself as a woman.

He asked then, "How long have you been living here?"

"Three years come April. William and I came out from Cleveland."

"When did he leave?"

"A few days after Christmas."

"You spent the winter out here, alone?" he asked sounding amazed.

She nodded. "I refused to go back to Cleveland like a whipped pup." Her rage at William's departure fueled her through the cold winter days and nights, and in many ways kept her from being afraid.

"Most women would have turned tail and ran."

"I'm not that smart, I suppose."

He smiled for the first time, and it served to ease the hard dangerous lines of his dark face, and some of the tension that stood between the two of them, also. "Can I see the fields?"

"Yes."

He followed her out, and she did her best to ignore the feel of his gaze on her back.

"You planted all this, yourself?"

"An acre a day was all I could manage. I'm hoping to do more next spring."

There were fat green ears of corn spread out on strong stalks as far as the eye could see. "You're a remarkable woman," he told her.

Elizabeth had to admit it felt good to hear such praise, even if it wasn't sincere. "As long as the weather continues to bring rain, I should have a fairly decent profit after harvest." She asked him, "You ever farmed?"

"Yeah. Grew up on my daddy's place in Texas."

That was good to hear as well. He'd be able to help from the start. She wanted to ask him how a man who'd been a deputy marshal wind up in prison because of a fight over a prostitute, but didn't. "I grew up on a farm, too."

"That had to be a help."

She nodded. They were making small talk. It was all they had for now.

"Any siblings?" he asked.

"Two sisters, both younger. You?"

"No. I gave my folks such a hard time growing up, I think they were glad I was the only one."

The amusement in his tone made her smile for the first time. When their gazes met, Elizabeth began to wonder if she hadn't made such a bad decision after all, but then reminded herself she'd known him less than four hours. It was far too soon to presume to know his true character. Redonning her distant manner, she said, "We can go back into town tomorrow for any personal items you might need."

"The warden gave me money when I was released. It's not much, but it'll buy me what I need."

"Good." She had no intentions of telling him about her own savings. It was a secret she'd kept even from William, just as her father had instructed when he opened the account in her name the day after she married. At the time, she and her father had argued over the ethics of the matter at the time, but now that William was no longer her husband, she was glad she'd taken her papa's wise advice and kept the details to herself.

"Anything around here you want me to do first?"

"I'd like to have a new barn by the time the snow falls. The windmill needs repair and the chicken coop needs a new roof."

"That all?"

She forced herself not to reveal her smile. She didn't want him to think she was promoting familiarity.

When she didn't respond he tossed out, "As long as you feed me the way you fed me today, I'll build you anything you want. Been a long time since I tasted such good cooking."

"Are you trying to flatter me, Mr. Yancy?"

"No, ma'am. Just speaking the truth."

Under his steady yet disarming gaze, the infusion of warmth Elizabeth had noticed before returned, bringing with it the realization that maintaining her distance from him might be more difficult than she'd first assumed. The distracting memories of his nudity were also bedeviling her.

"So you'll know, I'm trying to be as respectful and easy going as I can. If we're going to be on this place together, I don't want you to be afraid of me. I meant what I said about never harming a woman."

"Thank you. I appreciate your concern." And she did. Their relationship would be awkward enough without adding fear to the brew. Although she might be foolish for doing so, at that moment she genuinely believed his claim. "Would you like to see the rest of the place?"

"I would."

For the next hour, they endured the heat in order for him to first see the coop where she kept her hens and the rooster she'd named Douglass after the great Fred himself.

"Douglass?" he asked chuckling.

"Yes. My papa had a rooster he named Douglass. He said the bird strutted around just like Fred used to do. I'm simply carrying on the tradition."

Next was the windmill. As he looked it up and down, she told him, "I'd like to be able to irrigate my corn and bring water up to the house, but I can't if it doesn't work."

"You're right," he agreed, coming out from behind the wooden structure. He studied the steel vanes. "I'll give it a good look over in the morning."

When she saw him yawn, it came to her that he was probably exhausted. She felt safe in assuming a person didn't get a restful sleep in prison and by Sheriff Cody's account, Yancy had been incarcerated for close to three years. "If you'd like to spend the remainder of the evening resting, we can finish this tomorrow."

"Thank you," he replied with genuine gratitude. "I'm so tired I'm about to fall down."

"Then I'll see you in the morning, Mr. Yancy."

"Have a good evening, ma'am."

Elizabeth nodded and walked back toward the house.

That night as Jordan lay on the too-small mattress looking up at the stars through the large hole in the barn's roof, he thought about the woman sleeping inside the house. From a strictly male point of view, he'd been lucky. The wife he'd been forced to marry could have been a crone. Instead, he was hitched to a cat-eyed, chocolate-skinned beauty named Elizabeth. *Elizabeth.* Saying her name in his mind conjured up her face, her voice and her tall full body with its soft tempting curves. Her prim and proper ways drew him like a moth to a flame. That afternoon in the buggy she'd made it clear that she didn't plan on him sharing her bed. Jordan understood that; she didn't know him from a jackrabbit, and were he in her shoes, he would have said the same thing. However, in the eyes of the state of Kansas, they were man and wife, and as man and wife, they'd verbally agreed to stay together until death. Jordan had no intentions of sleeping in the barn until they put him in the ground, not when he was married to a woman as sensual as he sensed Elizabeth to be.

He found it hard to believe her husband had abandoned her though, and just before winter no less. Had the man found her difficult to live with? Did she harbor some deep-seated ways that drove him to distraction, or was William simply a cad? Jordan had no answers. All he knew was that because of her, he was no longer destined for the hangman's noose, and for that blessing, he would owe her for the rest of his life.

Chapter Two

The next morning, Elizabeth awakened in bed just as the sun began to rise. The air in the dark room was already stifling, which meant she had yet another sweltering day to get through. She dragged herself to the edge of the mattress. Sitting, she placed her head in her hands for a moment and swore she was just as tired as she had been last night before the heat and perspiration finally allowed her to fall into a fitful sleep. In truth, the smothering heat hadn't been the sole reason she'd tossed and turned all night. Thoughts about the man she'd taken as her husband and whether the decision had been a sound one plagued her until she closed her eyes. *Jordan Yancy.*

Elizabeth walked over to the basin and splashed the tepid water onto her damp face and neck. Using a towel to dry herself, she then stripped off her sweaty gown. Next came the camisole underneath and soon she was nude except for her thigh length drawers. Her skin sighed with gratitude and relief, and Elizabeth wished she could walk around just as she was. Even though the room was still warm and humid, she was no longer melting beneath the layers of clothing society mandated good women wear. Were she a hussy or a woman on the stage, she probably wouldn't care what society thought. Such women were headed for perdition anyway, or so she was told, so what was one more sin? However, good women guarded their nudity as if it were made of gold—even looking at one's body was frowned upon. With that in mind, she set the inappropriate desire aside and continued her preparations for the day.

After dressing, her first order of business was a trip to the chicken coop. If the hens had graciously laid any eggs, she'd be able to add them to breakfast. On the way there, she glanced over at the barn and wondered if Mr. Yancy were awake and if he had spent a restless night wrestling with the idea of their marriage, too.

There were four eggs; more than enough for her needs. Smiling, she bowed and thanked the hens for their largesse. With the eggs safely in her basket, she started back to the house, but slowed upon seeing him step out the barn and into the gray morning light.

"Morning, ma'am," he said with a nod.

"Morning, Mr. Yancy." The nervousness returned. She almost asked if he'd slept well, but such personal questions between strangers could be considered rude, so she said instead, "I'm just about to start breakfast. Come to the house when you're ready."

"Anything I can help with? Wood? Water?"

She shook her head. They were only a few feet apart, and she swore the temperature in the air had risen even higher. He was all she could see. The dark skin, the large frame, the intense potent eyes. He was wearing an old, tan double-breasted shirt, frayed denim trousers that rode his hips and thighs snugly, and on his feet, a pair of worn, short-heeled boots. He was the epitome of how she imagined a man from Texas might look. The outlaw beard seemed to accentuate the full lips. Aware that she was staring at those same lips, she swiftly raised her eyes and found him watching her with a hint of amusement. For a moment, he said nothing, causing the contact to lengthen and touch her, making her again aware of his maleness and its silent power.

He said to her, "Let me get washed up, and I'll be in to eat directly."

Heart pounding, she nodded hastily, then went on to the house.

Inside, she broke the eggs into a bowl. While scrambling them with a bit of cream from her icebox, she chastised herself for her gawking. It wasn't as if she'd never seen a man's mouth before, for heaven's sake. Next she'd be wondering what those lips might feel like kissing hers, and that would not do at all. Pouring the eggs into the hot skillet, she thought about William's mouth. His lips had been thin, and his kisses—well, she didn't know if they were good or bad. He was the only man she'd ever kissed; therefore, she had no others to compare him with. They certainly hadn't made her see the stars her cousin Felicity swore she saw each time she and her intended kissed. Then again, Felicity had always been fast. Kissing boys was all she ever talked about during Elizabeth's annual two-week summer visits to Felicity and her family in Toledo when they were young. Returning her attention to the now done eggs, she set them on a plate and bent to check the progress of her biscuits in the oven. Kisses were the last thing she needed to concerning herself with.

Yancy entered the house, savoring the sight of her and the tempting smells of bacon and eggs, but when he saw the pan of hot fresh biscuits she was removing from the oven with a towel-shielded hand, he had yet another reason to be thankful for his cat-eyed wife.

She placed the biscuits on the counter, then opened the door of the small icebox and took out a tin holding pale sweet butter. Her back to him, she silently buttered the bread, then said with a note of nervousness in her voice, "I'll—let you fix your own plate."

Yancy ran discrete but appreciative eyes over the flare of her black skirt and the trimness of her waist in the faded blue blouse. "That's fine, but only after you get yours. How about we eat outside on the porch. It's pretty hot in here."

She turned and the sheen of perspiration on her forehead was plain to see. "That might be best. A few more minutes in here and we may melt."

He waited until she was done, then stepped over to the stove to do his own plate. The biscuits were still warm. He fingered up some of the melted butter running up the sides and caught her watching him as he put his finger in his mouth. As she quickly turned away, he smiled knowingly to himself, then added a large helping of the eggs and bacon. When she led them outside, he watched the sway of her hips.

Outside, she took a seat on an old weather-beaten settee that was on the porch. Not wanting to crowd her, Jordan took a seat on the step. As they ate in the morning silence, he watched her discretely. He liked that she was tall, and not skin and bones. He preferred a woman who filled his hands. Soft curves won out over sharp bones every time, and from what he could see of Elizabeth's form, she was made for him to hold. Thinking about how shocked she'd be were she able to read his mind, she made him smile and return his attention to his food.

They were just finishing up their meals when they saw a lone rider approaching. Elizabeth stood and watched silently. "It's Sheriff Cody. I wonder what he wants?"

Jordan had a pretty good idea. "He's probably coming to make sure you're all right."

She looked his way.

"First night."

She seemed to understand that, and with embarrassment on her face quickly turned back to the sheriff's approach. Once again Jordan watched her knowingly. There was more going on with his new wife than wariness of him; she was scenting him like a mare scenting a stallion in heat, and like a mare that couldn't decide whether to allow him to approach or whether to flee. Yesterday, in the sheriff's office, the moment her eyes meet his he sensed that beneath all that primness was a woman inside that she probably had no inkling about; one waiting to be unleashed and introduced to all the pleasure he could bestow, but he'd have to gentle her first so she'd be comfortable when the time came for nature to take its course—because it would come.

The sheriff reached the house, then dismounted.

"Morning, folks," he said, walking up. Pulling a bandana from his pocket, he removed his hat and wiped at the sweat on his tanned leathery face. "Gonna be another scorcher."

Elizabeth, standing behind the porch railing, replied, "Good morning, sheriff. I'm afraid you're going to be right about the heat."

17

Cody turned to Jordan. "How's things, Yancy?"

"Fine, sheriff. The lady and I are finding our way."

Cody gave an almost imperceptible nod but asked Elizabeth, "How's things going, Miss Elizabeth?"

For just a moment, she glanced over at her husband, then away. "As he said, we're finding our way."

"Good." He looked between them. "Just thought I'd stop by. You folks have any problems, just let me know."

Elizabeth nodded. "Thank you, sheriff."

Jordan remained silent.

"I'll head on back to town then." He gave Jordan one last parting look, which was met with unreadable eyes, then the sheriff mounted and rode back the way he'd come.

In the silence that followed his departure, Elizabeth forced herself to glance his way. "I'll…take the dishes back into the house."

As she gathered up her own and stacked his on top, he said, "You could have told the sheriff something else and been free of me, you know."

She paused for a moment and then replied, "I do, but it wouldn't have been the truth. I'm still uncomfortable with our arrangement, but you've not given me any reason to want you gone."

"Trying to be real careful that I don't," he admitted. "I don't want you to be afraid."

She prayed that he was telling the truth, because if he suddenly turned violent or disrespectful, she'd have no defense against him unless she had a rifle in her hands.

As if reading her mind, he urged softly, "Don't worry. Nothing in this world would make me hurt you."

Unsure how to react, she looked away.

"I know this may sound like blarney, but I want to be a good man to you. You saved me from the hangman. It's the least I can do for being able to see the sun rise every day."

The sincerity in his eyes appeared so genuine that she wanted to believe him, and because she did, unnamed emotions flooded up and took lodge in her throat. Thinking about how lonely and isolated she'd been since William's letter, and how often she'd longed for companionship or just someone to converse with during the long winter months made her eyes sting with the tears she refused to shed. Instead, she did something that seemed unthinkable yesterday when she signed her name next to his in the sheriff's office, she whispered, "Thank you for rescuing me as well."

Taking the dishes inside, she left Jordan Yancy standing on the porch, her whisper echoing in his ears.

A moment later, she was in the doorway again. They stared at each other for a few intense moments, then she asked, "Do you still wish to go into town?"

"Yes."

"Then I'll change clothes and we'll go."

"I'll bring the buggy around."

"Thank you," she said quietly, then disappeared back into the house's shadows.

When she reappeared she was wearing a high-necked white blouse, a brown skirt and a large rimmed hat straw sporting a lone white flower in the back. The high button shoes shone like new.

"You look real nice."

Her cheeks warmed under the praise. "Thank you. I'm roasting, though," she admitted, coming down the porch steps.

"Do you want to drive?" he asked.

"No you should. We're going to cause enough talk as it is."

"Really?"

She nodded. "First my husband abandons me, then I have the audacity to turn down four marriage proposals from men I could not abide but decide to marry a felon instead? I wouldn't be surprised if they hissed me out of church on Sunday."

Reins in hand, he looked over at her seated beside him. "Four proposals?"

"Four, Mr. Yancy, and if you ever have a chance to meet them, you may understand why."

He stared.

"What's the matter?"

"Here I was thinking you were this quiet little mousy thing, but I'm getting the feeling that I'm married to a hellion instead."

"Is that troubling?"

Jordan looked at her ripe mouth, then up into the cat eyes. "No. Not at all. I like a woman with spirit."

"Then, me being opinionated and not at all docile won't prevent us from finding our way?"

"No. Might be real helpful, in fact." Jordan liked his women spirited and smart. A plumb dumb woman might be good between the sheets, but she was useless for any real conversing once the play was over.

"William never cared for those parts of me," she said, looking out toward the road and the vast prairie beyond. She went quiet for a few moments as if thinking back. "He said there was no such thing as a woman's opinion, so a woman should let her husband do all her thinking." She turned to him and asked, "Is that what you were raised to believe, too, Mr. Yancy."

Jordan sensed the weight of the question. His answer would be very important to her. Apparently, she and her William hadn't been equally yoked, and her need to be valued ran deep. He could read it in her eyes. He shook his head. "My mother was a schoolteacher, and my daddy said she had more opinions than a bear had teeth."

That made her smile, and his insides warmed as if touched by sunlight. "I like making you do that."

"What?"

"Smile."

Her head dipped and a smile peeked out.

"Doesn't seem like you've had much of that lately," he told her.

"Ever," she answered softly from beneath the wide brim of her hat. Then she turned away and stared out at the distance as if revisiting her memories. "He was thirteen years my senior. Joyless, pious and miserly."

"Why'd you marry him?"

"Because he was the only man who offered for me," she added quietly. "As you probably know, women my age aren't much sought after, and the older we get, the less chance we have. When he asked me to be his wife, I agreed."

"How long had you known him?"

"A year before we married. He was my pastor's brother."

"I see."

"But, I'm still astounded by the notion of him tossing me over to marry a woman young enough to be his daughter. Pious, godly, William? His sanctimonious family undoubtedly dropped dead en masse."

"Yet you're still standing."

"As best I know how."

Jordan wanted to slide his finger down her cheek to see if her skin was as soft to his touch as it appeared. "We're going to do fine," he told her with quiet conviction.

"Did you really mean what you said about wanting to be a good husband to me?"

"I did." And he wondered what it would be like to kiss her and feel her soft weight beneath him as he filled her and stroked her.

"Then, I shall attempt to be a good wife to you," she pledged, her voice hushed.

Jordan studied her in the silence. "And what does that mean?"

Elizabeth slowly sat back against the seat. What she needed to say wasn't something she felt comfortable discussing at all, but if she truly intended to be a good wife, the subject needed to be broached, even if she couldn't make herself look at him. "Marital relations."

"Ah," was all he said.

She plunged on, "I know men have certain needs, and it's a wife's duty to be accommodating."

"Duty?" he asked.

21

The soft humor in his voice intrigued her enough to face him. "Yes, duty."

"Is that what you were raised to believe?"

"Yes."

"Not all women feel it is a duty. Some actually enjoy themselves."

"Maybe saloon women and actresses, but not good women."

"Good women, too."

Elizabeth shook her head. "I didn't mean to turn this into a debate. I just wanted you to know…that I intend to…"

"Do your duty?"

Elizabeth didn't know how to react to the teasing light in his eyes. "Yes. And since I know you've been in prison, and it's probably been…" She couldn't continue. Every inch of her body was embarrassed.

He finished the sentence for her, "A long time?"

She nodded hastily.

"Yes, it has been, but I couldn't wish for a more beautiful woman to break my fast with." His voice was as intense as his eyes, and Elizabeth's was suddenly shaking like a leaf in the wind.

"Will you do your duty for me right now, Elizabeth?"

"Now?" she croaked.

"Now, darlin'. Nothing I want more than to take you in the house and please you a hundred times, catch our breath and start all over again."

Elizabeth's breath was caught in her throat. The inner heat she'd noticed before had returned, filling her with a stirring yearning warmth that made her body answer his heated request in ways it had never responded before. Her nipples were tight, and the secret place between her thighs felt full, damp.

"So will you come inside with me?"

She didn't know how to answer, but she'd told him she would, and she'd always been a woman of her word.

He stepped down from the buggy and came around to her side. When he held out his hand, she hesitated for a moment.

"Remember. I won't hurt you."

Placing her shaking hand in his, she let him assist her to the ground.

Hands still joined, they faced each other, and Elizabeth's heart was beating like an ancestral drum. He raised their hands, placed a fleeting kiss against the back of her hand, then used his finger to slowly and possessively trace the shape of her lips. Her eyes closed, her mouth parted, and she fought to keep from fainting away in response to the soaring sensations.

"You're a passionate woman, Elizabeth."

Elizabeth wanted to dispute that, but didn't because he'd picked her up and was carrying her into the house.

Chapter Three

In the silent shadows of her bedroom, he set her on the bed, and he was all she could see. Shaking, she removed her hat and placed it on the nightstand. When he sat down on the bed beside her, she wanted to flee, but forced herself to stay where she was. Again, she reminded herself that she'd agreed to this.

Jordan knew she was scared of him, and it occurred to him that she might be afraid of the act as well. He didn't know really, but the urge to finally sample her lips in earnest was one he could no longer deny, so he leaned down and kissed her gently, softly, letting her become comfortable with this first contact; letting her learn the measure of his kiss while he did the same with her. His only goal for now was to be gentle with her, and this initial taste of her sweet trembling mouth brought home just how long it had been since he'd had a woman. "Do you know how lovely you are?" he whispered against the shell of her ear in a voice as soft as the silence.

Elizabeth was having trouble breathing. The powerful sensations flaring from the touch of his lips were unlike anything she'd ever experienced. Her entire being seemed on the verge of catching fire. When he lowered his head and placed his kiss against the edge of her jaw then the bare stripe of skin above the high collar of her blouse, her eyes closed. She wanted to stop shaking but couldn't; not when his hot lips were against her jaw again, her cheek, and then brushing so heatedly against the skin beside her eye. As he kept up the soft teasing, her breathing became more pronounced and her mouth parted in passionate response. He put his lips on hers again, then gently nibbled her bottom lip. As inexperienced as Elizabeth was, she knew he was not. The tempting movements of his mouth on hers were teaching her passion. "Kiss me back," he invited in a hushed voice.

She was forced to admit, "I don't know how…"

"Relax," he whispered, "make your mouth soft."

So she did, and this time when he kissed her, she felt his need fully. Heat jumped from his lips to hers and he must have felt it too because he slid an arm around her waist and dragged her in against him and deepened the kiss. She was shocked when his tongue caressed hers, she never knew such things were done, but soon, she found herself mimicking his actions and he pulled her closer. Learning and letting him lead, she was soon pursuing his lips, flicking her tongue timidly over the parted corners of his mouth while he groaned sensually in response.

Jordan drew away slowly, wanting her now, but knowing it was too soon. Instead, he fed on her visually, wondering if she knew how sensual she looked with her kiss-swollen mouth and her lids heavy with passion. He traced the curve of her lips, then undid the top buttons of her blouse until her throat was bare. He kissed her there and tasted the scented flesh with his tongue. The hollow rippled, she gasped and he pressed his lips there again while his manhood swelled with its own rippling response. He slid a hand up the exposed skin of her neck and felt the dampness brought on by the humid, sultry day, then traced a finger over the rise of her breasts that were hidden beneath the layers of her clothing. "You have on too many clothes, darlin'. "

But when he moved to undo the rest of her buttons, she drew away and covered her exposed skin with her hand, her gaze wary. "What's wrong," he asked quietly.

For a moment, she didn't answer, then confessed, "I've never…William, never…"

"Never, what?"

"Opened my clothes."

Jordan found that to be the damndest thing he'd ever heard, but he didn't tell her that, instead, he asked, "Then how," he paused.

He could tell she lacked experience in this. Embarrassing her was the last thing he wanted to do, but he needed to know the extent of her inexperience. "Didn't he make love to you?"

"Yes, but we didn't kiss this way. When the need came over him, I'd lie on the bed, lift my skirts and pray he'd do his business quickly."

Jordan pulled her into his lap. She didn't resist, so he encircled her with his arms and while holding her close, tenderly kissed the top of her head. "William's an ass." Looking down into her eyes, he said, "There's more to you than just that sweet nest between your thighs. I want to make love to you everywhere, Elizabeth."

Elizabeth had never heard such scandalous speech, and the effects moved through her like liquid fire.

"I want to love your breasts, and your thighs, and the nook of your navel. I want to fill my hands with your hips and explore you like a man blind…"

Once again, she found it hard to breathe. He'd talked about pleasing her, and admittedly, she had no idea what that entailed, but could it really involve removing all of her clothing? She'd die if it did, she just knew she would.

"We'll go slow, and when you want me to stop for a minute, just say so…"

So the kissing began again: slow, teasing invitations that made her forget about her misgivings and his scandalous words. His manroot was hard beneath her hips, but as passion reclaimed her that worry too melted away. So many new emotions were running riot through her that her vision became hazy, and she lost touch with everything except his fiery kisses and the heat of her body leaning against his. When he started to undo more buttons, she wondered if she was becoming one of those wanton women she'd always been warned about because as he pressed his lips against each newly bared stretch of skin the glory of it all made her croon.

"Good girl," he whispered in a voice touched with amusement. Kissing his way back up to her ear, he husked out, "Forget everything you ever believed about having relations, and just let me give you pleasure…"

His hands began to tour over her corset-encased breasts, and not even the thickness of the fabric kept her from feeling them.

Jordan was a man. The realization that he would be the first to pleasure her set off a fire in his blood that could take a lifetime to extinguish. No other man had ever cupped her breasts while kissing her luscious mouth, or laid claim to the edge of throat. No man but him had ever released the hooks on the front of her corset, one by one, and seen the dark-nippled treasures come free so he could lick, bite and suck.

When he bit her and then took her into his mouth, Elizabeth's newly awakened body exploded, and she filled the silent room with her raw, low-throated scream. The shuddering that had her in its throes made her so mindless, all she could do was lean back against his solid chest and not care who she was or how she appeared. This was new, wicked, delicious.

He whispered, "Did you like that?"

Elizabeth was still spiraling. He could have asked her to run naked through the center of town and she would have complied. The heaviness between her thighs was so pronounced, she wanted to touch herself to try ease the ache. "What did you do to me?"

"It's called an orgasm, darlin'. When your body can't take any more passion, that's what it does. Some folks call it, coming."

She could still feel it echoing through her like a far off drum. She never knew such a thing existed. Now she did, and she wanted to know if it could happen again, but was too embarrassed to ask. Realizing her breasts were still exposed, she slowly drew the halves of her corset together and held it closed.

"I'm just going to open it again," he said plainly.

His gaze was hot; hot as the small bedroom, and because she knew what would happen when he did, anticipation sparked her desire. He ran a finger over her nipple and asked, "Do you want to come again, Elizabeth?"

She couldn't respond because what he was doing to her nipples made speech hard to form.

"Shall I lick you again? Suck you again. Would you like that?"

She dearly wanted him to, but she was too scandalized by her own needs to voice the desire.

He toured his palm over the tight buds and murmured against the silence, "You have to tell me, darlin'." He plied her nipples with a heated series of plucks and pulls that made her hips rise up from his lap and increased the tumult between her thighs.

"Say, suck me, Jordan."

Elizabeth was on fire.

"Say, lick me, Jordan."

"Ohhhh."

He leaned her back over his arm and took the nipple in his mouth and proceeded to do all the scandalous things she wanted him to do but was too inhibited to say. He took his time; dallying, teasing, using both his fingers and his lips until the sensual rhythm beating between her thighs spread to her hips.

Jordan knew that if he didn't have her soon, he would spill his seed like an adolescent boy, but he held off because he wanted her bursting with need before impaling her with his burning need. Wanting her with a hunger that surpassed every other woman in his past, Jordan began kissing his way down her body while his hands singed themselves on the feel of her legs and thighs hidden beneath the folds of her skirt. He pushed the fabric up past her knees, exposing her thigh-length cotton drawers. The heat of her skin seemed to radiate through the polished fabric and he forced himself not to touch her where he wanted to the most. Instead, he bit her nipples with passion-gentled teeth and while he lingered and played, he let her get accustomed to feel of him running his hands up and down the shrouded thighs and over the lush full hips. But the damp forest, so lustily accessible through the long slit in her drawers called to him like the siren to Ulysses, and he couldn't resist any longer. She was wet, slick and so thick with need that the initial touch sent her into her second orgasm and the pleased Jordan watched her come with glittering, passion-edged eyes.

Elizabeth didn't know such pleasure was possible. The orgasm had her twisting and rising and crying out. His fingers were still bewitching her and she parted her legs shamelessly so that he wouldn't stop.

He bent to kiss her mouth, murmuring, "Now, you're ready?" And because she'd lost touch with time, it seemed that only seconds passed before her drawers were stripped away, and he was above her, naked and slowly introducing her to his hard thick delight. And it was delight. Whatever William had been doing to her before could not compare to the feel of this man possessively easing his way inside. As he stretched and filled her, she crooned because it was so wonderful, so glorious, so wanton. Never before had a man lifted her hips so he could fit himself to the hilt and never before had she felt so greedy in response to his hot thrusting strokes. He was a big man everywhere but there was no hurt, just the urge to be stroked until tomorrow's sunrise.

Jordan gave thanks that her William was such an inept lover. One man's loss was another's gain, and as the measure of his strokes increased in intensity, he knew he had hit the mother load. She was virgin tight. Who knew she'd be so exquisitely responsive or that she'd meet each thrust with unbridled abandon? The sight of her and the feel of her surrounding him, rising and falling to his rhythm was threatening to make him explode. His prison-starved body wanted to complete this now, but he fought down his male self in order not to scare her with his overwhelming need. It was difficult however, especially with her nude body offering itself so lushly, and in the end, he gave up. Feeling his own completion welling up like the portent to an earthquake, he closed his eyes, lifted her hips and bore down hard. The wave of orgasm washed over him, and the years of prison celibacy released themselves with a mighty yell. He sensed her coming too. Working her like there'd be no tomorrow, his hips hammering like steam pistons, he held her roughly and stroked and stroked until she screamed, and he could stroke no more.

Later, the pulsating and sated Elizabeth finally opened her eyes. He was lying beside her, and when she turned her head to look his way, he was watching her. Then he smiled, and she responded with a shy smile of her own before moving her eyes to the ceiling above the bed.

Jordan had had no idea how she would respond to him now that it was all over, but he was buoyed by her smile. His eyes on the ceiling, too, he asked, "Wasn't that better than going to town?"

The question elicited a soft chuckle. "I think you're a very outrageous man, Mr. Yancy."

"Don't you think you ought to call me by my given name…considering?"

She looked his way, let him see her amusement, then went back to the ceiling. "I suppose I should."

Silence settled for a few moments, then she asked, "What do people usually do, after?"

"Start again. Talk. Sleep." He raised himself up on an elbow and looked down at her. "You choose. Although you may be a little too sore for us to start again, just yet."

Elizabeth wondered if she'd ever become accustomed to his plain way of speaking or to the subtle heat in his eyes. The memories of her scandalous behavior rose up with vivid clarity, bringing back the feel of him hard and thick between her thighs. She was a changed woman now. There'd be no going back to the prim sheltered person she'd awakened as this morning. Because of him, she'd taken her first full taste of passion and Lord help her, she wanted more. Had she been told at sunrise that she'd be lying naked in bed with him before noon, she'd have accused the person of being drunk yet here she was, sated, throbbing and savoring her lusty initiation to the word, orgasm. "I think I want to talk."

"Okay. Go ahead."

She asked the question that had been plaguing her since their first meeting yesterday. "Why did you go to prison?"

Jordan had been wondering when the subject would come up and supposed now was as good a time as any. It was best to get it out of the way. "A man got killed, and I took the blame."

"Willingly?"

"No."

"Who was he?"

"The black sheep son of a rich Texas politician. Man named Sullivan. He used a knife on a cathouse queen named Lura and cut her up pretty bad. I came to arrest him, but he wanted to fight, so I obliged him, then threw in him the town jail. Few days later, his daddy's lawyer bailed him out. Next night, Sullivan was found dead in his room. He'd been stabbed to death with the same knife he'd used on Lura. "

"And they said you did it?"

"Yep. According to the court, Lura was my woman, and I killed him out of revenge."

"Was she?"

He turned his head her way so that she could see his face. "No."

"Was the real killer ever found?"

"Funny thing that. Last month, Lura's old madam sent a letter to the judge. Said she was dying and didn't want to burn in hell for what she did. Guess she killed Sullivan because Lura had been her biggest moneymaker until he carved up her face. She couldn't earn a dime afterward."

"So that's why you were released?"

"Yes."

"Does Sheriff Cody know the truth?"

"No. Far as he's concerned, I'm a murderer."

Elizabeth sighed with the injustice of that, but at least she knew the truth now, and she sensed that it was truth, because it was hard for her to reconcile a man who'd been so mindful of her a few moments ago with one cold hearted enough to take someone's life.

Admittedly, she wasn't worldly; she'd only known him two days and he could be pulling her leg, but she didn't believe that to be the case.

Her dark serious eyes met his. "Thank you."

"You're welcome."

Jordan wasn't sure if she were thanking him for telling her the story or for the pleasure he'd gifted her with, but one thing was certain, they were finding their way. "I'm going outside to wash up."

She nodded in response. Their interlude had left her dewed with sweat and the need to clean herself, especially between her thighs was strong. "Would you like something to eat when you're done?"

"Yeah. I would."

"Okay."

He got off the bed, and although Elizabeth knew she shouldn't be staring at his nudity, she found it difficult not to. He had a beautiful frame: tall, muscular, dark. Memories of seeing him through the kitchen window yesterday returned, but having him so close and knowing what they'd just shared in bed made this time different. As he dragged on his trousers she wanted to touch him; run her palms over the well-formed shoulders and arms, slide her fingers over his strong back and the indentation of his spine. She hadn't touched him at all during their relations and now secretly wished she had so that she'd have those memories as well. Having been raised to believe that a woman's role in bed was to play no role and simply let the man do as he would, no longer rang true. His advice that she forget all that she'd been told before about what a man and woman did and did not do came back to her, and the words made sense now where they hadn't before. He had ushered her into a world that allowed her to do more than just lie there, and she wondered if it was possible for a woman to give a man as much pleasure as he'd given her.

Dressed in his denim Levis, he walked back over to the bed and looked down at her seated in the center. Leaning in, he kissed her softly and murmured, "Thank you for being my wife."

The words pleased her as much as the kiss. The contact relit her desire and as the kiss deepened, she cupped his beard-shrouded jaw and whispered, "You're welcome."

And then he was gone, and she was alone.

They ate a simple meal of sliced beef between pieces of the bread she'd made a few days ago, and washed them down with tall tumblers of sweet cold lemonade. As they sat across the table from each other, neither of them mentioned their heated encounter; it wasn't necessary; each had their memories. Elizabeth, not sure how to act around him in the aftermath of something so primal and so life changing, was reticent and uncertain even though every time he looked her way her nipples tightened and her thighs echoed with bliss filled remembrance.

As if reading her mind, he asked, "Uncomfortable again."

She nodded, then said to him, "I feel like someone else."

He smiled understandingly, "In a way you are, I suppose. William was a cad to use you the way he did, but I'm glad to be the man showing you it can be different. Even fun, if you let it."

"Fun?"

"Sure. Just wait, you'll see."

His eyes told all, and the anticipation made the drum between her legs beat louder. She looked away but her nipples were tight and ready.

A knock at the door interrupted them and Elizabeth excused herself to see who the visitor might be. Seeing Mathias Bolye's weasel-thin face on the other side of the screened door made her wish for the ability to make herself invisible so he'd turn around and go home. He was one of the men who'd been after her to marry and not someone she wanted to see. With him however was Reverend Smalls from the Turner AME church. She couldn't imagine why the two had come. "Afternoon, Mr. Boyle. Reverend."

33

"Miss Elizabeth," they said in unison.

She stepped out onto the shady porch. After having been inside the relatively cool house most of the morning, she found the afternoon air thick with heat. "What brings you two out on such a hot afternoon?"

"We came to see if the rumors are true," Boyle said.

He was well dressed as usual, in a crisp brown suit, white shirt and a string tie. He ran the town's newspaper, was a Howard College graduate and in his mind more learned and important than anyone else around. "What rumors are you referring to?" she asked looking from him to the Reverend Smalls who was taller and sported the mutton chops so popular in decades past.

"The ones saying you married a prisoner."

"And if they are true?" she asked, determined to remain pleasant in the face of their nosiness.

"Then I believe we need to talk," the reverend replied.

"About what?"

Boyle answered, "The soundness of your mind."

Elizabeth bit down on her anger and said coolly, "Why is that any of your business?"

The reverend said, "We care about you, Elizabeth. Surely something is wrong if you've chosen this stranger over the fine upstanding men of your own community."

"I'm fine, reverend."

Boyle said, "But, you were out here alone all winter. Such loneliness has been known to affect one's judgment."

"I assure you, my judgment has not been impaired by loneliness or anything else."

"Elizabeth what you've done is not the action of a sane woman," the reverend pointed out.

"Oh really?"

"Mr. Boyle and I are concerned enough that we've come to ask for your father's address so that we can write to him and get his opinion."

She studied each man closely. "You want to write to my father?"

The reverend said, "I believe it is warranted."

"And if I don't. What then?"

Before they could respond, she heard Jordan say from behind her. "I'd be interested in hearing the answer to that, too."

When he stepped outside, he stood there for a moment, looming over the five-foot six-inch Boyle like a dragon sizing up a sheep. Boyle's eyes widened in surprise, and he took a nervous step back. The reverend seemed a bit shocked himself but hid it well.

"Name's Jordan Yancy."

"Mathias Boyle," the newspaperman responded in an unsteady voice, then as if remembering his own self-importance said, "And this is the Reverend Smalls. We're here to see to Elizabeth's welfare."

"And I'm sure she's real appreciative, but she's doing real good on her own."

"That's debatable," the reverend replied. "Especially in the face of the choices she's made."

"You mean picking me?"

The reverend thrust out his chin and nodded.

Boyle added, "We're concerned that she might not be treated with the respect she deserves."

When Jordan came to stand beside her and placed his strong arm around her waist with a gentle possessiveness, Elizabeth hid her surprise. It was not a gesture she'd been expecting, but it felt as if he'd been holding her this way through time. In answer to Boyle's question, he looked down at her and asked, "Am I treating you with the respect you deserve?"

She gave him a simple, quiet, "Yes."

He grinned down, and she had to look away because the drum beats had started up again. She turned to Boyle's thin, hard-set face. There was anger in his dark eyes, but she met the hostile stare without flinching. "Would you care for some lemonade?"

In reality, she was enjoying standing close to Jordan this way, and she didn't want to leave his side. Although she didn't care for Mathias or the reverend right now, they were visitors and neighbors, two valued entities out here on the desolate Kansas plains, so she was expected to be polite.

"Yes, I would," the reverend replied, his eyes never leaving Jordan.

"I'd like some, too," Boyle added.

She made move to leave Jordan's side only to feel him give her waist an almost imperceptible squeeze before she walked away. Careful to keep her pleasure from showing on her face, Elizabeth went inside.

Chapter Four

Where you from, Yancy?" Boyle asked.

"Texas. Town called Churchfield near the Sabine River. You?"

"Atlanta. Came out here two years ago. I run the town's newspaper. Howard College graduate."

Jordan assumed he was supposed to be impressed, but he didn't respond.

"What did you go to jail for?" the reverend asked boldly.

"Murder."

Both his and Boyle's eyes popped with surprise, then they visibly calmed themselves. "Never heard of the courts setting a murderer free," Boyle said.

"They do when a man is innocent."

The men studied him as if trying to determine whether Jordan was being truthful or not, but Jordan didn't care what they concluded. The only opinion that mattered belonged to Elizabeth.

Elizabeth returned a few moments later, carrying a tray holding three short tumblers filled to the brim with cold lemonade, and she met Jordan's gaze with her now-familiar shy smile. After distributing the drinks, she took a seat on the old settee, and Jordan sat down beside her. Both men kept Jordan under scrutiny and viewed him coolly as they sipped.

The reverend then asked her, "What did your father have to say about your marriage?"

"I've not had time to write to him as of yet."

"All the more reason why I should write to him as well."

Elizabeth shook her head. "I'm a grown woman, Reverend. My father respects my decisions, and you should do so as well."

"Then you won't give me his address?"

"No."

His lips thinned. "I can't help you if you won't let me, Elizabeth."

"I'm not in need of help, Reverend Smalls. Jordan is my husband, and nothing you say or do will alter that."

Elizabeth knew the reverend didn't like to be challenged, but she refused to let him or Boyle meddle in her life when they had no legitimate reason or right to.

Boyle said, "I'd like to interview you for my paper, Yancy. Introduce you to the folks around here."

Jordan didn't respond.

Boyle said smugly, "Man like you probably wouldn't want his past known though, so I'll understand if you say, no."

Elizabeth met the newsman's mocking eyes with a frigid stare. "Why wouldn't my husband want it known that he was a Deputy Marshal?"

"Marshal?" Boyle croaked, choking on his beverage. He stared wide-eyed at the equally surprised looking Smalls.

It was her turn to be smug. "He was a lawman when he was rail-roaded."

The Howard College graduate now looked confused. "You didn't say that, Yancy."

"I haven't said a lot of things, Boyle," Jordan pointed out over his drink. He wanted the two men and their sanctimonious attitudes and questions to leave. Elizabeth was not a feeble-minded child in need of their direction on how to live her life. Jordan was pleased that she was sticking to her guns and not letting them intimidate her.

Elizabeth wanted them to leave, too. She knew the reverend was well respected and that his opinion counted for much, but she would not let herself be dictated to, so when they drained the last of heir drinks, she said, "I'm sure you both have other more important hings to do this afternoon, so my husband and I thank you for isiting. Please come again."

Jordan had to admit that every time she acknowledged him as her husband, his heart swelled with pride. As of yet, she still hadn't ddressed him by his given name, but he was certain he'd hear that rom her sweet mouth too, in time. "Nice meeting you, Boyle, Reverend Smalls."

"Have a safe trip back to town," Elizabeth said, doing her best o keep her voice even.

It was obvious the men weren't pleased about being dismissed ut neither seemed willing to take on the big man at her side. After andling her their tumblers they made their leave, got into Boyle's uggy and drove away.

As Elizabeth and Jordan watched the dust from the road kick up n the buggy's wake, Jordan drawled, "I don't think they're real happy with us, right now."

"I don't think so either," she replied. "The reverend means well 'm sure, but Boyle's a pompous little varmint. He's one of the four hat have been pestering me about marrying."

"I figured as much. Are the other three varmints, too?"

"Two are. The other one lives with his mama and doesn't get up n the morning without asking her permission."

"Sounds like a great catch."

"Only if the net is big enough to hold his mother, too."

Looking his way, Elizabeth wondered if other married couples had as easy a relationship as it appeared she and her husband were mbarking upon. She'd spent the years with William walking round on eggshells always afraid of doing something wrong.

"Penny for your thoughts."

"Just thinking about how different things seem to be now."

"In what way?"

She shrugged. "William and I didn't laugh. There wasn't much ompanionship between us."

"And now?" he asked quietly.

"I don't feel so alone."

He nodded understandingly. Being in prison had imposed its own dark loneliness, but being with her was putting sunlight back into his life. He hoped to be able to do the same for her.

"I can't believe they think I'm touched in the head."

He shrugged. "Like they said, you had some perfectly good prospects for your hand."

"That's their opinion. Not mine."

He smiled.

In spite of Boyle's and the reverend's opinions, she looked upon choosing Jordan to be her husband as one of the soundest decisions she'd ever made. "You should move your things into the house."

He looked into her feline shaped eyes. "You sure?"

She nodded. "We can't find our way if you're in the barn."

Jordan agreed, but he didn't want to rush things. "As long as you're comfortable."

"I am."

He leaned in to kiss her and she met his lips without resistance. Drawing on her ripe mouth made him remember this morning, and the fact that he'd not gotten enough of her. "I want you again, darlin'…"

Response rippled through her, and the familiar drumbeat started up again. She reached up to pull him closer and deepen the kiss. This was still new, but she knew more than she had this morning, so she let her desire rise.

He whispered, "Ever make love outside?"

She drew away with such surprise on her face, he chuckled.

"Guess the answer's no."

"Outside?"

"Yes, ma'am."

"Really?"

Jordan knew she had no idea what a joy he found her to be. She had just enough innocence to make him want to spend the rest of his life showing her the ins and outs of passion so she could fully release the sensual woman he sensed hiding beneath all that prim properness. He leaned closer and brushed his lips over hers. "Shall I give you a little taste?"

His kisses were moving over her throat and chin and his hands were moving over her breasts. "Will you do me a favor?"

Eyes closed, she answered, "I'll try."

"When we're home, leave off your corset."

Elizabeth's heart pounded in response to his bold request.

"I love undressing you, but it's in the way."

William had never undressed her, not even on their wedding night, but Jordan wasn't William, and as he slowly conquered the buttons of her blouse and undid the hooks of her corset, she was glad. The feel of his big hands pleasuring her made her forget she was outside on the porch, and sent heat simmering through her veins. Leaning back against the settee, she let him and his hot mouth have their way. He sucked and plucked and circled his tongue around the pleading buds until she arched for more and he readily obliged. He raised the dark-nippled twin globes to his lips so he could feast more intensely.

Elizabeth could hear herself crooning and grasping; could feel her hips rising as ancient rhythms took hold. Then, his hand was between her parted thighs, teasing her within the long slit of her drawers, and when he shockingly slipped his long finger inside the orgasm hit her like a kick from a mule and she stiffened, shouting her joy.

Jordan watched his lovely wife ride out her pleasure with her breasts bared and his hand between the legs spread so sweetly below her rucked-up skirt. He wanted nothing more than to satisfy his throbbing manhood, but he put off taking her for now. She had to be sore from the loving he'd given her this morning, and he cared for her enough to not want their lovemaking to cause her any discomfort.

Instead, he leaned down and kissed her passion-parted lips and whispered, "The more pleasure I give you, the more stamina you'll have. Pretty soon, you'll stop coming so quickly."

Elizabeth heard his words as if she were far away. She wasn't rightly sure she understood the meaning of what he'd just told her, but because of the pulsating orgasm, she didn't care.

When he slowly withdrew his finger, she groaned softly in protest.

His voice hot, he said, "Turning you into a greedy woman, am I?" So he slid it back in, added yet another and she gave a soft sound of satisfaction. "Open your legs wider, darlin'. I want to see if you can come again."

Elizabeth was running wet. His wicked fingers were moving in and out of her flesh the way he'd used his manhood earlier, coaxing her to rise and fall; making her slide her hips forward so she could better feel his silent commands. He worked her, impaled her and erotically schooled her until a second orgasm threw her forward and she came, holding onto his wrist and screaming rawly.

His lips on hers, he murmured thickly, "Good girl."

And to Elizabeth it was good; his kisses were good, the feel of his tongue on her damp nipples was good, but the hand now moving gently between her thighs was marvelous.

When she opened her eyes, he was above her and smiling down.

She told him, "You're far too good at this. . ."

"Can I have my hand back now…unless you're still using it, that is."

She was embarrassed to her toes.

When he gently broke the contact, his fingers came free slick with her essence. He brushed them clean on his denims. "Told you this could be fun." He kissed her, then slowly, possessively and so thoroughly she moaned.

Satisfied with her response, Jordan pulled away, then closed her gaping blouse. "Go on in the house and do whatever it is you'd be

doing this time of day. Soon as I can walk, I'll go see what's ailing
our wind mill."

Elizabeth face filled with concern. "Why can't you walk?"

He chuckled softly in response to her serious curiosity. "When
a man doesn't get relief, it's kinda hard to move."

"Is there any way I can to help you," she asked anxiously.

"Yes, you can take that tempting body of yours in the house so
can calm down."

No man had ever said such a thing to her in her life.

He stroked her cheek. "To get relief, I'd have to make love to
you again, and not with my hand, if you catch my meaning."

She did, and was embarrassed all over again.

"So go on inside," he said affectionately. "I'll be all right in a
few minutes."

"Are you sure? You can show me what to do."

"Woman. If you don't go on, you're going to find yourself bent
forward over that porch railing with your skirt up around your
neck."

Elizabeth couldn't help herself. She looked over at the porch
railing, then back into his glittering humor filled eyes. "We can do
this, standing up?"

He threw back his head and laughed loud enough to be heard
in town. "Go!" he said pointing to the door. "I'll give you that lesson
some other time."

Unable to keep the smile from her face, she stood, then obeyed.

For the rest of the afternoon, he worked on the windmill and
he began clearing the bedroom of Williams' things. Most of his
clothing was still in the dresser drawers, and a suit hung in the
armoire. Even though she knew he wouldn't be returning, she'd
been reluctant to donate them to the church or to throw them away

because of the finality the act would represent. No woman wanted a failed marriage, no matter how lifeless the union may have been, but she felt no such reluctance now. As she placed everything into an old unused trunk, there were no feelings of sadness or regret. In spite of his perfidy, she bore him no ill will now because she was embarking upon a new life too; one filled with companionship, passion and porch railings, of all things. Closing the trunk, she stood, then left the bedroom to start dinner.

After dinner they were sitting on the porch discussing the problem with the windmill—it need new steel vanes, and getting to know each other better.

"Republican or Democrat?" he asked her.

"Republican," she replied, "but I'm convinced more members of the race will be voting Democratic in the future.

"You might be right, but this man will be loyal to the party of Lincoln until they put me in the ground."

"William said women would never be given the vote. Do you believe that, too?"

He shrugged. "My mother says he's wrong, and when you live in her house, you either agree or eat outside with the dogs."

Elizabeth thought that was funny, and wondered if she'd ever get to meet his formidable mother. She'd like to think the two of them would get along nicely. "Do you miss home?"

"I do. Missed it a lot when I was in jail. Not so homesick anymore."

His dark eyes met hers and she felt her heart swell at the compliment. "I've never been to Texas. Can we go visit sometime?

He shrugged. "Sure, but let's get us settled in first."

She thought that a wise suggestion and found herself looking forward to settling in.

Soon the sun was setting with vivid reds and oranges, signaling the end of another day.

Jordan said, "Been a long time since I've sat on a porch and watched the sun set. Pretty powerful sight."

She agreed. Elizabeth had never considered what a person might miss being imprisoned, like sunsets—sunrises, too, she supposed. What else had he been deprived of while serving time for a crime he didn't commit? She could only imagine the anguish he must have suffered over the injustice. "I like the sunsets, too. Most evenings, I'm sitting right here."

"Then I say we meet here, same time from now on." There was a glint of humor in his dark eyes.

"I say you have a deal."

"You can sit closer, you know."

Enjoying his playfulness, Elizabeth scooted over.

"Closer," he coaxed.

About six inches separated them on the settee. She moved nearer then he draped an arm across her shoulder and eased her into his side.

"Much better," he proclaimed.

Elizabeth had never felt sheltered by a man before but found it to her liking. She leaned her head on his shoulder and made herself comfortable because it seemed like the natural thing to do.

Night fell, then the moon and the stars came out. The mosquitoes did too, so they reluctantly rose from the settee and went inside. Because of the lack of windows in the small frame house, the interior was stifling.

Jordan told her. "First thing tomorrow, more windows."

"Really?"

The house was dark but they were bathed by a swath of moonlight pouring in through the open front door.

"Can I get carpenter tools in town?"

"Yes."

"Good."

When they entered the bedroom, Elizabeth told him, "Stay here a moment. I'll light the lamp." Because she knew her way around in the dark, she had no trouble finding the flint and setting the spark to the wick in the oil lamp. Soon a shadowy light danced around the room and he stepped in to join her.

In spite of all they'd shared today, she was a bit nervous knowing she'd be sleeping in the bed with him, but she hoped the shadows in the room would keep him from noticing.

It didn't.

"If you're not ready, I can sleep in the barn."

"No. Please. I'll be okay. Still finding my way," she confessed. "Sleeping together is a natural way to end the day, don't you think?"

"I do."

"And we are man and wife."

"We are."

When she was married to William, she'd always gone to the kitchen to undress and get into her night things. Even though William and Jordan looked upon the physical aspects of marriage differently, she felt more comfortable undressing alone. In light of being half naked outside on the settee, and being taken until she screamed in the very bed they were going to share now, her reticence was silly, but she was still a modest woman and old habits die hard. "I'm going to put on my gown in the kitchen."

He nodded. "Whatever suits you."

She took her night things down from the hook on the door, then hastily left the room.

In the kitchen she took off her blouse and skirt and then the corset she'd promised him she wouldn't wear when at home with him. Her body felt different. Where before she had no knowledge of the sensual power lurking within, her new husband had brought it to the fore. She was now aware of how her nipples could harden when they were kissed and that the right touches between her legs could start a fire there. Realizing that she was exciting herself just by thinking about all the pleasure she'd had today, she put on her sleeveless nightgown, gathered up her clothing and headed back to the bedroom.

When she returned, he was already in bed. There was a kindness in his eyes that calmed her. Buoyed by it, she crossed the room to douse the light and plunged the room into darkness. She crawled into bed and lay there stiffly in the silence. She felt him behind her but didn't know what to say or do. He took care of things. Scooting over, he fit himself against her, placed an arm across her waist, then kissed her hair. "I'll see you in the morning, Elizabeth."

And before she could reply, he was asleep. Content, Elizabeth made herself comfortable, then closed her eyes.

Chapter Five

The next morning, Elizabeth awakened in bed alone. Puzzled, by the empty space beside her, she sat up and listened for his presence in the house. When she didn't hear anything, she left the bed and grabbed her wrapper. Had he taken off for parts unknown during the night? Had yesterday with all its pleasures been nothing more than a dream? Entering the kitchen, she heard the loud distinctive ring of an axe. She went to the window and there he stood out in the yard shirtless and splitting the wood that had been stacked up in the barn since winter. For a moment, she watched silently and feasted her eyes on the sheer magnificence of his dark form. After deciding she was a lucky woman indeed to have such a man in her life, she stepped outside.

"Morning," she called.

He stopped and looked up. "Morning."

"You're up awfully early," she said walking out to where he was working. She had to force herself to stop staring at his magnificent chest and arms.

"Did it because there's something special about making love to a beautiful woman first thing in the morning, and we're supposed to be going into town today."

Her body reacted instantly and she wondered how many other wives had husbands who began tempting them before sun up. "We do need to go into town," she said amused.

"Which is why I'm out here and not in bed with you. You can be real distracting, you know."

His eyes were full of his meaning and she felt the touch of them like a hand. William had never been amorous in the morning, and until Jordan came into her life, she never knew that couples could ake love anywhere or at any time of the day. She thought it only ook place in the bedroom at night in the dark. "I'll start breakfast."

He nodded then went back to his chore.

Watching her go, Jordan definitely found her distracting. He'd wakened this morning hard and ready, but she'd been sleeping so oundly, he hadn't the heart to disturb her dreams. Last night, he'd lanned to make love to her one more time before they went to eep, but her bed was the first one he'd slept in since being impris- ned, and as soon as he pulled her close, the years of weariness ame down on him all at once, and next he knew, it was morning. Ie brought the axe down on the logs and made a vow to make love o his distracting wife just as soon as they returned from town. Thinking about that made his manhood tighten. He hefted the axe or another strike and smiled.

He drove into town with the primly and properly dressed lizabeth seated at his side on the buggy's black leather bench. It vas already hot, so he kept the horses at a reasonable pace to keep om being overtaxed. "You think folks are going to be mean to you or marrying me?"

Beneath her hat, Elizabeth shrugged. "Some will, especially if Mathias Boyle fans things up with his newspaper. I know he's going o write about us and he won't be kind."

"I don't care what he says about me, but if he slings any mud at ou, I'll be feeding his nuts to the nearest squirrel."

She laughed softly. She'd never had a champion before. She ked it.

They entered town and Elizabeth directed him down Main treet to the general store owned by Wexford Anderson. The short, lump, black-skinned Anderson, stocked a wide variety of goods; verything from sewing needles to saddles. The opening of his store st year had been a blessing because now folks in the area didn't ave to make a two and a half hour drive over to Nicodemus to do eir shopping.

Jordan tied the reins of the horse to the post, then went around to help her down. Having been a lawman, he instinctively looked around to get the lay of the place. He cast a passing glance at the sheriff's office sitting on the other side of the street. The town was small, and there were only a few businesses lining the main street but there were buggies and wagons moving up and down the road and more than a few people on the plank walk. Most were people of color and most were staring curiously.

Elizabeth saw them, too. She supposed that by now everyone around knew the circumstances surrounding her marriage, but she wondered how many knew that Jordan had been an innocent man.

The interior of the store was crowded with farmers buying supplies and women buying dry goods for their household. Children were eyeing the penny candies on display and a group of old men were sitting around the cracker barrel, drinking lemonade and playing dominoes.

The muted sounds of many conversations filled the air, but when the shoppers noticed Miss Elizabeth and her new husband one could hear a pin drop on cotton. Elizabeth's lips thinned. She had no idea how they would be received but she prepared herself for the worst.

Then in the silence Mr. Anderson's froggy voice rang out "Marshal Yancy! Is that you?"

Jordan turned and upon seeing the familiar face a wide grin split his face. "Well, I'll be damned. Wex! What are you doing here?"

The two smiling men shared a hearty handshake, then Anderson called out, "Folks, this here is one of the finest marshals ever born in Texas. Got himself railroaded to prison but everybody in town knew he was innocent."

Then he turned back to Jordan. "Welcome to Kansas."

Elizabeth could have kissed Anderson on his bald head. Where before the faces of his customers had been skeptical, they were now smiling and viewing Jordan with interest.

Anderson said to Elizabeth, "Morning, Miss Elizabeth. I heard you'd married up but didn't know it was the marshal. You got yourself one fine man here. A fine man!"

"Thank you, Mr. Anderson."

Her husband was smiling down, and for Elizabeth the day suddenly felt much brighter.

Wex then asked Jordan in a more serious tone, "When'd you get out?"

"Few days ago. One-Eyed Peg confessed to killing Sullivan."

Anderson shook his head at the news. "Should've known she was involved. She was mighty mad after what he did to Lura's face."

"So how'd you wind up here?" Jordan asked. Wex had run a general store back in Texas, too.

"Came up here to visit my brother after my mama died in Houston last year and been here ever since."

He and Jordan then moved off to talk and fill the list of supplies Jordan had written down, while Elizabeth drifted over to the dry goods.

"Mighty handsome fella you got there Elizabeth."

She turned to the speaker, Adelaide Henry one of the women from the Turner AME church and the town's leading matriarch. "Morning, Miss Addie. Yes, he is."

"A girl could do much worse," Adelaide said knowingly. "Bet Mathias is fit to be tied."

Elizabeth smiled. "I'm sure he'll have something sensational to print about Jordan being in prison."

"Didn't Anderson say your man was innocent?"

"He did and he was."

"Well, then don't worry about Mathias. If he prints any lies, he'll have me to answer to."

"Thank you, Addie."

"Just make sure you bring him to church on Sunday. Only the Good Lord can make a man that handsome, and I'm sure all the ladies want to see His handiwork."

Elizabeth chuckled. "Yes, ma'am."

Adelaide moved off and Elizabeth continued making her way through the store.

Elizabeth felt more relaxed on the ride home. Going into town she'd been apprehensive about the reception she and her husband would receive; but after Mr. Anderson's ringing endorsement of Jordan's character, and Adelaide Henry's favorable words about Jordan's handsome looks, Elizabeth was no longer worried. She was sure there would still be a few people whispering behind their hands, but she wasn't going to let that bother her. Not now. Now, all she had to worry about was building a life for her and her remarkable man.

"That sure was something running into Wex after all these years. Imagine him being here, of all places," he said to her.

"I'm glad he spoke so highly of you. Folks respect his opinion. Maybe you won't have to feed Mathias's nuts to the squirrels after all."

Jordan laughed so long and so hard, Elizabeth became concerned. "What's so funny?"

When he could speak again, he said with humor in his eyes, "Just hearing the word nuts coming out of your proper speaking mouth, is all."

Elizabeth stared confused.

"Do you know what nuts are?"

"Well yes, but…"

"No, darlin'. Not nuts like pecans or walnuts."

"I know, but I'm assuming it's a metaphor for his brain or something."

He started laughing again.

"Jordan!"

"I'm sorry. You are just so sweet sometimes."

And when he told her what nuts really referred to, Elizabeth was mortified. "Oh my word! I feel like I should wash my mouth out with soap. Oh, my word!"

Jordan shoulders were shaking as he laughed.

"It's not funny, Jordan Yancy."

With a smile on his face he stopped the buggy.

Elizabeth asked, "Why are we stopping."

"To commemorate something."

She wondered if he'd been in the sun too long. "What?"

"That's the very first time you've called me by my given name."

Elizabeth tried to think back. "Really?"

He nodded. "I liked the sound of it."

"Then it is an auspicious occasion."

"Pretty big word, auspicious."

Elizabeth had never met a man who could seduce a woman just by the tone of his voice and the look in his eyes. "I like big words," she responded softly. Once again, he was all she could see.

"And I like you."

He kissed her then, the first one of the day and the sweetness of it made her melt. For a few silent moments they reacquainted themselves with the tastes, feel and passion of each other. He loved the scent she wore and she loved the way he kissed her, as if she were precious, valued, needed. Soon his hands were roaming and hers were moving up and down his back, and the kiss deepened.

He husked out, "You've got this damn corset on again."

"Don't swear. Good women wear corsets."

Placing his lips against her jaw and ear, he asked, "Can I take it off?"

She forced herself to deny him, "You're not going to undress me out here in the middle of the road," she whispered, her voice husky with arousal.

He leaned his head down and bit a nipple through her layered clothing. His caressing hands followed and he murmured, "You sure..."

Elizabeth wasn't sure of anything at that moment. Warmth that had nothing to do with the sun overhead was undermining her defenses. The buggy's roll top canopy sheltered them somewhat from it and prying eyes, so when he boldly began to undo her buttons, she let him have his way.

"I'll let you keep it on, but I want it open so I can touch you."

Elizabeth almost came there and then. She knew she should be scandalized by his actions, but she was too busy soaring to care. The hooks of her corset were undone and as the slight breeze drifted over her bare skin, he leaned her back against the seat and feasted lustily. "Ohhh."

Once again, the word marvelous came to mind. His mouth, his hands, his tongue, all had her panting, and hot between her legs. As if he knew she needed to be touched there too, he placed his hand on her through her skirt and worked the spot lightly.

"Ohhh."

"Like that, do you?"

She did, very much, and widened her thighs so he could tease more of her.

"Let's make you come, then I'll take you home and make you come again."

Her breath was stacked up in her throat. She could feel the heat of the day drying away the dampness on her tightened nipples left by his mouth and tongue, and she could feel her skirt rising up her legs. Then, his fingers were there; touching, sliding, impaling, and her hips rose greedily for the prize.

He bit her nipples and moved his fingers in and out with such slow and seductive expertise that the orgasm soon buckled her, and she was gasping and twisting and arching, and not caring that she was shouting his name outside, and in the middle of the road.

For the rest of the way, he kept her ripe and running with stolen kisses, licks for her breasts and further magical forays beneath her skirt. By the time they reached the house, Elizabeth was in such need he could have laid her down on the porch steps and taken her there, but he led her into the bedroom and after a hasty removal of clothing, he eased in his hard promise and she groaned with the glory of it all.

Jordan was finally where he most wanted to be and feeling her muscles seal around him, wondered if a more perfect woman had ever been made. She was so beautifully responsive he could make love to her until the sun became the moon, and not be satisfied. The long firm legs wrapped around him, the softness of her breasts in his hands, her ripe full mouth so primed for his kisses made him increase his strokes. He was so hard and ready, his desire refused to let him go slow or take the time to linger over her lush curves. He wanted her now, right now, and he lit into her like a man long denied. The orgasm gathered from a place deep within, and when it erupted he gripped her hips and pumped until he roared.

When the echoes of his orgasm finally faded away, Jordan felt boneless. To keep her from being crushed by his weight, he turned so that she was lying atop his chest. He hugged her close, then sent a slow hand down her satiny spine and over the comely curves of her behind. Nothing on earth could have compelled him to move. He kissed her head and said, "We're not going to get much work done around here if you don't keep your clothes on."

She raised up. "Me? You're the one making me engage in all this scandalous behavior."

He grinned. "And I'm having the best time. How about you?"

"I think your head's large enough as it is. You don't need any flattery from me."

He gave her a soft smack on the butt. "Sassy woman."

Then he was kissing her and when he began to swell inside of her, Elizabeth drew back a moment in confusion, then she looked down at herself.

He asked, "Something wrong?"

"You have me at such sixes and sevens I just realized where I am."

"What do you mean?"

"I'm on top."

He gave her a few languid strokes and said, "Yes, you are."

Moving in response to his bewitching commands, her eyes slid closed, and she whispered, "More scandalous behavior?" She had no idea a woman could be on top.

"At your service."

Her positioning gave him easy access to her breasts, hips and mouth, and he took full sensual advantage. Elizabeth soon realized the benefit of being above him, because she could take in as little or as much of his prize as she craved, and she could control the pace. In spite of her inexperience, her body instinctively knew what to do, so she gave it its head, and under his erotic tutelage she wantonly rode her husband until orgasms claimed them both.

As she lay on him in the aftermath, she savored being held close and would have laid there for an eternity, but when he snatched the sheet up to cover her and she heard him snap, "Who the hell are you!" she rose up and looked behind her to see William standing in the doorway. Her eyes went wide. "William!"

He barked back, "What is going on here?"

Jordan answered, "Go wait in the parlor."

William looked ready to burst. "That is my wife! How dare you—?"

"Outside! Now!"

Elizabeth was now huddled next to Jordan. What was William doing here?

"William, do as he says, please."

That he was furious was plain, but he finally spun on his heel and left them in the room alone.

Jordan watched the exit with an equal amount of fury. "Why'd he come back?"

Elizabeth slid from the bed and began to dress. "I have no idea." This was all happening so fast, she was finding it hard to think. "Maybe he came back for the last of his belongings. I don't know." She did know that she didn't want him there. Not now. Not after she and Jordan were trying to build something with each other.

"I'll respect the man enough to let him talk to you alone. I'll be out directly."

"Thank you." Dressed, Elizabeth left.

William was pacing when she entered. He looked her up and down contemptuously. "You didn't waste much time replacing me in your bed, did you? Who is he?"

"My husband."

He stared.

"Yes, William, my husband. After you tossed me over, I went out and got myself another man. Why are you here?"

"Malinda turned out to be more flighty than I cared for."

"So you thought you'd come back here, and do what?"

"Pick up where we left off."

She found it hard to be civil, but she tried. "There is no, *we*, any longer, William. Jordan is my husband now."

"Not if you're still married to me, he isn't."

She stilled. "I sent back the divorce papers, just as you requested."

"But I never signed nor filed them," he said smugly. "So we're still married."

Jordan who was standing in the doorway saw the horrified look on Elizabeth's face and wondered how long it would take him to beat William to a pulp. The man was much shorter and thinner, so Jordan was pretty sure it wouldn't take more than a few minutes.

William shot Jordan a triumphant look. "Now, with that said, you may leave."

Elizabeth said, "No, William. You may leave."

"This is my house."

"Not anymore. The deed belongs to me now."

He looked between the two of them. "I'll take you to court."

"Why? You left me, remember. File the papers so we can both get on with our lives."

"And if I refuse?"

"What can you possibly hope to gain by forcing me into a court of law to tell the world that I no longer want you as my husband?"

"You are my wife!"

"Only on paper." Elizabeth had had enough. First Boyle and the reverend, and now this.

"Say the word, darlin' and I'll put him out."

Elizabeth didn't have to think twice. "Put him out."

That said, she went into the bedroom and slammed the door.

In the charged silence that settled after her exit, Jordan said, "I suggest you saddle up and ride on."

"She's my wife."

"Not anymore, so your choices are to leave like a man or can I toss you out like yesterday's trash."

"Touch me and I'll get the law."

"That's your choice. Since Sheriff Cody married me and Elizabeth, you might have a hard time getting him to back you."

William's lips thinned. He picked up his hat from the chair. "You haven't seen the last of me."

Jordan didn't respond.

William stormed out.

Jordan stepped outside on the porch. After watching the man ride away, he went back in and locked the door.

When he entered the bedroom, Elizabeth was pacing angrily. "Is he gone?"

Jordan nodded.

"Can you believe this? He abandons me, then has the gall to return and want to pick up the pieces. I should have socked him."

Jordan chuckled softly. "Come here."

She went to him without protest, and he sheltered her in his arms. "He says he'll be back, but I don't think we have anything to worry about. No court in the land is going to honor his claim once they find out the truth about his leaving."

"I will not go back to being his wife, Jordan. I refuse."

"You get no argument from me. Took all I had not to pound him into meal." He looked down into her angry eyes. "Texans don't take kindly to back east pip squeaks trying to lay claims to their women."

"Good." She just hoped William knew that, too.

Later, Jordan was outside tossing feed to the chickens, and as they pecked away at it, he asked the rooster Douglass. "Where were you when that snake snuck into the house? If you can't keep varmints away any better than that, I may have to replace you with a dog."

The rooster eyed him balefully, then strutted away. Jordan shook the last of the feed out of the tin bucket and headed back to the house just in time to see Wexford Anderson drive up on his delivery wagon. In the bed were all the supplies Jordan had ordered this morning from the store, including new vanes for the windmill and carpentry tools. Once the men got everything unloaded and into the barn, Wexford climbed back onto the seat, and with a parting wave drove off to continue his deliveries.

"Where do you want the new windows?" Jordan asked her at the table over dinner.

She was still brooding over William's surprising return. "How about the bedroom and the parlor?"

He nodded and forked up a piece of the tastiest roast chicken he'd had since leaving his mama's table. He knew she was thinking about her other husband, and he wanted to tell her not to worry, but rather than bring up the subject again, he said, "You're a real good cook."

"Thank you."

Shaking off thoughts of William, she focused on Jordan. In spite of all their bouts of scandalous behavior, Elizabeth noted that she still knew very little about him, but was looking forward to finding out all there was to know once this mess with William was cleared up. "How long do you think the windows will take?"

He shrugged slightly. "Day or two at the most. Maybe one day we'll be able to afford real glass but right now, we'll make do with the screening."

"That's fine. The air will come in but the skeeters will stay out."

He toasted her with a fork full of mashed potatoes. "Amen!"

So for the next two days, Jordan worked on sawing in the frames for the new windows, and she tried not to think about William as she resumed her daily routine of tending her crops during the day and working in the house when it got too hot to be in the fields. Drought and insects were the bane of farmers, and Northwest Kansas had plenty of both. It hadn't rained in days and because the windmill still had to be repaired, she was forced to flood the irrigation ditches between the rows of wheat and corn by hand. It was back-breaking work carrying bucket after bucket, then walking back to the pump to start all over again, but it had to be done.

"Why don't you let me do that?" Jordan asked, coming out to the field that morning. The corn was almost harvest ready, but the husks were beginning to show the effects of the drought.

She shook her head. "You finish the windows. I'm fine."

He looked her over. She was wearing a hat, a long sleeve blouse and a long skirt. Just thinking about how hot she must be under all those clothes made him want to wilt. He was also willing to bet she had on that damn corset, too. "Then let me pump your water for a while so you can catch your breath. You're going to get sun stroke out here."

"I'm fine, Jordan. Who do you think did this after William left and before you came? I'm not a hot house flower."

"No, you're not, but you're not made of stone, either. Stop for a minute."

He heard the frustrated sigh and he shook his head. "Am I married to a stubborn woman as well?"

Her chin went up.

"Answer's yes. Okay. When you fall out, send Douglass or one of the chickens round to get me. I'll be finishing up the windows." And he strode away.

Grumbling to herself, Elizabeth went back to the pump.

That evening, Elizabeth's monthly started. She went to the bedroom for her rags, and after pinning one to her drawers, she laid down. She'd had very little to say to Jordan after that morning's spat at the pump, but he'd been right, she'd pushed herself too hard, and now she wished she'd listened.

When he entered the bedroom a few minutes later and saw her lying face down on the bed, he came over asking with concern, "What's wrong? Are you okay?"

She met his eyes with a small smile. "Is this the type of marriage where the wife can talk to her husband about her monthly?"

He sat down on the bed, then gently rubbed her back. "Yes, it is."

"Then that's what's wrong with me."

He leaned down and kissed her cheek. "Anything I can do? My mother always had my father make her tea. Do you have any? I'll make you some."

"In the cupboard in the kitchen.

"Do you have any bourbon?"

Elizabeth turned and stared. "Bourbon."

"Yes, he always put a shot or bourbon in it. Mama said it helped her sleep."

Elizabeth had never heard of such a thing, but if bourbon would relieve the cramping enough to let her sleep, she'd drink a bottle. "Look in the sideboard in the parlor. William always had a bit of liquor to toast the New Year, but I'm not sure what kind."

"I'll check and be right back."

As he left the room, she called to him, "Jordan?"

He stopped and turned back. "Yeah?"

"Thank you."

He winked. "You bet."

Chapter Six

Saturday morning, Wex Anderson rode out to their place. Elizabeth and Jordan who were seated on the porch having breakfast greeted his arrival with a smile.

"Morning, Wex," Jordan said setting his plate aside.

"Morning, marshal. Miss Elizabeth. Sorry to bother you folks so early, but thought you might want to see this."

He handed Jordan the latest edition of Boyle's newspaper. Filled with foreboding, waited as Jordan read silently. When he was done, he handed it to her and said, tersely, "Good thing I'm not allowed to carry a firearm."

Elizabeth read:

The scandal surrounding Elizabeth Franklin heightened today with the return of her true husband, Mr. William Franklin. Contrary to popular belief, Mr. Franklin did not leave his wife last winter never intending to return, but was merely back East seeing to family business. He was outraged to learn of the lies his wife has spread about him and furious to find her living with another man she now calls her husband. When this reporter and the Reverend Smalls approached Mrs. Franklin about her decision to take convicted prisoner Jordan Yancy into her home, we were given short shrift by her and her prisoner lover and sent on our way. Such sinful conduct should not be tolerated in the God-fearing community of Turner. Mr. Franklin plans to have Yancy removed from his home by the courts if necessary.

Elizabeth had never experienced such anger. She looked into Jordan's wintry eyes and knew that his fury equaled her own. "So are they going to run me out of town?" she asked Mr. Anderson.

"Boyle should be the one," he told her. "But yes, some folks are talking about shunning you until this is settled."

Elizabeth's tight jaw showed her mood. "Boyle is a liar and so is William. I have William's letter to me as proof."

"You may have to show it around to stop all the talk this is going to cause. Boyle's out delivering the paper now."

Jordan said, "Thanks for bringing it by, Wex."

"You're welcome, marshal. Hate to see your name dragged in the mud after all you've been through. You, too, Miss Elizabeth."

"Thank you, Mr. Anderson."

"I need to get back to the store. You two stay well."

With a wave, he drove off.

"My fists want to have a talk with Mr. Howard College."

"How can William lie that way?"

Jordan shook his head. "I don't know. Maybe I should move out until this is settled."

"No. You are my husband. William can make all the claims he wants; I have his letter. That has to mean something."

"I don't like you being maligned this way."

"Neither do I, but the horse is out of the barn. Whether you stay or leave won't matter to the gossips."

"Are William and Boyle friends?"

She looked down at Boyle's paper. "Apparently so."

"What do you want to do?"

"Keep finding our way."

He pulled her into his arms and held her tight. "Then I'll stay right here by your side."

Elizabeth smiled.

They went to church on Sunday. Elizabeth, dressed in her best green dress and matching hat could see the parishioners straining to get a good look as she and Jordan found a seat in the pews. The Turner AME church wasn't large in size or in members, but it served as the spoke of their small community and everyone attended. She saw William seated up front and thought that a good place for such a sinner to be.

As the service began, the reverend looked out into the pews, and when his eyes met Elizabeth's his lip curled with disdain. She didn't cringe or drop her gaze because she had done nothing to be ashamed of in spite of what he seemed to think, but what he thought came out in a fiery sermon on the wages of sin and a woman's duty to her husband. Everyone knew whom the sermon was directed at, and it took all Elizabeth had inside to sit there in silence while being so publicly humiliated.

After the service, she and Jordan stepped outside to drink punch with the rest of the congregation during the social hour, she refused to tuck tail and run, but very few people came over to introduce themselves to Jordan or to say hello.

Mathias Boyle strolled over and said, "Morning, Elizabeth."

"Mr. Boyle."

"How're things, Yancy?"

"Just fine," Jordan lied. "How's the newspaper business?"

"Doing well as you probably read."

Elizabeth said coldy, "How can you print something filled with so many untruths?"

"I don't print lies, Elizabeth. Are you not married to two men?"

"No, Mr. Boyle, only one."

"According to William, you are."

"So you've decided to take his word over mine?"

"Of course he has," William said, walking up behind them. "A woman's word isn't worth much, now is it?"

Jordan growled, "Move along, both of you."

Boyle smiled. "Sure." Whistling, he walked away.

William stood there for a moment, then he smiled and moved on.

"Little varmints," Elizabeth said. She could see folks watching and whispering. "Let's go home."

"I'm more than ready."

And he was. Jordan wanted to take a bullwhip to William, Boyle and the damned preacher Smalls. Hearing Smalls publicly berate

Elizabeth and not be able to do anything about it was the hardest thing he'd had to do since walking into the penitentiary. It was plain whose side the reverend was on, and it was plain that most of the congregation supported his view. Once again, he thought moving out would be the best thing.

As he drove them home, he said, "You might want to reconsider my offer to take a room in town."

"No. Isn't your parole contingent on being married to me?"

"I'm sure it is, but folks are treating you this way because of me."

"Folks are treating me this way because William is lying, and I will not give them credence by having you move into town."

Jordan had to admire her spunk.

"Do me a favor?" he asked.

"What is it?"

"Promise me not to mention William or Boyle anymore today, and I'll promise you the same."

"You have a deal."

"Thank you."

The sky was clouding up by the time they reached the farm, and it looked as if all the prayers for rain were about to be answered. After changing out of their church clothes, they went to the barn to bring out the four large barrels she used to collect rain water for baths, washing her hair and irrigating the crops during dry times. They'd been empty for weeks now, but she hoped it would rain enough to refill them. After getting them positioned, and securing the animals, Elizabeth and Jordan sat on the settee to watch the storm roll in.

Storms were another manifestation of nature Jordan hadn't seen much during his time in prison and this one would be his first as a freed man. In the distance dancing streaks of lightning flashed in the sky, followed by the faint booms of thunder. Dark clouds continued to form and were making their way across the plains. He found the sight almost as moving as his need to make love to his wife. It had been four long days since her monthly came to town and after they'd made their pact he'd spent the rest of the ride home from church trying to come up with a tactful way to ask if things were back to normal. Although they hadn't been man and wife for very long, he'd become accustomed not only to her company, but to touching, kissing and teasing her into participating in scandalous behavior.

Elizabeth enjoyed being held close to his side and the companionable silence. The air was electric with the approaching storm and being near him was making her senses stir. Her monthly stopped its flow last night, so they were free to resume their lovemaking. She'd debated with herself whether to tell him or not, but because she didn't want to seem forward, she'd kept quiet. Now, as the storm drew closer and the wind began to blow across the porch, she decided to come right out with it. "My monthly left last night."

His hands shot up. "Hallelujah!"

She laughed. "You are the most outrageous man."

"And I'm ready to make you do the most outrageous things."

The promise in his voice coupled with the intensity in his eyes set off a flare in her blood that warmed her everywhere. "Oh, really?" she whispered.

"Yes, ma'am."

The sky was now as dark as evening, and the lightning and thunder were doing Mother Nature's version of call and response. A particularly vivid shard of lightning struck the ground about a mile away and the low growl of the thunder shook the house. Jordan ran an adoring finger down her brown cheek, then over her lips. "We should go inside. I'd love to have you out here in the rain, but not with all these fireworks."

She nodded and let him lead her into the house.

Their bedroom was airy and cool thanks to the storm and the new screened window. He eased her against his tall hard frame and kissed her with a desire pent up for four days. She met him with a longing of her own and the embrace deepened to the sounds of raindrops pelting the roof.

Fueled by the urge to touch him, Elizabeth began to undo the buttons on his shirt surprising both herself and him with the bold move. When she finished, she toured her hand up and down his strong chest, then leaned up and kissed him passionately. He pulled her closer, infected by her nearness and flicked his tongue against the parted corners of her mouth while circling his palm over her hips.

They moved to the bed where he spent an inordinate amount of time removing her blouse and then her skirt. He gave her breasts their pent-up tributes, then worked her drawers down her hips and off. For the very first time, he viewed in all of her nude beauty and she let him look, touch and kiss because she was no longer ashamed of being the lover he wanted her to be. The hand now between her legs cajoled her to open wider and she complied willingly. He teased fingers through her damp hair, sending her desire higher and when he leaned over and slid his tongue around the recessed whorl of her navel, her body arched in shimmering response.

He loved how wet she was. It was an indication of his ability to please her and how much she was enjoying this. "Ready for more scandalous behavior?"

Her body answered by rising greedily to his play because a verbal reply was beyond her at that moment. He rubbed a slow thumb over the swollen pulsing bud at the gate of her core and she purred deep in her throat and spread her legs wider. He couldn't resist. Bending low, he planted a kiss on the tender inner skin of her parted limbs then gave her the most carnal kiss of all.

She froze and backed way all in one quick motion. Her eyes wide with shock met his smiling ones. "No." she declared in hushed surprise.

"Yes," he countered with knowing amusement. "Didn't I promise to love you—everywhere?"

She was staring at him as if he'd suddenly grown another arm. "But—?"

"But what? Come here, darling'." He put his hands on her hips and brought her back down the bed. She looked up at him with the same wonder on her face and he couldn't hide his smile, "Trust me," he told her. "If you don't like it. I'll stop."

Outside the storm was raging with wind, thunder and rain, while inside a more sensual storm was brewing. To make her ready again, his mouth and his hands worked their magic down the front plane of her body, stopping to make sure her nipples stayed hard and tight the way he liked, then with his fingers between her thighs invited her to open for him. She complied just as willingly as she'd done before because her desire would not be denied.

When he tasted her this time, she didn't pull away, the sensations were too intense; too dazzling. The loving was raw, hot. Never in her wildest dreams would she have imagined an act like this and soon all thoughts melted away as she rose and fell to his magnificent conquering. She was gasping, twisting, crooning. Nothing could have prepared for his wicked feasting, his sucking, his tongue. She felt delirious, feverish and when he took that tiny nubbin of flesh into his mouth and then circled it with his tongue, she didn't even feel the fingers he was impaling her with because she was screaming and coming and shuddering.

He thrust himself inside of her and savored with his eyes closed the feel of her still rippling flesh tighten around him. She was so hot and wet he began thrusting immediately. There was no room for tenderness and care; this was pure hard lust, and he stroked her with the rumbling power of his own inner storm. When the orgasms shattered their world, not even the noise of the storm raging outside could mask their loud cries of release.

The storm outside moved on, leaving behind the sounds of the rain softly hitting the roof to mingle with the bedroom's silence. Elizabeth and Jordan were lying side-by-side, spent and content. He turned his head so he could look into the passion lidded eyes of his wife, then asked, "So, am I going to have any more trouble out of you the next time I want to do that?"

Still reeling from his wicked kisses, she chuckled quietly. "No, sir."

"Good, because I plan on doing that a lot."

The promise in his voice made her thighs tighten in anticipation. "More scandalous behavior."

"Until death do us part."

Her eyes were serious. "You mean that?"

"I do. When we're old and gray, I'll still be tossing up your skirts looking for treasure."

Shaking with humor, she shook her head. "What am I going to do with you?"

He reached over and pulled her on top of him. "Don't rightly know, but I know what I want to do with you."

Easing his manhood inside the tight sweet path to paradise, he then spent the rest of the evening proving his point.

The next morning, they went out to see if the place had incurred any damage from the storm. They were pleased to find nothing more serious than a few shingles blown off of the roof. Jordan was up there making repairs when Sheriff Cody rode up. Elizabeth set aside the bowl of peas she was shelling and stood to greet him. "Morning, sheriff. "

He touched his weather beaten hat. "Morning, Miss Elizabeth."

"What brings you here?"

"Need to talk to your man."

Jordan called out. "Morning."

The sheriff acknowledged him, then reached into his saddlebag and removed a long brown envelope. "Got something for you, Yancy. Or should I say, marshal?"

Jordan came down the ladder.

The sheriff asked. "Why didn't you tell me you were a lawman?"

"Would it have mattered?"

Their eyes met for a long moment, but Cody didn't answer. "This came for you today."

Jordan took the envelope. As he opened it and withdrew some documents. the sheriff said, "Copy of your pardon. They sent me one, too, along with this." Cody handed him a brand new marshal star. "Took a while for all the paperwork to come together I guess."

While Jordan looked down at the star in his hand, and contemplated what it meant, Cody asked, "Why didn't you tell the warden you'd been pardoned?"

"After the guards brought me back from meeting with the judge, I did, but the judge didn't give me anything to show the warden so the man didn't believe me. Judge said the papers would come in a few days, but they never did far as I knew."

"Somebody must have known something," Cody replied. "Otherwise, your name wouldn't have been placed on the prisoner marriage-law list. Sounds like someone was trying to cover up all the mistakes that got you railroaded in the first place."

Jordan didn't know or care. All he could see was the star in his hand. Because of the pervasive Jim Crows blanketing the country he might never have the opportunity to be a marshal anywhere ever again, but the star represented his honor and not even Jim Crow could negate that. He looked up at his wife. He couldn't wait to celebrate. Maybe they'd dip into William's holiday liquor and toast his now official freedom. William would probably throw a fit, but who cared about him?

Cody's voice broke into his reverie. "You can start carrying a firearm any time you like, and according to those papers, you can leave the state if you so choose."

Elizabeth felt ice form in her heart. Would he leave now that he was no longer mandated to stay? Rather than deal with that issue now, she needed answers to another matter that was equally as important. "How does this affect the titling of my land?" she asked. "You said that by my agreeing to the marriage, the land would be mine free and clear."

"Judge says it's yours whether Yancy stays or not."

That gave her a modicum of relief, but the question remained. Would Jordan stay?

Jordan saw that the light had gone out of her eyes. He knew what was worrying her and he planned to talk it over with her just as soon as he could. Turning to Cody, he said, "Thanks for bringing this out. Changes a lot of things."

Cody glanced over at Elizabeth for a moment then brought his attention back to Jordan. "I'm in need of a good deputy. If you want a job, it's yours. And no offense to Mr. Boyle, but I don't believe everything I read in the papers.

Jordan nodded. "Thanks."

Elizabeth asked, "Has William been to see you?"

"Yes, ma'am. He asked my opinion. When I told him I'd seen the letter he sent to you asking for the divorce, he stormed out. You folks have a good day."

He rode away.

Jordan and Elizabeth were left contemplating each other. She broke the silence first. "Now you have solid proof of your innocence."

"Grateful for it, too."

So that there would be no confusion, he said, "This pardon won't change what's between us Elizabeth."

The searing emotions closed her eyes. Having him stay meant she would not have to return to a solitary life on the plains and endure the awful loneliness. "Good," she whispered.

He held out his arms and she went to him and let herself be enfolded against his heart. "Til death do us part, remember?"

She looked up with tear-bright eyes and nodded. It came to her then that she was in love with this man. Even though she hadn't known him long, she loved him as if they'd been together throughout time. She slipped her arms around his waist and hugged him tight. If he never returned her feelings it wouldn't change how she felt. He cared enough to remain at her side and for Elizabeth that was enough.

That night as they lay in bed, she asked, "Are you going to take the sheriff up on his offer?"

"I don't know. Times are changing. In some places, marshals who look like me aren't allowed to enforce the law against people outside of the race. I'll ride to town tomorrow and see where he stands. Be nice to have work so I can start taking care of my wife."

She decided to tell him about her nest egg and his response surprised her.

"Glad to know that, but you keep the account in your name. Never know what the future holds. I could get hurt, die and you'd maybe wish you still had those funds to call on. We'll use them only if we have to. Okay?"

She nodded. His unselfish attitude made her love him all the more.

Later, as Jordan held his sleeping wife, he realized that being here with her had become his life. The courts had given him sanction to reclaim his star, to strap on a firearm and to leave Kansas if that was what he wanted, but what he wanted he already had—Elizabeth. With her big words, good cooking and innocent ways, she'd given him a home. She'd also given herself when there was nothing that demanded she do so. The day he left prison who knew she'd be waiting at the end of the line? From her biscuits to her corset, she'd become his entire world. Leaving her never crossed his mind. No matter the challenges ahead, he would always be at her side. *Til death do us part.*

Prisoner

The next morning, Elizabeth pulled out her soaps and wooden tubs in preparation for wash day. She and Jordan didn't own a lot of clothing but when one added in the sheets, pillow slips, towels and tablecloths, it became an all-day task. She had on one of her oldest gowns, and she didn't look forward to the sore red hands she'd have because of the lye soap, but clean clothes were a necessity. Jordan had already left for town to see Cody about the deputy job, and as she scrubbed one of his double-breasted shirts on the metal washboard, she hoped the discussion would go well.

It did. Jordan returned home later that afternoon as the newly appointed deputy of Turner, Kansas. He was so anxious to tell Elizabeth the good news that he yelled her name excitedly just as soon as he set the brake. He ran around to the back of the house thinking she was still doing the wash, but all he saw were the clothes lines filled with laundry drying in the breeze.

So into the house he went. Still calling her name he barreled into the bedroom and the sight of her languishing in the big claw foot tub, froze him in mid step. "My, my, my," he whispered appreciatively.

Elizabeth dropped her head. She had not intended him to find her this way. The wash hadn't taken as long she'd thought, so she'd treated her sweaty body to a tub bath and followed it up with this second tub of scented water just to soak in. She could smell the fragrance of the salts permeating the room, and she assumed he could as well, just as he undoubtedly could see the way her nipples had blossomed the moment he appeared in the doorway.

A delighted Jordan walked over to the tub and took a seat on the narrow edge. He ran admiring eyes over her glistening skin then sent a finger over the rounded silk of her shoulder. "I took the job."

"That's wonderful news."

"I start in the morning."

The finger lightly traced the bones at the base of her throat before tracking down to an already berried nipple. Leaning in, he sucked at it softly before moving over to treat its twin to the same silent, hello. Her head back against the lip of the tub, Elizabeth purred as her desire awakened and rose. The finger commenced its traveling, over and around her breasts, then down the space between to tease her navel hidden just below the water line. It slipped lower and she shamelessly parted her legs to facilitate its exploration. He rewarded her famously, and before she knew it, she was panting and rising in response to his hypnotic underwater coaxing.

"Stand for me," he invited quietly.

She complied and the scented water cascaded down her legs. He ran a lusty hand over her wet hips and up her back then back down over her hips. He moved his touch between her legs and asked, "Do you want to be made love to…"

Elizabeth was melting, and yes, she wanted him.

The hand between her thighs was doing marvelously scandalous things and she didn't know how much longer her legs would support her trembling weight.

"Then say, Jordan make love to me."

"Jordan…please…" She could feel her orgasm gathering.

"Please what…"

Impaled she rippled. "Make love to me."

She was wet and ripe, and Jordan was hard as the branch of a hundred year old oak. "Think I'll taste you first. Would you like that?"

Elizabeth wondered if she'd ever become immune to this. She prayed she would not.

"You have to answer me, darlin'. " He put his tongue against her navel and showed her just how he planned to sample her sweetness. To further entice her, he began moving his fingers in and out with a lazy erotic rhythm that made her gasp. "Say, taste me, lick me…"

In the end, Elizabeth said that, and more, so he carried her to the bed and laid her down. When she spread her legs, he gave her everything she'd asked for.

Chapter Seven

In the weeks that followed, Elizabeth and Jordan settled into a relationship of ease and contentment. He spent his days in town as the new deputy and she worked on getting the crops ready for the upcoming harvest. At night they concentrated on each other and engaging in scandalous behavior. William had supposedly left town to go to Lawrence to see a lawyer. Elizabeth refused to let thoughts of what he might really be up to ruin her happiness.

That afternoon while Jordan was away at work, she was surprised to see Adelaide Henry drive up. "To what do I owe this pleasure?" Elizabeth asked.

"Sheriff Cody says you have a letter?"

Elizabeth went still. "William's letter?"

"Yes. May I read it?"

"Come on in."

After seeing Adelaide into the parlor, Elizabeth went into her bedroom for the letter. When she returned she handed it over, and Adelaide read it, then gave it back. "So he and Boyle have been lying to everyone."

"Yes, ma'am."

"Then on behalf of the town, please accept my apology."

"That isn't necessary."

"Of course it is. Gossip has attached itself to your name like fleas on a dog, but once I am done it will stop."

"What are you planning to do, if I may ask?"

"You may. I will begin by shutting down Mr. Boyle's printing press."

"Can you do that?"

She nodded. "Those presses belonged to my late husband. He ran the paper before I hired Mr. Boyle, and as of today, Mr. Boyle will be looking for other employment. I will not have the paper I own used for nefarious purposes."

"I thought he owned the paper."

"That's because you haven't been living here long enough to know. Boyle is an employee." She stood. "Again, Elizabeth. My apologies. Mr. Boyle's last act as my employee will be to publish a retraction and an apology. Tell that handsome husband of yours he has my regards."

"Yes, ma'am."

Adelaide drove away and left a grinning Elizabeth standing on the porch.

The retraction was printed in the next edition. Boyle apologized for his part in the trashing of Elizabeth's reputation and begged her forgiveness. He didn't mention he'd been fired, but neither Elizabeth nor Jordan cared.

Two days later, Jordan finally received a response to the letter he'd written to his parents right after receiving his official pardon, and they wrote back to say how happy they were to learn he'd been freed, and how much they wanted to meet Elizabeth.

"When do you think we can go and see them?" Elizabeth asked him one night as they lay in bed after yet another memorable bout of lovemaking.

"Spring maybe, so we can avoid having to travel during the winter weather."

"I'd like to go to Cleveland to see my father and sisters, if we can. They're anxious to meet you." She'd written to her family about her new marriage, and they'd all sent back their blessings.

"Don't see why not. Looking forward to meeting them, too."

She smiled and cuddled close. "You're a good husband, Jordan Yancy."

He kissed the top of her head. "Told you I would be."

A few minutes later, they were both asleep.

Harvest was a community affair. Gangs of men and machines traveled from farm to farm across the region, lending assistance to those needing it. Every year when the last crops were sent to market, Adelaide Henry threw a party to celebrate. It was a gathering started by her late husband Martin, one of the town's founders, and after his death she'd kept up the tradition.

"So everyone's invited to this shindig?" Jordan asked as he put on the fancy string tie that Elizabeth had purchased for him as a gift a few weeks back.

"Everyone," she echoed as she slipped into the matching skirt and high collared jacket she been sewing on for the past two weeks. The wives of some of the wealthier farmers would be decked out in their sequins and jewels, but since Elizabeth had neither she settled on a pattern for an outfit she could also wear to church. Like most of the women in the area, she didn't have the funds to invest in a dress she would only wear occasionally.

"You look nice in blue," Jordan said to her.

"Thank you. You look pretty fine yourself." And he did. In his newly purchased suit and new boots, she was sure he'd be the most handsome man there.

"Got you something." He took a small velvet box out of his pocket and handed it to her.

The small heart shaped locket inside was the most beautiful keepsake she'd ever seen. Moved by his sentiment, she looked up and said, "Thank you, Jordan. It's very beautiful."

"Here. Let me help you put it on."

He did the clasp for her and she moved her fingers over its shape as it settled into place.

"I had the man put your initials on the back."

She turned it over and saw E Y monogrammed in a flowing script. Raising herself on her toes, she gave him a warm kiss of thanks and declared herself the happiest woman in Kansas.

On the ride out to Adelaide's, Jordan debated with himself whether to tell Elizabeth whether he loved her or not. He'd never said I love you to a woman before, and he knew that some men would rather have a case of the clap than utter the phrase, but he loved her like he loved breathing. She was spirited, smart and so confident, she'd done her own negotiating for the price of the crops she'd sent to market. She was good in the kitchen, uninhibited in the bedroom and when he added all of those attributes together, how could he not love her? What he didn't know was whether she felt the same way about him. He sensed that she did, but he didn't want to put a fly in the ointment of a perfectly fine arrangement if he turned out to be wrong. So, he kept his feelings to himself.

Just as Elizabeth had predicted, everyone in the area was at Adelaide's for the annual Harvest Dance. There were fiddlers and dancing, and the succulent smell of the meat cooking on spits and in pits filled the air. Children played tag and had foot races. Men lined up for the annual horseshoe competition while the women tended the many dishes of food and desserts spread out over the two long trestle tables. Prizes were awarded for the largest vegetables, the tallest sunflower and the best tasting pies and jams. Elizabeth and Jordan waded through the crowd, stopping here and there to greet the people they knew, and like everyone, had a great time.

When it was over, they drove home under the light of a fat full moon. Elizabeth was cuddled against his side and wondered if there was any way possible she could be any happier. "I think I ate too much."

He grinned. "Probably all that pie."

"And ham and string beans, and cake and ice cream. It usually takes folks a few days to recover after Adelaide's wing ding."

"I can see why." He looked down at her, "Do you have my blue ribbon?" He'd won the horseshoe toss.

"I do indeed. Planning to display it prominently on the mantle. Now everybody knows that in addition to being a top notch lawman, you can fling a horseshoe to Texas."

He chuckled. Jordan had been puffed up with pride squiring her around the gathering. When she planted a kiss on his cheek for winning the horseshoe toss the envy he saw in the eyes of some of the single men had stroked the male in him. All in all, he'd had a good time, and he knew just how to make the day complete. "Ever made love in a buggy?" he asked slyly.

She laughed. "No."

"Would you like to?"

She dropped her head and her shoulders shook with humor. "And if I said, no?"

"Then I guess I'll just have to stop driving and see if I can't convince you."

As always, Elizabeth thought he was the most outrageous man she'd ever known, and she loved every Texas inch of him. No longer reticent about their physical relationship, she reached down and took hold of that portion of his anatomy that she found the most satisfying. Moving her hand over him just the way he liked, she felt him swell and harden in sensual response.

He sighed pleasurably.

"Like that, do you?"

He leaned back and the reins slipped from his hands. The mare stopped, but Elizabeth didn't. Nimble fingers undid the placard of his pants, then giving her husband a sultry moonlit smile, she lowered her head to his lap. He groaned but that didn't stop her either. With her hand grasping the thick base and the velvety hard top in her mouth, she treated him to some very scandalous behavior indeed; behavior that closed his eyes and put a rhythm in his hips. "Damn, woman…"

"Don't curse," she admonished with a smile, then resumed her conquering.

Jordan could have spent the rest of eternity right there on the seat, but there was something he wanted more. Pulling away from her hot little mouth in order to keep from coming, he said thickly. "Come here…"

He made her stand, then raised her skirts. The first touch made him freeze. When he looked up she was smiling serenely in the moonlight. "Elizabeth Yancy, where are your drawers?"

She straddled him on the seat and the slowly lowered herself on the hard dark root she'd prepared so carnally. "I must have forgotten to put them on," she whispered in reaction to the bliss she was taking in.

"And you call me outrageous."

No more words were shared. They were too busy rising and falling. Somewhere along the way, her jacket was opened, then tossed aside. Her corset cover went next and there she was riding her husband with her torn open corset and her breasts in his mouth and hands. She screamed out her pleasure when the powerful orgasm grabbed her and as she rippled and shuddered in response, he clutched her hips and worked her until his male roar rolled across the empty plains.

And he wasn't done. Making her switch places, he filled her as she sat on the seat, then took her again as she stood with her back to him. Each orgasm surpassed the last with its force and strength, and when they'd finally, finally gotten enough of each other, Jordan kissed his scandalous wife, then picked up the reins and drove home.

Lost in the haze of desire, Elizabeth didn't protest when he reached in and picked her up. She didn't care that her breasts were exposed by her ripped corset. She was too busy savoring being held close to his heart as his strong arms carried her up the steps and into the house.

They indulged in yet more scandalous behavior and when they were done, he held her in his arms. Jordan was happier than he ever imagined he could be and knew he'd shoot William personally if the man tried to mess up what he and Elizabeth had found together. "You know. I'm not sure when it happened, but I'm real in love with you, Elizabeth Yancy."

She could hear the strong beat of his heart beneath her ear. "Are you?"

He nodded, saying, "Yep."

She hugged him tight. "Good, Because I love you, too."

"Hot damn!"

"Don't swear," she responded with a laugh.

"Can't help it. It's what a man does. Name a better way."

Leaning up, she kissed him so soundly, and with so much passion Jordan seriously considered never swearing again.

The next morning as Elizabeth put the final touches on the breakfast she and Jordan would be sharing before he went off to work, she wondered how William had fixed his mind to believe she'd want him back? It wasn't as if he was a prized catch. She valued her rooster Douglass more than she did her former husband. She placed the biscuits in the oven and turned over the miniature hourglass that served as a timer. Now that she knew Jordan loved her, and she had confessed her love to him, she didn't give a bean about William; not red beans, or string beans, or beans of any kind. Jordan was her husband, and nothing on earth would change that. Nothing.

As Jordan fed the chickens, the knowledge that Elizabeth loved him was going to keep him grinning all day, but William's unexpected and unwanted arrival was not amusing. Showing up like he had upset Elizabeth, and Jordan found no humor in that, either. He wanted their marriage to be as free of anguish and distress as possible; especially now that they'd declared their mutual love. The last thing they needed was to have William find a way to cast a pall over their happiness.

They were seated at the table having breakfast when they heard the sharp knock on the door. Jordan stood to go answer the summons, and the curious Elizabeth fell in behind.

It was William, and he had with him Sheriff Cody.

Cody nodded from his side of the screen door. "Morning, Yancy. May we come in?"

Jordan opened the door and the two men stepped inside. Cody nodded politely at Elizabeth. William simply glared.

She said, "Let's go into the parlor."

After everyone was seated, the sheriff spoke. "Mr. Franklin wants to swear out a complaint against Miss Elizabeth for bigamy."

"Bigamy?" Elizabeth echoed skeptically. "Does that come before or after *abandonment* in a court of law?"

William visibly flinched under the force of her scathing tone, and Jordan smiled inwardly. He wondered how long it would take the man to finally realize that this version of Elizabeth was not the same woman he'd married.

William said, "You can't be married to two men at once."

"Then you should have filed those papers."

"How dare you snap at me that way? First I find you rutting on him like a whore—" Before he could utter another word, Jordan snatched him up and dragged him close.

Elizabeth was pleased to see William looked properly terrified.

"Apologize! Now!" Jordan snarled.

William nodded like a puppet. "I didn't mean that. I'm sorry. I am."

Jordan threw him back him into the chair with such force, the small man bounced.

Elizabeth's features were encased in ice and she was tapping her foot angrily. She came to a decision and she stood. "William, do you really want a woman carrying another man's child?"

Jordan's eyes almost popped out of his head. He stared at Elizabeth and she gave him a saucy little wink, then not caring that they weren't alone, she tossed out, "With all we've been doing, I'm probably carrying a litter of little Texans."

"Hot damn!"

Cody grinned.

William's face was livid, but Elizabeth paid that no mind. "Now, William. You should probably head back East and get those papers filed because if you don't, I will."

She saw him cast an ugly look at her still flat belly then he stood. "I'll send the papers. Let's go, sheriff."

He stormed out.

Cody stood. "Congratulations, you two. Your child is going to have a couple of fine parents."

Elizabeth was pleased by the compliment. She took a seat while Jordan walked the sheriff out to the porch.

When Jordan returned, he came and sat beside her on the parlor settee. "Are you really having a baby, or did you just say that to get William to leave?"

She shook her head. "I'm really having a baby. Your baby. Our baby. Probably late spring if my calculations are correct."

He pulled her onto his lap folded her in and she leaned back against his strong shoulder. He then placed a tender hand over her stomach. "Is there anything I need to do, should be doing?

The concern in his eyes and voice made her reach up and cup his cheek. "Nope. Right now, your only job is to love me."

He took her hand and kissed the palm. "Hell, if that's all, we have this maverick licked." Then he waggled his eyebrows. "Speaking of licks…"

She laughed and gave him a long kiss. "Behave yourself, we're going to be parents."

"Not right now, we're not."

So Jordan carried his laughing wife into the bedroom and as he placed her on the bed, Elizabeth knew she was going to love this outrageous man for the rest of her life.

GUNNS AND ROSES

by

Katherine D. Jones

Acknowledgements

To the wonderful folks at Parker Publishing, thanks a million for this opportunity. A big, big thank-you goes out to Deatri and Angelique. And also to my writing buddies Maureen Smith, Angie Daniels and Gwyneth Bolton, thank you for the late-night critique sessions! Can't wait to read your novels.

I'd also like to thank Officer Sabrina King for technical assistance and for eighteen years of friendship. To my family, of course, none of this is possible without your love and support.

Last, but certainly not least, to my fans and readers, thanks punches for your encouragement—keep the emails coming, I love the feedback.

H is hands and mouth were everywhere, touching her, caressing her, bringing her pleasure. Stephanie loved being with a man who knew how to make her feel good. She felt the moisture between her legs dripping lazily down the sides of her thighs. The scent of sex permeated the air, arousing her even more. She felt his tongue lick up the juices that flowed freely from her, then move from her thighs to her engorged lips. She shuddered in sweet agony. "More," she whispered as her body pulsed and quivered.

His laugh tickled her ears. She could tell that he enjoyed making her feel good. "Greedy, aren't you?"

Her response was buried in his kiss as he moved upward to cover her lips with his own. She tasted herself on his tongue as it searched her mouth, and she liked it. He brought her to new heights of ecstasy. She kissed him back, hard, showing him just how much she wanted him.

With him, she felt free. He had this habit of making her feel freaky—almost nothing was off limits. He knew how to play, how to bring her to the brink of sexual madness, then set her back down safely. He stroked her sensitive nub with his fingers until Stephanie moaned in pleasure. The heat continued to build between them until she neared her first orgasmic release.

The only sound in the room came from their lovemaking. She heard the slap of body against body. She felt his bare chest, rippled with muscles, close to her bare breasts. Her nipples were taut from his tongue loving them. She called out his name as her body began to shake with the involuntary shudders of her next climax. Then she heard his cries of love and devotion as he fell over the same satisfying edge.

Sweat soaked and panting, Stephanie woke. Her shoulder-length hair was a wild mess. She'd have to do the best she could to tame it into a decent ponytail. She turned her head to look at the clock; in less than an hour she'd have to get down Interstate 880 to Palo Vista Correctional Facility.

Biting back a few choice curse words, she attempted to jump out of bed. Stephanie wanted to move quickly, but her body betrayed her. This was just what she needed—to be late again. Her body still throbbed with need and desire. Why did Bryant Wilson invade her dreams nightly?

Bryant cringed as he read the sign. Palo Vista Correctional Facility. Each time he saw the sign, he felt a stabbing pain in his heart. This was one place he never thought he'd be.

He reached the visitor receiving area, an unwelcoming cramped room set up to hold people while they were processed. He resisted the urge to fan himself, as it wouldn't have done any good in the stifling heat of an Oakland summer. The current high temperatures that gripped the city, in an uncharacteristic heat wave, blanketed everything in searing heat.

He was thankful for the blowing air conditioning. Even though it didn't cool the place off to a more comfortable temperature—it was better than being outside.

Observing his surroundings, he didn't think he would ever get used to being a visitor here. Feeling self-conscious about his summer weight, black pin-stripped Armani suit and Cole Haan shoes, Bryant stood to the side. *I look like a lawyer*—a thought that made him shudder.

Women with babies attached to their hips waited impatiently in line. Some were dressed in their Sunday best, others were dressed in their Monday worst. It was easy to spot the ones who were tired of visiting their men in a jailhouse.

Hushed tones of English, Spanish and occasionally other languages filled the room. Finally, after what seemed like an eternity, an attractive female officer approached him. Her cocoa-brown slim-shaped beauty, especially in a place like this, struck Bryant. He'd seen her a few times in passing, but not as she conducted orientation. Usually, her uniform was crisp and pressed, but today her uniform looked as though it could use a touch from a warm iron, and she wore her hair in a ponytail. When he'd seen her before, her hair was always in a nice blunt bob style. He smiled inwardly. He knew about women and ponytails; she must have been running late.

He tore his thoughts away from her personal agenda and back to the business at hand. His days of visiting the facility would be ending soon enough.

"For those of you who may be visiting this location for the first time, my name is Officer Gunn. For those of you who have been here before, you know the drill. Please empty your pockets and remove your shoes. Place the items in one of the baskets provided for you, and then proceed one at a time through the metal detector. Please do not bunch up, as this will only cause a delay in your visitation."

Efficient without being cold, she performed her job very well. Bryant put on his best smile, designed to charm and disarm any woman. He recognized the officer as one he'd seen during his time of coming to visit his brother, but they'd never carried on a real conversation. She appeared to keep him at arm's length.

Officer Gunn arched a brow in response, but continued her spiel without missing a beat. She wouldn't give in to her carnal desire to get naked right in the middle of the room. She convinced herself to act as naturally as she could. Yes he was fine, yes she wanted him, and yes it was wrong to fantasize about an inmate's friend or relative. But damn what's right! She was hot and horny and all she could think about was satisfaction—and he was the one to give it to her. She inhaled deeply, then exhaled, forcing her thoughts back in control. Once she felt better, she continued with her duties.

Stephanie kept her voice low. "You will proceed downstairs to the visitation room. Make sure that you have your paperwork with you before entering the room, and make sure you adhere to all the rules posted around the room. Thank you for your attention, and have a good day."

Bryant watched the young woman with obvious interest. Despite her unflattering uniform, her curvaceous figure was perfectly evident. He studied her the way he would any woman, but she didn't seem too flattered by his *appreciation* of her.

Bryant put his paper down to shake her hand.

"Sir, I need you to keep moving in order not to hold up the line, thank you."

Bryant gathered his pride and proceeded through the processing area. He didn't know why she always rebuffed his attempts to be friendly. He'd been to the jail at least half a dozen times. This was the fourth time he'd seen her, too. He was interested, and that's all he wanted her to know.

"Gunn, someone left his visitation paper. Will you check the name so that they won't have to call up here?" Officer Eason shook his head. "How many times do we have to remind them?"

Stephanie read Wilson, the last name on the paper. "I'll take it down there," she volunteered.

Eason smirked. Stephanie was not known for being the type to volunteer—at least for no reason.

The visitation room was large with few windows. Not cheery or homey by any stretch of the imagination. Old tables with even older cushioned gray metal chairs performed their function and nothing more. Stephanie had never been fond of the space, but it was all part of the job. One day she would work in a beautiful environment, someplace with life and happiness, she thought. Stephanie sighed. But it wouldn't be any time soon. According to her watch, she had two more hours until the end of her shift.

At the doorway, she watched as Mac and his brother talked. She hated to admit it, but Bryant was one fine male specimen. *If you like thugs*, she reminded herself. But still…there was something strangely appealing about his shoulder-length dreadlocks, his tall stature, well-muscled lean body and sensual brown eyes. When he'd attempted to flirt with her earlier, it was as if he had the ability to look right through her. He could never know his effect on her though, how she fantasized about being with him every night.

A feeling of slight disappointment washed over her. He must have coaxed one of the other guards in charge of visitation because without his paperwork, he shouldn't be sitting across from his brother right now. Disgusted, she thought, *yet someone else in the jail that didn't follow policy.* Stephanie shook her head, and took a deep breath.

Mac noticed her approaching him. His wide face lit up as he did. Stephanie pushed the air out of her lungs. Macklin Wilson was the kind of guy who had it all, but threw it away on fast women, fast cars and fast cash. He had a basketball scholarship to be a Duke Blue Devil, but after one semester he was back home at his parents' house waiting for the next golden opportunity to fall into his lap. Mac had talent, good looks and charm, but the work ethic of a slug.

Stephanie had watched him during his incarceration. He still treated everyone as his personal servant. Still ran game from the inside, and everyone knew it. Despite the fact that officers were supposed to be able to remain objective, she despised Mac. His kind made her life miserable. The drugs, the peddling in human flesh, the complete disregard for human life—Mac stood for what was wrong in her Oakland community.

Worse yet, he was one of the lucky ones—he'd had it all in his younger days, and the fact that he had *chosen* to throw it all away in favor of instant gratification rankled her. This was his third incarceration for drug dealing amongst his other charges.

Bryant tried to focus on his conversation with Mac. He had to let the fact that he was in jail again roll off his back, but anger tinged his tone anyway. His little brother, who had at least two inches on him at six foot-five inches tall, was going on and on about how he had to get him out.

"Mac, you've got six months left. Why are you making such a big deal now? With your history, you could do six months standing on your head."

"Bro, I'm telling you, there's something not right about this place. Maybe you can get me on work furlough or something? I don't need to be here all day. I've heard rumblings."

Bryant wanted to be patient, but he was tired of driving from jail to jail to visit his brother. "Mac, I'll see what I can do. But after this, you're on your own. You know I love you, man, but you're breaking my heart. This is the last time I'm coming to some damned jail to talk to you. Six months—then never again. This is killing Mom and Pops."

Mac looked down at his massive hands. His normally well-manicured fingernails were now bitten down to jagged edges. "Binky, you know I wouldn't ask if it wasn't important."

Bryant glared at his brother. "I ought to knock you out of that chair. You know you're never to call me that in public. You must really be desperate." After a moment of thought, he blew out a breath. "What exactly has you so nervous?"

Mac wasn't the type to scare easily. Maybe he should listen more carefully. He started to say something more, but then he caught a whiff of the perfume that had distracted him earlier. She must be close. Bryant closed his eyes as he discreetly inhaled. When he opened his eyes again, Mac smirked at him.

"Don't even think about it, big bro. She's off limits. Besides, I don't think she's into men, though I'd like a chance to show her what she's been missing."

For reasons he couldn't quite understand, the remark made Bryant livid. He didn't even know this particular C.O., but he didn't relish the thought of her being disrespected by his brother and the other inmates in the facility. Palo Vista wasn't exactly for the hardened criminal, but these guys were no boy scouts either.

After he calmed down, he finally responded, "Fast women, expensive cars and quick money are what got you locked up in the first place. What's going to be different in six months, Mac? You still gon' be Big Mac, the man to beat on the streets? God, man, how long are you going to play this stupid ass game? You've got three kids that need you and a whole slew of other family that want you to be successful without getting into trouble. If you don't want to do it for yourself, just think about us."

Mac rubbed his hands over his jaw. "I've had plenty of time to think since I've been here, and I've thought about all that. I won't make any promises, but I don't want to see the inside of these walls again either. After I settle a few things, I'm done. For good this time, I swear."

Bryant listened as he turned around to locate the sweet-smelling officer. She had never given him the time of day before, but he hoped between now and the time that his brother's sentence was up, he'd be able to change her mind.

"You forgot this upstairs. Normally, you wouldn't have been allowed to enter the visitation room without your sheet, but I see that didn't happen today. Remember to keep this with you every time you come to visit your brother or anyone else in the facility."

Stephanie handed the piece of paper to Bryant who clasped her hand in his as he took it. The electric spark that passed between them sent awareness spiraling through their veins.

She stepped back, almost losing her balance in the process. Bryant stood up suddenly to help steady her. His large hands held her firmly in place. She felt heat creep up through her face. She couldn't be this close to him—he was going to make her lose her job.

Stephanie scrambled out of is embrace. "Thank you," she barely mumbled as she scurried out of the room.

Before she left, Stephanie stole another glimpse. *Yeah, too damn bad, he's just another thug.* She squeezed her thighs together, and scolded herself for the throbbing between her legs just from looking at the brotha. *Damn,* she thought miserably, *it's going to be one of those nights.*

"Officer Gunn, you've got to count before you get off shift."

Stephanie groaned inwardly, but walked back toward the cells. It had been a long day, and all she wanted was to jump in the shower at home to wash it all away.

Seeing Bryant after dreaming about him had unnerved her. Then adding a little contact made it worse. Soon enough, she wouldn't even be able to look at him.

Caught up in her thoughts, she was distracted while doing the inmate count. She hadn't even noticed that Mac had stepped slightly out of line. "Officer Gunn, I need to speak to you privately."

Stephanie held her clipboard out a little further to put as much distance between her and Mac as she could. He was definitely an imposing figure with his height, but she wanted him to know that she was not intimidated. "Inmate Wilson, we don't have anything to say to each other. Now back in a straight line, *please.*"

A few of the other inmates watched in amusement. Many had tried to get under her skin, but no one had been successful.

Mac scowled but remained silent for a few seconds. Finally, when no one else paid any attention to them, he approached her again. This time he tried to give her a piece of paper.

"Mac, I told you before we can't take anything from you guys. I'm not going to lose my job over you. Now get back in line and stay there."

Mac moved back into the line, but not before making one last attempt to gain her attention. "Officer Gunn, my brother doesn't believe me. I need your help. Give this to him. He'll know what to do. Please."

Stephanie finished her count, and then looked around nervously. "We shouldn't even be having this conversation. If you want to spend the next seven days in solitary, keep messing with me. Have I made myself clear?"

Mac shook his head. "Perfectly. You're just like all the other correctional officers—and my brother thinks you're different. Never mind, lady, I'll take care of this myself." Macklin glared at her as he skulked back to position.

His intensity was disconcerting, which gave Stephanie pause. Maybe she should listen to him, but he was a convict. The only time they didn't lie was when their lips weren't moving. Her thoughts were already enough to put her on thin ice, she couldn't allow her actions to complete the job.

"Inmate, that ought to tell you something. If your brother doesn't believe a word out of your lying mouth, why should I try to convince him otherwise?" She stared right back at him to let him know he didn't scare her. Finally, she said, "Now, I've got work to do."

Stephanie shuddered involuntarily under the intensity of his menacing glare. His nickname Big Mac was more than appropriate. Ordinarily, a strong, big man like Mac would turn her on, but not in this case. He was a threat to society and deserved to be exactly where he was—behind bars.

Stephanie finished the rest of her administrative functions, and went to the locker rooms to change. It was time to get out of her monkey suit. Sometimes she felt as much like an inmate than the actual inmates did. Her conversation with Mac had disturbed her.

Not so much because she felt threatened by him, but more because in some ways she felt as if she was losing herself. There was no enjoyment in her job or her life for that matter.

She changed, then closed the locker after she'd hung her uniform on her hanger. *Maybe you just need a good lay, girl. You're attitude seems to be getting worse with each day.*

Stephanie found the drive home shorter and much more pleasant than the drive coming to work. This time she wasn't worried about being late, traffic, or anything else for that matter. This was her time and relaxing felt good. It seemed that her body had been holding more tension than she'd realized. She turned up the radio, which she always had on her favorite XM station, Suite 62. Cayman Kelly's smooth baritone voice broke through the night air.

Just then her cell phone rang, interrupting her pleasant reverie. She scowled at the little contraption before she flipped it open. "This is Stephanie."

"Well, I hope so, 'cause I've been calling you for two weeks."

Stephanie sighed. "I know, Laurie. But in my defense, I've been so tired after work, I haven't been able to do anything after I get home but crash in front of the television."

"Okay, well enough of that, no television for you tonight. I have a special invitation to this new chick bar, Happitini, tonight, and I demand you go with me. As far as the friend thing goes, you've been awful, but I'm giving you tonight to make it up. Say you'll go with me and all is forgiven."

"Laurie, do we have to? I have to be up so much earlier than you do. Can't we do this another time?" She already knew her answer, but decided to ask anyway.

"No, because you say that every time. Besides, if you do this with me, I won't bug you for at least three or four more months."

Stephanie momentarily brightened. "In that case you've got yourself a deal. Just give me enough time to change."

Laurie giggled. "I'm on my way over to your place right now, so I'll wait while you get ready."

"Subtle, girl, very subtle. You just want to make sure that I don't back out. I told you I'd go, but come on over anyway. I guess it will be good to hang out with you. I have to admit I've been in some sort of funk lately. Maybe this is just what I need to pull myself out it."

She hung up the phone as she pulled into her driveway.

After a quick shower to wash off the day's dirt, she sat down at the vanity in her bathroom. Stephanie wasn't one to wear much make-up, but to go out, she would do her best to look the part. Her foundation and lipstick would be minimal, only enough to accentuate her positives, but her eyes would be dramatic and alluring. She wanted to make a statement, even if she didn't know who she would be seeing this evening.

She wondered what her friend would be wearing, knowing her, it would be something that left little to the imagination. Stephanie went to her closet to see if she would have anything comparable, a feat that required she delve deep into the crevices of the space.

Laurie arrived about twenty minutes after Stephanie and made herself at home. When Stephanie came down the stairs, her friend was already helping herself to some cold fruit.

She smiled inwardly. Laurie's outfit was exactly what she'd expected. Her shoulder-length hair was pulled into an updo, with black tendrils cascading down the sides of her face. Her M.A.C. makeup was flawless, and she'd added about three inches to her five foot nine height with her black strappy heels. Her dress, which gave new meaning to the notion of a little black dress, hugged every curve and dip of her body. She looked hot and she knew it.

Stephanie breathed out slowly. But tonight she would give the girl a run for her money. At the foot of the stairs she twirled around to give Laurie the full view; she was pleased with her friend's response.

"Wow! You look fantastic. Now, that's what I'm talking about. You've outdone yourself with that outfit, girl. Little skanky, dontcha think? Ooo wee, we're gonna to have all the fellas chasing us tonight."

Stephanie smirked. "Don't you get it, girl. I don't want to be hounded by two legged creatures acting like four-legged ones. I'm not looking for a relationship. I'm taking a much needed break."

It was Laurie's turn to smirk. "I didn't say anything about a relationship. I'm talking about *sex*, pure and simple. The kind of sexercise that has you swinging from the rafters, soaking the bed with sweat, and calling out his name in wild guttural tones. Hell, it don't even have to be his name, just call somebody!"

"Issues and problems," Stephanie responded. "That's what you have. Now, let's get out of here before I change my mind."

"Maybe I do, but at least I'm not hiding away in some jail. I'm living my life to the fullest. When are you going to give that job up anyway? You need to be in a corporate setting where you see positive men. Not those damn jail birds."

Oh where are the violins? This was the same conversation she carried on each week with her mother and brothers.

"Once I finished my degree I thought I would have moved on, too, but for right now, this is where I am. I'm comfortable there, and my coworkers leave me alone for the most part. If I move to another job, there's no telling what kind of drama I'll find there." She sighed. "So, you just do your thing and I'll do mine." She added a little more emphatically before her friend could get on her soapbox. "Now, let's go, or I'm taking off this dress and watching Lifetime movies before I go to bed."

Laurie smirked, but kept her opinion to herself. She took the hint and a few minutes later, she and Stephanie were on the way toward the city.

"Are you sure this is the place?"

Laurie laughed. "When have I ever let you down? Of course this is the place. Now quit being so lame. We're going to have a great time. I demand it."

Stephanie didn't quite know how to respond to her friend. Yeah she was always good for a laugh. But Stephanie didn't know if she wanted to be the next good-time girl like her. "You've been doing a lot of demanding lately. So tell me, what's gotten into you?"

"Girl, I'm just spreading my wings. My company has been trying to work the black off me. I suppose I want to get out more…have some fun before my life passes me by. Know what I mean? This year I'll be the big 3-0. I'd like to feel as if I have something to live for or at least like I've accomplished something. I'm not trying to get all deep and philosophical here, but I want more." Laurie smiled. "No, I demand more."

"I do know what you mean." Stephanie nodded her head. "Sometimes I get depressed about my life. I don't do anything but work, eat and sleep. I know why I got into this rut; it's just hard trying to get out of it. The prison system is safe for me emotionally. It doesn't cost me anything, but my time. I mean, I can go to work, I can do a double shift, I can get cussed out or cuss out someone, and it really doesn't matter. I thought by this age I would be doing more with my life, too."

"But that's the thing, girl, you can. Stop playing it safe. Do something wild and crazy. That's why I brought you here. The rest of your life starts now. No more goody-two shoes. From now on, we live on the edge."

They exited the car and walked into the building. The elevator ride to the fourth floor was uneventful, though they did run into several ladies who also looked their hoochie best. Stephanie read the bar sign. *Happitini: Where we've served 450 types of Martinis…and counting.* The sign blinked as they approached. The area surrounding the sign was very modern; it appeared to be much more than a *chick* bar. It had at least two dance floors and looked like a super lounge from what she could see from the foyer. The large windows provided a perfect view of the Bay.

Laurie produced her invitation, and then they were led in all the way. A chipper hostess in a black mini skirt and white collared shirt greeted them as she showed them to a table near the stage—a stage with *poles*.

Stephanie looked directly at her friend. "All right, spill it. What kind of place is this?"

The blaring of a whistle and the bumping beat of the entertainment's theme song drowned out Laurie's answer. The light show began to alternate several different colored lights that seemed to pulse with the loud music. Stephanie's heart raced with the beat. All the women in the club rushed toward the stage. Stephanie's eyes widened as wildly cheering ladies crowded their table. After a few seconds of the music playing, Stephanie learned why—and his name was *Chocolate Freak*.

A female singer, covered Rick James's song "Super Freak" with the words changed accordingly. Chocolate Freak was definitely not the kind of guy who you took home to mother! The dancer gyrated his pecan-brown complexioned hips and bare thighs down the stage in perfect choreography to the music.

A black mask covered his eyes and the majority of his face. And what little there was of his costume, sparkled amid the lights and smoke. His brown hairless chest was barely covered by a black rhinestone studded vest, which topped off a black studded G-string.

"He's a super freak, super freak" played as he came up to Stephanie to dance exclusively for her.

She found herself getting into the spirit. As he began a slow grind up and down her body, she laughed and squealed in delight. It wasn't until he took his chocolate covered penis out of his costume and put it an inch in front of her lips that she gasped in surprise. *Umph, wonder if this is what Magic Shell had in mind for their product?* She thought. Stephanie involuntarily flicked her tongue over her lips, but didn't take it any further than that despite his open invitation for her to take a lick. "Whoa, whoa, whoa, big fella. You gotta do that to someone else," she said in protest. A few more sips of her drink and she wouldn't be responsible for her actions.

The dancer smiled, then turned his back to her so that she could get a generous look at his tight muscular ass. Stephanie fanned herself as the other women in the room laughed…some in delight, some in jealousy.

Chocolate Freak moved on, freeing Stephanie to ogle with the rest of the crowd. "Now that was a nice piece of man candy!" She waved her hands in front of her face.

"You got that right," Laurie added. "Now, why couldn't I get a bite of that chocolate?"

Stephanie took a sip of her complimentary chocolate martini. Still fanning, she replied, "Because you would eat him up in one sitting. I keep telling you—moderation girl." She paused. "And I'm not even mad at you for bringing me to a nudie show. This has been too much fun. I really needed to step out and do something wild for a change. I won't doubt you again."

Laurie raised her glass. "Okay then, a toast to new and exciting adventures."

Stephanie nodded in agreement. "To a new you and me." She licked her lips, tasting the sweet chocolate from her glass. Damn, he was a serious piece of eye candy. She envisioned the ten inches of chocolate madness doing her just like Laurie had described earlier. She felt a bead of sweat begin between her breasts. This was not good. Especially once she began to imagine Bryant Wilson licking it up. She would be his chocolate freak any day of the week. He could suckle the sweet perspiration off her nipples and from her navel and then from…

"Ooo wee, I haven't seen that look from you in a while. What's his name?"

Stephanie blushed. "That obvious, huh?"

Laurie shook her head. "Yes, dear, I'm afraid so. That come hither stare into space and the way you keep licking your lips. I'd say you might need to go to the restroom soon. Or better yet, you might need a *private* session with Chocolate Freak."

Not with him, but there is someone else I wouldn't mind seeing in a G-string.

"I almost forgot who I was hanging out with. Okay, let's just calm down here. We're grown women, not horny teens." Stephanie gathered herself. "One more drink, and then I've got to get out of here. But this time, no chocolate. I need something a little less dainty." She waved her hand for a server. "I'll take a Sour Apple Martini, please."

As she waited, she noticed the change in music. The deejay was now playing "Candy Shop." The dancer's name fit him, too—Now-Later. One look and Stephanie was fanning again.

He was so long and well endowed that you could have some *now* and *later*!

Stephanie and Laurie said in unison, "Dayum!"

They were still laughing as they left the building. Laurie had her arms around Stephanie so they could steady each other as they walked toward the car.

Bryant was saying goodbye to his sister-in-law when he noticed the noise coming from the two women. Surprise and shock registered on his face once he realized the gorgeous woman in the tight red dress was none other than Officer Gunn. His body reacted instantly to her seductive appearance. What was it about a long-legged woman in red that drove him so wild?

He was about to pull the car out of the lot, but changed his mind. He had to say something...

He stepped out and walked toward them. Laurie saw him first, but after being hit on most of the night, she wasn't in the mood for anymore.

She turned toward him. "Whatever you're selling, we ain't buying, and no you can't watch us. I hope that answers all your questions. Good night and good luck."

Stephanie turned to see whom her friend was dissin' this time. "Oh damn! Laurie, hush. I know him."

"Oops." Peals of laughter erupted from both women—as much an effect of the alcohol as the circumstances.

Stephanie appeared mortified. "Mr. Wilson, what a surprise. Just ignore my friend. We've been hanging out a little too much. But if you're interested, there are some pretty horny women upstairs, and you just might get lucky. The dancers are whipping them into a frenzy."

Bryant's eyes grazed over her body, in the same way he had earlier in the day. "Are you sure you should be driving? Seems like the two of you had a *really good* time up there. My guess is you went to that new place on the fourth floor? My sister-in-law just started working there as a bartender. Her car's busted, so I dropped her off—that's why I'm here. So, how about I make sure you ladies make it home safely before I go to pick up Lisa's car?"

Laurie took a good look at him this time. Then she whispered in Stephanie's ear. "Now, that is a candidate for your new sexercise program. Girl, you betta hit it before I do."

Tension rolled within her belly at the thought of him with someone else, but she couldn't let her know that. Stephanie's gaze locked onto Bryant's. "I don't think that will be necessary, Mr. Wilson. We were just having a little fun, but thanks for the offer. I guess I'll see you the next time you visit your brother. Have a good night."

Bryant smiled. "Then tomorrow it is, Officer Gunn. Be careful out there. I'll be thinking about you until then."

Gunns and Roses

It was a warm starless night in Oakland—the kind that left one breathless with its beauty. He drove his Saab convertible with the top down to enjoy the wind whispering through his dreads. He'd thought about cutting them in the past, but moments like this reminded him why he enjoyed them so. He never felt more free.

Just thinking about his freedom made him feel a twinge of guilt about Macklin. Why that boy did all the wrong things, he would never know.

Everything came easy to Mac. He could get good grades without studying, and he was always the life of the party—as he was blessed with the gift of gab. Mac had it all: good looks, charm, brains and talent.

Bryant excelled in most areas, too, but the difference was he had to work for his accomplishments. Nothing came easily, and he didn't want it to. He liked feeling like he earned his station in life. He built his company from the ground up, with nothing but long hours and determination to thank. Nothing was just handed to him...not like with Mac.

His cellular phone rang, which brought him out of his thoughts and back to reality. It was the phone call he'd been waiting on from one of his boys. "What's up, man?"

His friend Tony Snowden spoke as if it were ten A.M. instead of the late evening. "I just wanted to let you know that I finished Lisa's car. You know you owe me for working past 10:00 P.M. on a Thursday night."

"Uh huh, but as long as we're calling in markers, I can think of a few."

Tony's hearty laugh reverberated through the phone. "All right, I guess we're even. You want me to drop by the club so you can go on home? I can have Margie ride with me."

Bryant was thoughtful for a moment. "No, it's late. Ride with me, and we can do it. Let Margie do her thing. Besides, isn't she about ready to drop that load?"

"If you mean, isn't she about due to deliver my son? Yes. I see that before you can talk with my wife again, I'm going to have to take you through some sensitivity training. Do you know that a hormonal, pregnant woman will kill you if you say the wrong thing?"

Tony's laugh was infectious, and Bryant heard himself joining in. "You gotta point, bro. I'll be there in about thirty minutes. Lisa's got a couple more hours before she'll need the car. Do you have time to listen to a brotha?"

"Uh oh, what's her name?"

"I didn't say it was about a woman."

"You didn't have to. Every one of our quality time moments has to do with women or a woman. I'll get the beer ready."

"You got a deal, but after I come back from dropping off the car."

"That's fine. I'll see you soon. But don't expect me to play any violins. You need to stop playin' and settle down."

Bryant was quiet for a few seconds. His remark hit home more than Tony knew. After a long exhale of breath, he responded, "Just hear me out. I'll be there in a minute."

Bryant finished his errands, dropped off Lisa's car at the bar, and then he and Tony rode back from Jack London Square to Tony's place. He cleared his throat. "How did you know that Margie was the right one?"

Tony looked at his friend curiously, because this was the first time that they'd had this particular conversation. He bit back a sarcastic reply to answer honestly. "I took one look at Margie, and it was magic. I felt so comfortable with her; she was immediately under my skin. I mean, it sounds crazy, but after about only a week, I went to bed thinking about her and woke each morning with her on my mind. She told me she had felt the same way. We've been married five years, but the courtship, if you want to call it that, was less than a month. I couldn't deal with the thought of being without her, so I made an honest woman out of her, and we got married."

"Just like that?"

Tony rubbed his chin thoughtfully. "Yep, just like that. There was no reason to agonize over it. I knew in my gut that it was the right thing to do. We connected when we talked, you know what I mean? When she smiled at me, I knew that all would be right in my world. There was no reason to take a chance on losing that kind of relationship. It was the best decision I ever could have made. And now she's just a couple of weeks away from delivering our child. Not to get all mushy, but I don't think I could love her more. We're at the perfect stage of our lives together. I know a good thing when I have it—believe me."

"I've always enjoyed watching the two of you. But I have to admit, I wasn't too interested in finding someone before. I mean, my life has been about building my business. And the few times I've tried to combine business and a personal life it has turned into a disaster." Bryant paused. "But things are better for me now."

Tony waited for Bryant to finish his sentence, but knowing where he was headed amused him. He smiled his easy smile. "And now there's someone who's caught your eye."

"Yes. There's this correction's officer at Palo Vista where Mac is…man, she is fine. She won't give me any conversation though."

"Uh, probably because she would lose her job." Tony's tone dripped with sarcasm. He shrugged his shoulders. "You might want to be real careful with her—that's a sticky situation for you because of Mac, but especially for her."

Bryant took off his jacket and tie, then raked his hands through his hair. "I know, I've thought about that, too. Mac only has six months left on his sentence. If I can just get her to acknowledge me, I can wait until his release to pursue anything serious. But I don't know…I'm not trying to be whipped."

Tony nodded. "If she's who you think you want to spend the rest of your life with, then there's only one choice, bro."

Bryant finished his beer while they talked on the porch. A couple of hours later, exhausted and drained from his long day, he headed home.

The talk had given Bryant some food for thought. He didn't want to spend his life running from woman to woman. Maybe Tony was right. The short drive from Tony's place gave him the opportunity to think about his advice.

As he approached his street, he was reminded about how much he had going for him. Bryant enjoyed living in the Grand Avenue Promenade area. It provided him with the benefits of living and working in Oakland. He had a lot to offer a woman, he knew that, but he wasn't about to get played. Stephanie held his attraction, but if she continued to rebuff his attention, he would have to admit that she wasn't the one.

He was so distracted by his thoughts that he missed the dark colored sedan that had been following him since he left the club.

When Bryant arrived at his building, he took the private elevator to his unit. He passed by the afro-centric decorations in the living room to head straight to his bedroom.

Once there, he stripped down to his silk boxers. Heat from outside and heat from desire suffused his body.

Bryant grabbed a Heineken out of the refrigerator. Beer in hand, he walked back into his living room to look out over the city.

One of the best parts of residing in his part of town was the view outside his big bay windows. He had a breathtaking view of Lake Merritt and the revitalization of this part of the city. Seeing the beauty that surrounded him should have been enough to calm his troubled soul, but with a bit of irony, he realized he would stay true to his word.

His thoughts drifted back to visions of Stephanie in her tight red dress. Her dark hair graced her shoulders, looking soft and smelling sweet. Officer Gunn, he thought, with her long legs in those high-heeled pumps that added inches to her already seductive height. He could just picture dancing close to her. With the added inches they would be cheek to cheek.

During the night, he tried many ways to relieve the bulge between his legs, but it seemed there was only going to be one way to soothe the ache. He needed the object of his desire, Stephanie Gunn between his muscled thighs.

Stephanie arrived at work the next morning to pandemonium. She asked one of her coworkers what the heck was going on, but the minute she heard the answer she regretted the question.

"During this morning's bunk check, Mac Wilson was found dead in his cell. Apparently, he hanged himself."

The lump in Stephanie's throat threatened to close off her airway. This couldn't be right. She had just talked to him yesterday. "What did his cellmate say?"

The young woman shrugged her shoulders. "I don't have any more information. The warden's been dealing with the paperwork all morning, as you can imagine. I only heard about the hanging because I was delivering something to his office. They have to release a statement to the press, so right now, just about everybody has been called in. And his brother…"

"Shit!"

Officer Green raised her eyebrows. "What's that for?"

Stephanie shook her head. "I'm sorry. I was just thinking about deaths. The families usually come storming in here like the inmates are a step away from sainthood. I just don't relish the thought of seeing his brother again. He'll want all the answers that we don't have right now."

"You've got a point there, but that's the warden's problem. That's why they get paid the big bucks. Well, I've got to do my count. I'll catch you later."

"Yeah." she responded absently. Stephanie experienced a myriad of thoughts and feelings at once, but guilt was the major one. Mac had reached out to her. Why hadn't she listened to him? He was obviously troubled about something.

Bryant…How would she ever be able to look him in the eye again?

"Gunn, the detention supervisor needs to speak with you."

"Thanks, Eason, I'll head there now. Tell Green I had to leave the floor," Stephanie responded.

The detention supervisor was second to the warden. It was never good to have to see him. As she walked toward the administrative offices, her heart jumped into her throat. What kinds of questions would be asked? Did someone report her talking with the inmate?

She'd worked herself into a nervous frenzy by the time she reached the door. What she overheard made her hand freeze in mid air just as she was about to knock on the door.

"I don't care what it looks like. It's going to be ruled a suicide. We don't need anybody breathing down our necks over another homicide in the facility. This goes down the way I say it does, and I don't give a damn about the real circumstances. Big Mac was a two-time loser. Once he finished his time here, he would be coming back. As far as I'm concerned, somebody did him and us a favor. The only thing we need to find out is if he said something to Gunn. Now, go and find her, I want to get this over with."

Stephanie's mind went blank. What was the administrator talking about? She'd known Paul Neal since her first day on the job nearly five years prior. He always struck her as fair and decent, but he sounded like a totally different person now. She had to find out more, but she couldn't get caught snooping.

Stephanie backed away from the door a few steps and started walking back toward it in a rush. After almost bumping into the assistant administrator, Gus Winthrop, she appeared to have just rushed down the hallway.

"Whoa there. Where's the fire?" he said smiling. He held on to her just a little too long for comfort.

Stephanie appeared flustered. "Oh, Gus, I'm sorry. I just heard that Neal was looking for me. I didn't want to keep him waiting, so I was scooting down the hall as fast as I could. I just heard about inmate Wilson, too. Man, that's a shame."

Winthrop regarded her carefully before he nodded. "No problem. We were just finishing up in there. I'll just let him know that you're here. I've got another meeting to attend now. It's been a madhouse, as you can imagine, but I'll check back with you if I need any information."

"Sure. Whatever, just let me know," Stephanie responded with false confidence. Her stomach performed back flips during their conversation. She found it hard to concentrate and had to force her mind to focus.

Winthrop reappeared in a couple of minutes. Stephanie wiped her brow feeling sticky and sickly hot.

"He'll see you now. Hey, are you okay?"

She mumbled her response. "Yeah, just rushing. It's been a crazy day already, and I just got on shift. I'll be fine though. It's not like this kind of stuff doesn't happen in other institutions all around the country." She paused to gauge his reaction. He didn't seem to suspect that she'd overheard their earlier conversation, so she continued. "I'll see you later. I'll head back to the floor as soon as we're done."

He nodded in response and headed back toward his office.

Stephanie gave a courtesy knock on the door before she walked into the administrator's office. "You wanted to see me, sir?"

Neal smiled and he waved her in. "Yes, come in, Officer Gunn. I'm sure you've already heard about Wilson's death this morning. I've been trying to figure out exactly how this happened. To that end, I'm talking to anyone who may have had contact with inmate Wilson prior to his death. By the logs, I can see you processed his last visitation. I need you to tell me more about that."

Stephanie sat in the chair after Neal motioned her toward it. For a few additional seconds of calm, she cleared her throat. "Well, there's really not much to tell. I conducted orientation, and all the visitors went downstairs to the visitation room. The only unusual occurrence was that I had to take Mr. Wilson's papers to him. We spoke for about ten seconds—then that was it." She paused as she thought about Mac's behavior. "Inmate Wilson wasn't inappropriate or acting suspicious in any way. He and his brother seemed to be having a normal visit. There was no heated debate or obvious tension between them. After I completed my errand and Mr. Wilson had the visitation paperwork, I returned to my duty station."

Stephanie shifted in the chair, uncomfortable with recounting Mac's last hours. "Later in the evening while I was doing count, Wilson wanted to talk, but I reiterated the rules about not engaging us in conversation and walked away from him. The rest of my shift went without incident, so once I finished, I went home. That was about it, sir."

Neal seemed satisfied with her explanation. They spoke for a few more minutes, and then she was released to return to duty.

"I just have one question. What happens next?"

He seemed to consider his response. Neal's tone and voice were measured and slow. Something that grated on each of Stephanie's nerve endings.

"If I need to, I'll call you back in my office for more questioning. For right now we have to contact the people on Wilson's emergency contact list. Once the medical examiner releases the body, then I'm sure that the family will make their own arrangements. Since he had six more months before release, he'll be buried in a state cemetery, unless his family contacts the higher officials. That's typical with prison deaths, especially suicides. Most of the time the family doesn't have enough disposable cash to pay for a burial their insurance won't cover."

Stephanie nodded in understanding, though her mind was working overtime to figure out what they were doing. Her immediate thoughts were on Bryant. Was it fair to let him think that his brother killed himself when there could be the slightest chance that he didn't? She would have to find out what they were doing or her conscience would never let her rest. She wasn't fond of her job, the work environment, or the inmates for that matter, but she did believe in justice...and Mac deserved that...no, Bryant deserved that, even if he was no better than his brother.

The difference between them was that he was locked up and the other wasn't. She decided she would do what she could for him.

The walk back to the desk area where she worked seemed interminable. Disturbing thoughts ran through her head as she tried to talk herself out of doing something stupid. Maybe something that could jeopardize her job and way of living. Something like taking it upon herself to find out what really happened.

If Macklin had been in real danger, and she didn't do anything to protect him she would never forgive herself. Stephanie felt that as an officer of the law she had a solemn duty. A duty, despite her complaining, she intended to uphold until the day that she walked away from the job.

Her pace quickened as she neared the front of the building where she monitored the inmates.

How was she supposed to act "normal?" Bryant Wilson was the last thing on her mind during the night and the first thing on her mind this morning. How would he react? He and his brother appeared to be close. Regret twisted her insides. *You should have done more.*

Objectively, she knew that she didn't owe Macklin Wilson anything...so why did she feel so damned guilty?

Bryant arrived at the Palo Vista facility at his usual time. He hadn't really planned to see Mac again so soon, but to have a chance to see the sexy and vivacious Officer Gunn, he would visit his brother everyday for the next six months.

Bryant was ushered through the gates and to the visitation room without incident. As he passed through the metal detectors, he felt his spirits rise. Why was this woman he didn't even know causing such a reaction?

It was Friday afternoon, and the lobby was surprisingly clear. He was at the counter to sign in, in no time. "Bryant Wilson to see Macklin Wilson." He smiled brightly at the clerk.

The clerk looked down at the paperwork, and then back up to him. "I'm sorry, sir, who are you here to see?"

Bryant spoke louder. "Macklin Wilson. M-a-c-k-l-i-n," he spelled out.

"Um," she said. "Maybe you'd like to talk with one of our administrators."

What the hell is going on? "I don't need to see an administrator. I just need to see my brother. I realize these are minimum wage jobs, but I think that I've made myself pretty clear." His tone turned condescending as he lost the battle to maintain his patience. "Just type the information into your little computer and sign me in."

As Stephanie rounded the corner to return to her station, she heard the last part of their conversation. She was horrified by what she overheard.

Gloria, the clerk stood up, placed a hand on her hip, and spoke in the same condescending tone as he had. "If you'd really like to see your brother, I'm afraid you are in the wrong section of the jail. You need to go down the hall and follow the signs that say. Allow me to spell it for you, m-o-r-g-u-e."

Bryant felt the blood drain from his face.

"I told you never to call me on my job. You're not taking me down with you." Eason's harsh whisper conveyed his meaning beyond misunderstanding. He was into it up to his neck, but he still had enough bravado to bluff.

There was a snort of disgust on the other end of the phone. "Keep me informed, and I won't have to call. I want to know what the warden wants to do next. I should know his next move before he does. Understand?"

"This has gone way too far." He ignored the man's previous comments. "I want out," Eason demanded.

"Fine, you can go out just the way that Macklin Wilson did. In the meantime, I expect results." There was a chilling pause. "And so how is little Sabrina? I enjoyed her last soccer game; she's turned into quite the athlete. I had to admire the way her six-year-old legs carried her down the field. She's very quick, but I wonder…could she outrun Buster Smith? It would be a shame if that convicted child rapist were given directions to your home…or to her school, huh?"

Eason nearly choked. "You leave my daughter out of this, you coward. Don't you ever threaten my family or me again. Whatever issue you have with me, stays with me. And don't think you're the only one with reach. Remember, I know a little something about your family and financial dealings as well."

"Eason…Eason, calm down, there's no need for such a vile attitude. I'm just a businessman trying to protect my interests. We have a good thing going here." He cleared his throat. "And we both know that our arrangement has been profitable for both of us. It's been a good thing that our recent interference tried to mess up. Now that our little Mac Wilson problem has been solved, we can move on." He exhaled. "As a gesture of my good will, I'm willing to excuse your comments, as I realize that they were expressed in the heat of the moment. I'll expect an update in a couple of hours."

The line went dead; causing a small shiver to creep up Eason's spine. He never intended for this to go wrong. He would have to talk with Neal. And he wouldn't like what Eason had to say.

Stephanie pulled Bryant back away from the counter. "Just stop, Gloria. I'll handle it from here. Mr. Wilson, come with me. I'll help you."

Bryant looked from the receptionist to officer Gunn with a dazed expression on his face. She took note of it and gently led him away from the area.

She found a quiet corner in the hallway before she spoke again. "Mr. Wilson, this isn't usually how things happen. I'm sorry to be the one to tell you this, but your brother was found dead in his cell early this morning. He died of an apparent suicide, but we won't know until we have all the information. If you'll come with me, I'll escort you to our supervisor's office and he can go over what needs to happen next. Again, I'm sorry for your loss."

She studied his face, which alternated between expressions of pain and disbelief.

He blinked several times before he uttered, "Um, Officer Gunn, how did this happen? I just saw him yesterday. You know that. How could he commit suicide in a facility with four thousand people in it? I don't believe this."

She reached out to him in an unplanned attempt to give him comfort. Her head told her to back off, but her heart wouldn't let her. "Mr. Wilson, I know this is tough, but if there is anything that I can do, I will. Follow me now and we'll see Mr. Neal. He's the administrator of prison services, similar to the warden."

Bryant followed behind her, mute as he apparently tried to process what he'd heard.

Stephanie felt her heart breaking with each step they took. He may be no better than his brother, but death was always tough to deal with…and made especially tougher when you have such a close relationship with the decedent.

Stephanie kept her voice soft and reassuring. These next few minutes would remain in his memory for a long time; people that couldn't remember what they had for dinner the night before remembered the details of the day a loved one passed.

There were several stares and whispers as she passed her coworkers in the hallways. Bryant bore a striking resemblance to his younger brother. It didn't take too much brain power to realize that the recently deceased's brother was in the building.

The rumor mill had cranked into high gear. By the time she and Bryant arrived in the administration hall, she saw Winthrop, the same assistant that she'd seen earlier.

He introduced himself and extended his hand toward Bryant as he spoke. "Thank you for escorting Mr. Wilson, Officer Gunn. I'll take it from here."

His oily smile made her skin crawl, but she would do as ordered. As she turned to tell him goodbye, Bryant held out his hand.

"No, I need her to stay." His stance toward Winthrop indicated that the subject wasn't up for discussion.

Stephanie opened her mouth to protest, but after seeing the look of anguish in his eyes, she closed it without voicing her opinion. There was something so vulnerable about him…something that defied her assessment of him as a man. Maybe he had more character than she gave him credit for…maybe he wouldn't try to set up a gangsta funeral where all the homies would tip a forty to their fallen brother. Stephanie sighed inwardly. He was complicated.

"That's highly unusual, sir, but we'll make an exception in this case. If you'll come with me, we'll get started."

Stephanie and Bryant walked into Neal's office behind Winthrop. He covered his surprise at seeing her again with an overly enthusiastic welcome of Bryant. He was a fish out of water.

Stephanie regarded him carefully. Her normally unflappable supervisor appeared to be suffering from apoplexy.

For reasons that she would analyze later, she enjoyed seeing Neal squirm. *This is going to be interesting…*

Bryant glanced at Stephanie briefly before he spoke. Once he turned his attention toward Neal, his direct and brusque tone warned those in the room that he wouldn't accept the runaround. He wanted answers.

"First, tell me why I didn't find out about my brother until I arrived here? Second, tell me why the hell I had to put up with some foul-mouthed clerk in order to learn that my brother was in the morgue? What kind of place are you running here? I'm not leaving until I hear some answers."

Neal sputtered. "Sir, I'm sure it is just the emotion of the situation that has you so upset. Believe me, we're all working to find out what happened."

"If that's true, then what do you know so far? And don't try to sell me some lame story about my brother committing suicide. Macklin would never do that—that's not my family's way."

Neal started to respond, but was silenced by Bryant's icy glare.

"I'd like to see the coroner's initial report as soon as possible. These are the numbers where I can be reached." Bryant passed his card to Winthrop to whom he was sitting closer, and continued as if he were running a board meeting. "Now, in the meantime, I'd like to see my brother. I assume his body is still here?"

"Yes. The medical examiner is still working on the case," Neal responded. "But you have a right to see your brother's body and to begin making arrangements. You won't be allowed to transport his body, however. Our policy is very firm. As long as he still had time on his sentence, he'll remain here. Once the proper amount of time has passed, at your own expense you can petition to move the grave site."

"What are you saying? I have no intention of keeping my brother in this God-forsaken place. I could care less about policy. He may have made mistakes, but I'll be damned if he's going to be buried here— and away from his family. Just tell me the price, and I'll pay it."

Stephanie looked toward Neal to gauge his reaction. His eyes appeared to light up once money was mentioned, but he didn't address what could possibly be construed as a bribe.

Instead, he returned her gaze before he spoke. "Officer Gunn, if you'll be so kind as to escort Mr. Wilson down to the morgue level, I'm sure we'll both appreciate it. Once you're finished, Mr. Wilson, I'll have papers for you to sign. Again, we extend our condolences for your loss. I understand that Mac had a bright future ahead of him once. I'm just sorry that he ended up here at our facility despite all of his talent."

Bryant stood without saying a word. Stephanie had to scramble out of her seat to catch up with him. His six-foot-plus stride immediately put him several steps in front of her.

Finally, she called out to him. "Mr. Wilson, I'll take you there, but I really think that this is something you need to do on your own. You haven't contacted your other family members. Was the sister-in-law you were helping the other night, Mac's wife? I really think this is a private affair, and I shouldn't intrude. I'll do what I can to explain procedures to you though."

The only response she received was him walking faster. At first she wondered if he had even heard her.

"You're right. It is a private matter, but I want you with me. I need answers, need someone who can tell me when I'm wading hip deep through bullshit. I know my brother did not commit suicide, and even though this coroner's report will probably indicate evidence to the contrary. I've made my living by being able to read people, and I know that I'm not wrong about you. Unlike most here, you have a good heart. You're *going* to help me get to the bottom of this. I'm not going to let those people," he pointed toward the administration hall, "get away with murder."

"Whoa, Mr. Wilson, that's a pretty strong word. I think that you should just slow down. Deal with one thing at a time and allow yourself to grieve. This is a terrible situation."

Bryant stopped walking, which caused Stephanie to nearly topple into him. He held out his strong arms to steady her.

"You have no idea how much I've lost. My brother meant a great deal to me and the rest of our family. All I need from you…" he paused as he stroked her arm, "is to be willing to help me when the time comes."

Stephanie closed her eyes. What was he trying to do to her?

"Mr. Wilson," she breathed out. "Um, let's make our way to the office. I still have a lot of work to do."

Bryant's smoldering eyes had turned almost a fiery golden brown. "I'll accept that…for now."

His words held an air of expectation that nearly made Stephanie quiver. She felt guilty again—not about Big Mac, but about the way Bryant made her feel inside. They way he made her forget all of her responsibilities and made her want to throw caution to the four winds. They were at her job for goodness sakes!

Stephanie looked around to see if they were being watched and she regrouped as quickly as she could. If she didn't regain control of her emotions and her hormones soon, she'd beg him to take her right there in the middle of the hallway. Surely, the real thing would be better than her fantasy.

Bryant stroked the side of her face with the pad of his thumb. "This is not the time or place. But soon…"

They finally arrived at the proper hallway. Bryant stood outside to gather himself. The nameplate on the door had etched on it six letters that would irrevocably change his life.

Stephanie gathered her belongings from her locker. All she wanted to do was get home to hop in the shower. She could almost feel the stream of piping hot water sluicing down her back, cascading over her tense and tired muscles. This day had started out badly and finished worse.

She needed music. Whenever she had a bad day, music made her feel human again. With Suite 62 on her satellite radio blasting on the car stereo, she made the drive down the Oakland highway in less time than normal. Once she pulled into her driveway, some of the day's tension oozed away.

Gunns and Roses

Stephanie was half way to her door when she remembered to go back for her uniform. As she pulled it from the back seat, a slip of paper fell from one of her pockets. She recognized it instantly as the same note that Mac had tried to give her yesterday. Shocked, she stood rooted to the same spot for several minutes as though the paper would move on its own.

How in the world did it get there? What should she do?

Bryant had fallen asleep in the wee hours of the morning from pure emotional exhaustion. He'd returned home from the jail, called his parents and begun to make the necessary arrangements.

After calling his secretary to cancel all his meetings for the next week, he considered the rest of activities he would have to do. Mac's ex-wives and children would have to be taken care of too.

A wave of nausea overcame him. He sat up in the king-sized black leather-accented bed and swung his long legs over the side. His bedroom had always been his sanctuary, but right now his heart ached with a loss so deep that he found pleasure in nothing.

He walked into his oversized spa bathroom to splash cold water on his face. Bryant gripped the side of his white porcelain sink, his light brown hands contrasting with the shiny finish. He stared down at them, desperate to focus on anything aside from the traumatic event of seeing his baby brother lying cold…pale…lifeless on a slab. He released his breath slowly as he came to terms with the painful realization that Mac was really gone.

He'd been holding on to so much emotion during the entire course of the day. His hands shook as he struggled to maintain control. He stared at his face in the mirror. How could he have let this happen? Guilt tore at his gut. He would have a tough time facing his parents with the knowledge that he'd failed his baby brother. Mac had asked for his help, practically begged him, and he'd ignored his plea as just another game. Why hadn't he realized that this time was different?

Bryant was the responsible one, the one who was supposed to watch out for Mac. He was supposed to make sure that he stayed out of trouble. A tear rolled down his face, which he wiped away angrily with the back of his right hand.

Bryant made a silent vow to make this right. Whomever did this would pay.

Stephanie woke up in a panic. She turned her head toward the clock—3:00 A.M. She sat straight up in her bed. The paper, unread, sat beside her on the nightstand. She needed to do something. Read it, throw it away, or give it to Bryant as she'd been asked to originally. She couldn't just let it sit there. The thought that she could have helped Mac before…before he was killed, upset her.

Would Bryant ever forgive her? Should she tell him about her part in his brother's death?

Her career was over at Palo Vista, she knew that, she would never trust Neal or Winthrop again. Confusion made her head pound.

But what should I do next?

Bryant lay awake in his bed, staring out of the bay window that gave him a clear view of the night sky. It was a beautiful night by all accounts. A night for love. After a year of self-imposed celibacy, he needed physical release. Bryant had chosen this time to focus on his business and his family. A relationship meant distraction, and right now he didn't know if he could keep everything in his life in balance. If he were totally honest with himself, he wasn't sure it wasn't an excuse not to become involved with anyone. But he hadn't found anyone until now who could change his mind.

He still had at least six hours before his first appointment. He was knee deep in the process of making his brother's arrangements, and with a clear schedule, he could devote himself to the challenges ahead.

His restless mind drifted back toward Stephanie Gunn. If she hadn't been there with him earlier today, he didn't know what he would have done. She was the lone bright spot in an otherwise trying day.

The vision of her face and body in the red dress she wore the other night floated through his mind, causing his body to react in a most uncomfortable manner. He tried to push such thoughts of her out of his mind, but it was too late. His head and body disagreed about the timing and whether or not it was right.

He slid his hand down to his silk boxers to massage his thick erection and breathed out heavily. *This shouldn't be happening*. His body ignored him.

Stephanie Gunn had gotten under his skin. He had to ask himself, would she really be there to help him? She'd indicated as much, but she did work for the prison system. He wanted to trust her, but he had to think about it. What did he really want from her? Was it purely physical? Did he want her as much as he craved her naked body straddling his right at this moment? Did he want her help in figuring out what happened to his brother, and then it would be over?

Bryant began to stroke himself under the boxers with purpose. His hand kept a firm grip around the head of his penis as he worked it up and down, massaging his testicles in the process. He imagined Stephanie bringing him pleasure, first with her hands. Then he imagined that her mouth encircled his engorged member.

His body shook the bed as Bryant pumped more vigorously—breathing in and out in ragged gasps as he brought himself to completion. An orgasm ripped through him, causing his body to shudder and pulsate. Hot liquid covered his hands and shorts. When he was finished, he grunted in disgust; he had ruined another pair of silk underwear. He needed to stop fantasizing about Stephanie and make a move.

He had so many thoughts swirling around his head. He just wanted relief; he didn't want to think…to feel…he just wanted to be. He waited for his body to return to normal before he walked into the bathroom to take a cold shower.

Fifteen minutes later, he settled back into bed, and fell into a deep sleep. His thoughts were never too far from the sexy and vivacious Stephanie Gunn.

Bleary eyed and grumpy, Stephanie made her way to her kitchen for her one vice—coffee. She didn't smoke or drink heavily, but she had to have her coffee in the mornings in order to feel like a person. Her inability to sleep made her angry and even grumpier. She had enough going on in her life without having to deal with insomnia.

After working six days straight, she would be off for the next three days. Stephanie cherished the time alone, but now she had a decision to make. She picked up the phone to call Bryant, he'd made sure she had his number after they'd left the morgue.

She dialed the digits, listened to it ring one time and then hung up quickly. "I can't do this," she mumbled to herself. She wasn't ready to face him.

After coffee with French Vanilla creamer, half and half, and plenty of sugar, she bound up the stairs to take a shower.

Just thinking about Bryant had her body singing in anticipation, but she successfully ignored her desires because she needed to stay focused.

Her decision was costly. Stephanie knew that going in, but it was her only true choice.

She finished her shower, moisturized her body with one of her favorite body lotions, dressed and then headed back downstairs. Whenever she wanted to figure something out, she usually started by grabbing a piece of paper and a pen.

Stephanie crossed the kitchen to her modest family room. It contained among other things her favorite chaise. She sat down with the pad and began to write. On the top of the paper she wrote her heading.

Macklin Wilson

Suicide or homicide?

Facts: Convicted pimp, drug user and drug dealer.

Questions: What was he afraid of? Who did he think was after him? Why would someone kill him? Who would kill him?

The rhythmic tapping of the pen on the paper was the only sound in the room, until the sound of the doorbell broke her concentration.

She nearly jumped clear out of her skin. She looked at her kitchen clock. At 1:00 P.M. it could only be her friend, Laurie.

She hurried to the door. Her friend could be very impatient, and she didn't want to totally lose her train of thought. She yanked open the door without bothering to use the peephole.

"Oh my God!"

Bryant gave her the barest hint of a smile. "Well, that's a nice reaction, but not one I get often. I'm sorry to barge in on you, but need to ask you a couple of questions. Don't worry, I won't take long. And I promise I won't make this a habit." This time his smile reached to his eyes, making their unusual brown twinkle even more.

Stephanie stood at the door, staring at him for several seconds. When she was finally able to gather herself, she stuttered through her invitation to let him in the house.

Bryant seemed amused by her.

"I'm afraid you were a victim of my endless Google-ing. I put your name in the computer to find out where you lived. I know this is intrusive, but believe me, I wouldn't do it unless I felt that I had no choice."

"Uh…okay…well, uh, have a seat in the kitchen. Can I make a cup of coffee for you or would you like a soda?"

"Water would be fine. I really just came here to talk. I don't want to impose." He walked into her kitchen to take a seat at her table.

Stephanie looked around the room. Thank goodness she was a relatively neat person, she thought. Otherwise, this could have proved embarrassing.

She smoothed the white T-shirt down over her form-fitting blue jean capri pants. She was no glamour puss, but she was alone in her own home in a comfortable outfit. So it was wrinkled, but it was clean.

Meanwhile, Bryant looked as if he had stepped out of an ad for Men's *Vogue* magazine. His designer navy blue suit was impeccably tailored, right down to the last detail.

He sat down quietly as he waited for her to return to the table.

Stephanie pulled a bottle of water from her refrigerator. She spotted a couple of limes and grabbed those, too. A minute later, she was serving the water with sliced lime in a tall glass.

"Thanks. This is great, but I don't want you going to any trouble for me."

Stephanie smiled. "Unfortunately, trouble is all I've got." She sighed. "I need to show you something. It's probably going to upset you, and you may never want to speak to me again, but I can't deal with this on my own."

She moved to leave the table, but he held her hand to stop her.

"Bryant, what are you doing?"

"Stephanie, I came here because I need your help. I don't care what deep dark secrets you have. I want to find out what upset my brother so much. I had all night to think about things and to beat myself up about not listening to him. I want to make it right now. I need to find out the answers so he can rest in peace and my parents can have closure. They're up in age, and I'm afraid this could tear them apart. So, I'm begging you, let's leave the personal drama until after."

Stephanie blinked several times. "You can be one arrogant SOB, you know that? What makes you even think that what I wanted to say had anything to do with personal drama? Look, I know you're hurt and you're still in shock, but we need to keep it real. Don't make assumptions about me."

He treated her to an icy stare. "Oh, like you've made any about me? I know why you were so standoffish at Palo Vista, and it has nothing to do with your job. You took one look at me and decided who I was and what I was about before you even knew my name. I see the old double standard is alive and well in your book."

Her eyes flashed in anger. "How dare you come into my house and talk to me that way. You were coming to visit your brother in jail, what else was I to think? And quit trying to fix it up for yourself, it wasn't just another facility, like visiting a loved one in the hospital— your brother was a criminal."

Bryant stood up and began to pace the room as he talked. "Dammit, don't you think I know that? I hated everything that Mac had become. But I loved him. And this guilt by association is a bunch of bull. My parents are fine people and raised us right. Don't you dare condemn us all for the choices he made.

"Mac wasted everything, destroyed almost everything that he touched. I've spent my entire life trying to steer him in the right direction. It tore me apart to see him caged in that damn jail like an animal. He was everything that was wrong in our family. Our parents, through example, taught us how to achieve. They took pride in their boys, loved us unconditionally, gave us what they could." Bryant rubbed his fingers against his throbbing temple. "But nothing cut it with that boy. He always wanted more, like he was owed something special. During college I worked my butt off, holding down a job and maintaining my grades."

He stopped to regain control of his raging emotions. "When I decided that I wanted my own business, I gave up whatever I needed to in order to make it work. I've been the CEO of Wilson Marketing for almost ten years now. I started the company right out of college, actually, in the basement of my parent's home. Nothing came easy. But I'm not complaining. My life is richer for it. I'm not saying that I'm perfect, I'm certainly no saint, but my sins have usually involved not calling back a beautiful woman or going too fast down the highway. I've never been in trouble with the law, and I'm not some drug-dealing thug."

Bryant released a long breath. "I am proud, I am arrogant. I'm whatever you want to call me, but I loved my brother and I want to find out the truth. So, Ms. Gunn, whatever you know, whatever you have, I'm begging you…share the information with me."

Stephanie looked down. She was ashamed to admit to herself and to him that she had been judgmental. She'd let her preconceived notions about Bryant get in the way without knowing anything about him. She thought, *how shallow to crave his body, fantasize about him, yet know nothing about him or worse yet, assume he was no better than his brother.*

"I owe you an apology. Maybe I've been working around the criminal element so long that I don't know how to read people any longer. I did prejudge you, and for that I'm truly sorry. I've been fighting my attraction to you since practically the first time I saw you, but I didn't want to believe good things about you. That made it easier for me to resist you, and you deserve better than that from me." Stephanie walked to where she had been sitting before Bryant came over, picked up the pad and the note from Mac, then walked slowly back to hand over everything. "I think you need to see this."

"Thank you, Stephanie. Now I know that my faith has not been misplaced. Can I share something with you?"

Stephanie sat down next to him at the table. "I'm listening."

He kept the papers in front of him, but didn't look at them. "I've been attracted to you since the first time I saw you at the jail a few months ago. There was something so sexy about the way you fill out your uniform. I have to admit that you invade my dreams almost nightly…you are becoming my obsession. If it weren't for this ordeal, I might be tempted to do something…well, something inappropriate."

The desire she saw in his golden-brown eyes burned a hole through her and ignited her own passion. Her total inability to control her wanton cravings for him stormed back in full force. Stephanie tried to move away, but like a magnet, he pulled her into him. She didn't know if it was real or another one of her fantasies. When she felt his arms embrace her and his lips upon hers, she knew that it was real. It was everything that she imagined. The papers lay on the table, temporarily forgotten.

His large hands caressed her back as he held her close. She opened her mouth to him, inviting his tongue in for a passionate taste. Stephanie kissed him back hard. They dueled for control, each taking turns giving more than the other.

He stopped. "Do we know what we're doing?"

She began to pull her shirt over her head as she responded. "No, but let's hurry up before I change my mind. I don't think that I can look at you any longer without being tempted to beg. Despite my misgivings, I've been a little more than attracted to you, too. I didn't want to give in to my desires because I didn't want to take the risk. This is a major step for me."

Bryant smiled as he slipped off his shoes, and then dispensed with his lightweight jacket and pants. "For me, too." He brought her close again.

Stephanie kissed him again, long and hard. As his body pressed against hers, she felt his erection pulsate against her abdomen. With no shoes on, he had at least four inches of height on her. Stephanie smiled inwardly. A shiver of anticipation flowed through her as she noted Bryant's immense size.

Stephanie helped Bryant unbutton his crisp white and blue pinstriped shirt. He helped her loosen her pants in excruciating slowness. She wanted to move faster, but he kept the pace. Bryant's eye raked over her, which should have made her uncomfortable, but she enjoyed his open admiration. After a few minutes, her frustration with his deliberate behavior abated. She wanted the experience to last as long as possible.

Bryant planted kisses along her neck, taking the time to nibble on her every now and again. His long hair graced her bare chest, sending ripples of delight through her. He was the fantasy, and then some…

After both had stripped down to their underwear, she made the suggestion through clenched lips that they continue in a more intimate setting than the kitchen. "How about we take this upstairs?"

Bryant stopped kissing her briefly to say, "I thought you'd never ask."

He bent over to retrieve their clothing, which he gathered into his arms as he followed her upstairs. Stephanie was amused by his tendency toward orderliness—she would have done the same thing if he hadn't first.

She felt more comfortable upstairs in her bedroom. She didn't want anything to stop her from enjoying every second with him. When they stood next to her queen-sized bed, she asked, "Now where were we?"

Bryant swept her into his arms in response.

Giggling, they tumbled onto her bed. He slid his hands effortlessly along the band of her bra before he unclasped it. He freed her firm breasts from their lacy captivity and was awed by their beauty. "Damn, you're fine," he said in a husky whisper.

Stephanie grinned. "Ditto." She ran her hands through his locks. "How long have you been growing them, they're wonderful."

"Four years now, but enough talk. Let's get back to action. I want to love you; hear you scream my name. I want to feel those long legs wrapped around my waist. I've been jonesing for you for too long."

Stephanie lifted her hips up to slide off her lace bikini panties. Bryant's willing hands made the process much faster. Once she was naked on the bed, she demanded the same from him. "Fifty-fifty, sir."

"Now that's what I like to hear from a woman. Let me see how I can accommodate," he answered as he retrieved a condom from his wallet. He kissed her again, sliding his tongue deep into her mouth. He began to explore her again, gently teasing and nipping her with his teeth.

She moaned in pleasure as she gyrated her body against his, feeling his heated skin against her own. She enjoyed the feeling of his maleness between her legs.

Bryant moved from her mouth to her perky breasts. He caressed them with his hands until each nipple stiffened into a tall peak. Damn, he made her feel good, she thought.

His hands slid lower, coming to a stop on the smooth, clean-shaven skin of her center. He liked the feel, and began to stroke her with gentle, insistent movements. Up and down on her clit until he felt her wetness on his fingertips.

His own erection grew harder because she excited him in every imaginable way. While his hands worked their magic down below, he kissed her long, hard and deep. He could tell she liked it that way by her reactions. The harder he pressed, the more excited she became. He felt her body begin to convulse from his actions.

Stephanie took his engorged penis in her hands. She massaged and teased him until a small amount of liquid came from the head. She moved him over until she could angle her body to take him into her mouth.

He released a strangled cry after she took him to the back of her throat. He leaned over her to give her full access to him, which she took greedily. His hands never stopped giving her pleasure though as he continued to worry her clit until he brought her to the edge of orgasm. He didn't want to lose control though; he wasn't ready. Bryant removed himself from her mouth and moved down to her slick core.

His mouth replaced his fingers; he laved her labia, bringing moans of ecstasy from her lips. Stephanie was in another world now. His long dreads swung back and forth as he moved his mouth on her, but she didn't see that. The music played, but she didn't hear it. He peach nectar candles burned, but she no longer detected the fragrance. All she knew was Bryant making her feel good, exciting her and taking her to new heights.

"Oh my God, Bryant, I'm going to cum. Oh baby, you feel so good."

She entwined her fingers in his locks to move her body along with his. He delved deeper, his tongue became more directed; he knew that she was close. He played with her clit until her eardrum-splitting screams of passion flooded the room.

"That's right scream for me, baby." Bryant moved Stephanie to the missionary position. He made sure the condom was in place before he entered—slowly, to allow her body to become used to his large size. Once he was all in, his strokes were shallow and teasing. He allowed Stephanie to dictate the pace since this was their first time together.

She started slow, too. He took her breasts in his hands, rubbing one nipple between his fingers and the other he sucked into a stiff peak again. He continued sucking until he felt her body react. Then in a swift motion, he went deep inside her. Stephanie gasped in surprise, but she took in all of him. Her hips matched his stroke for stroke. "Put your legs around me, baby."

Several acrobatic moves later, sweat soaked and exhausted she lay on his chest. Their lovemaking was all she had imagined and more.

"You realize that this threatens our operation? I want you to search her locker. I want this done right—no sloppy mistakes this time. We're already in deep shit because of the brother. Why didn't someone check out this Bryant guy before we eliminated Mac?"

Neal stared at the blank faces of his officers. They were a good-for-nothing lot if he'd ever seen one, he thought. Scratched heads and silence were his only reply.

After he dismissed the staff, Neal picked up the phone. He needed to call the very person that he didn't want to talk to—Chester Smoot. "We need to talk," he said.

"We don't talk unless there's a problem. And I know there aren' any problems associated with our operation because I've been assured that everything was on schedule."

"Sir, we ran into a small problem. One of our inmates wa: nosing around and wanted to be involved with the operation. We've taken care of him, but of course there's an inquiry into his death We're going to handle that, as well as a slight snafu with hi: brother."

"We don't have 'snafus,' Neal. How did this happen? You neec to look into leaks on your end. How could an inmate even find ou what's happening. Furthermore, who did he tell? We can't afford tc have flapping jaws! Each day that our operation is down costs us ter thousand dollars. You're going to ruin us."

As much as she enjoyed being with him, she had to bring hin back to business. They needed to go through the information. She took a deep breath. "Bryant, you have to look at the information tha I have. Mac wrote something down on paper he wanted you to see I was working on it before you came over to my house. Not that I'n complaining about the interruption," she added with a grin. "Since it was written for you, I'm sure you'll know what to do with it Everything points to a major drug operation going on in the jail— One that might include the supervisors or even the warden. I over heard a conversation the other day that still bothers me. I know something is going on, but I'm not sure exactly what it is yet. Prison are notorious for the contraband that gets in…we probably have a bigger and more organized drug trade in the system than on the outside."

Stephanie hesitated, "Bryant I can't tell you how sorry I am that I didn't believe Mac. After putting this together, I honestly believe he was murdered."

Bryant sat up the bed, looking at her incredulously. "Did Mac tell you that he was in danger? And you didn't do anything?"

His accusatory tone threw her off guard. She didn't expect it after what they'd just shared. Stephanie stuttered. "I told you that he tried to talk to me—"

"But my question is, did he tell you that he was in danger?"

Stephanie swung her legs off the bed. "I think this was a mistake. You should go now."

Bryant gathered his clothing, shrugging on his suit as quickly as he could. His body shook in anger. "The only mistake was you ignoring my brother's pleas for help. I thought you were an officer of the law! How could you?"

The Isley Brother's Bedroom Classics crooned in the background as the tears fell down Stephanie's face. She reached her hand toward him. "Bryant I've told you how sorry I am. I would never knowingly let this happen. Your brother deserved as much of a chance—"

"As the next inmate," he finished for her. He moved out of her reach as he walked toward the bedroom door.

Neal tried to ignore the sweat forming on his upper lip. He fought back the bile that threatened to escape his throat as the barrage continued.

They had agreed never to meet in person, but here he was in the flesh. They had a silent partnership, one that included invisibility as well. There was no reason for a city councilman to visit a state-run facility. He may be in charge, but he was jeopardizing their entire business with his presence. Aside from being nervous, Neal was livid.

Thanks to Smoot's indiscretion, people would talk.

"Set up a meeting. We need to tie up this Wilson thing once and for all. I don't like loose ends."

"But, sir, don't you think we should lay low? We don't want to call anymore attention to the facility."

Smoot banged his hand on Neal's desk. "When I want you to think, I'll let you know. Handle it before I do." The command was issued just before the door slammed.

Neal slid down in his chair. This couldn't be happening. Stephanie and Bryant would get them all killed if he didn't take care of her first.

Bryant looked back toward Stephanie's house. *How could you have been such an idiot?*

He put his Chrysler 300 in reverse, barely missing the vehicle that was pulling into her driveway. He recognized the woman as Stephanie's friend Laurie. After she noticed him, she waved enthusiastically.

Bryant was in no mood to be sociable, so he simply ignored her as he drove away. There needed to be as much distance between him and Stephanie as possible. He wouldn't be responsible for his actions, otherwise. Disappointment about what had just transpired between them wasn't even close to the emotion he felt.

It was getting late, but he had no intention of going home. He didn't want to be reminded of his slip-ups. "How many times do you make the same mistake?"

Miles passed and he didn't have a destination. He drove until the hills became mountains; the mountains became distant blurs. His mind was such a jumble that nothing registered.

He thought about calling Tony, but he didn't want to disturb his friend with more of his love-life drama. This really hurt. He was genuinely falling for Stephanie. For the first time in a long while, he was sincere in his intentions for a woman. This was no casual relationship, not like his others. This time he was willing to go all the way to make it work.

He cursed into the wind. Why did he have to fall in love now? With all the emotional upheaval he felt, falling head over heels wasn't in the plan. He had been so content to maintain casual relationships—the kind where no one got hurt, because no one was serious. It was all about fun, flowers and fantastic sex. Feeling this way about Stephanie was the very thing he was trying to avoid.

Stephanie Gunn had rocked his world—and she didn't have to do much to accomplish that goal. He'd never wanted to be with someone like this before…never found anyone who could make him forget about everyone else on the grid.

Bryant swallowed into a dry throat. The taste was bitter in his mouth. He thought about her nubile body feeling so good under him as he thrust powerfully into her, and then her soft lips on his mouth. Then he became angry.

What was her game? All that talk about wanting to help…was it from the guilt? Would she have given a damn if he hadn't shown up at her townhouse to beg for her assistance?

He placed his right hand on the steering wheel, while the left hand rested on the car window. He thought back to what she'd said. Her words came back to him in haunting clarity—*I need to show you something. It's probably going to upset you, and you may never want to speak to me again. But I can't deal with this on my own.*

Bryant talked to himself as he drove. He had a lot of feelings to come to terms with. He'd let down his parents and his brother. Was it really fair to make Stephanie responsible for his failure? He wanted to be angry with her, blame her for everything that went wrong, but what did she owe him or Mac? She had a responsibility, which she met.

Bryant exhaled loudly. *She was trying to be upfront with you, man. Maybe you're the one who let mistrust get in the way? Why are you so willing to give up a relationship that you want?*

Now he really felt like an ass. How would she be able to trust him if he flew off the handle like this? Several miles later, tired and almost bleary eyed, the world began to make a little more sense.

In the end, he had to ask himself why he was so upset. Was it because Stephanie hadn't listened to Mac or because he himself hadn't? He made the decision to call Stephanie as soon as he made the long trek back to Lake Merritt.

By the time he pulled into his private garage, he was cursing himself for his stupidity. This time though, it was for doubting Stephanie in the first place and also for driving so damned far. After his earlier lovemaking, he was exhausted.

Laurie banged on the door until Stephanie answered. Her tear-stained face told Laurie all was definitely not well in her friend's life. The facetious greeting she'd planned died on her lips. Instead, she barged through the foyer after she shut the door behind her. Laurie didn't utter a word until she was filling the kettle with water for coffee.

After sitting down, she said, "All right. What gives? I expected to see some 'damn that was good bliss' up in here. Instead I see him driving away pissed off and you standing in that 'even the cat hides from it' robe. Tell me what happened before I have to go chasing the brotha down."

Tears streamed down Stephanie's cheeks. "Laurie, I think I've lost him."

"Lost who? Don't tell me you were serious about him."

Stephanie pulled the belt around her waist tighter on her yellow terry cloth robe. "Yes. I am…I was…" She sat back in the chair. "I don't even know what I'm saying. Girl, he is everything I've been looking for in a man. I was all wrong about him. And he's not at all like his brother. I mean, I expected him to be some lowlife, some con man, but he's nothing like that. He stormed out of here because he realized that I could have done something to save his brother Mac, but I chose not to. He has every right to be upset with me. But, I just don't know how to make it up to him," she finished quietly.

Laurie considered what she'd heard. The water was ready, so she went back to the stovetop. In the middle of the coffee-making process she blurted out, "You're serious?"

She poured hot water over the dark roast grounds in two cups, and then brought them to the table. "This is so crazy. Tell me everything that happened. And don't leave out the part where he made your hair stand straight up."

Stephanie walked to the family room to grab a box of tissue from the room where just hours before she was kissing Bryant. "Where do I even start?" After telling Laurie all the details about Mac, she shared what happened between her and Bryant.

Stephanie exhaled as she gathered herself together. "He's the one, girl. Despite my best efforts, I've known it from the moment I laid eyes on him. I've dreamt about this man, fantasized about this man and now finally loved this man. But I think I ruined everything by not acting quickly enough."

Laurie reached over to hug her friend. "I won't tell you that I'm not surprised by these new developments, I had no idea that you were already *jonesing* for someone when I invited you out to the Jappitini. But, if this is the way you feel about him, girl, don't give up so easily. He looked mad as hell when he left you here crying, but if there's that much passion going on between you two, it's gotta be worth saving".

She shrugged her shoulders. "Give him a minute to calm down before you consider the relationship a loss. And next time, no keeping secrets from your best friend. I should be mad at you, but considering the circumstances, I'm going to let this infraction slide." Laurie sipped her coffee.

"Okay, now that I've been a good friend, can we talk? Damn, he's fine! Woo wee, if he walked away from me, I'd be crying too! And at six foot something, I know he's got to be hung, right?"

Stephanie smiled for the first time since her friend had come over. "Laurie, if it weren't all true, I'd kick your behind out of here, but the sad truth is, he's all that and more!"

She stood up. "I've got to head back over the Palo Vista. There's got to be more information there that can help us. Bryant may have given up on me, but I'm not finished yet. If there's a way to help him figure out what really happened to Mac, then I'm going to do it."

Laurie regarded her skeptically. "I know that you want to help, but you have to be careful. Maybe killing an inmate was no big deal to them, and if they were willing to kill once, maybe they won't hesitate to do it again. Think about what you're doing before you go off half-cocked. Maybe you should wait to talk this over with him."

Stephanie crossed her arms over her chest. "No. I've made up my mind. I have to do this if I'm ever going to be able to face Bryant again."

"Neal may have become a liability and you know that I don't like weakness. Palo Vista is a cash cow that I don't intend to give up. So, I've decided to give him until tomorrow to rectify the situation. If he doesn't, then I guess Oakland will lose one of its veteran officers. Such a shame," Smoot added with a malicious sneer. "But on the bright side, Eason, it looks like you're going to be promoted." Smoot clipped the end of the cigar he held in his beefy hands.

As city councilman he catered to certain businesses, not all of which were best for city development, but as long as they lined his pockets, he was satisfied.

He spoke on the phone to Eason from one of his favorite hangouts, The Golden Kitty, which was an adult entertainment venue in the heart of downtown. This was another part of his *personal* economic development plan.

Chester Smoot was a man known for his indulgences and penchant for the exotic.

Smoot hung up with Eason, and then motioned for one of the strippers to come to him. She had been waiting patiently for her boss to finish his business so she could give him a lap dance—one of his weekly treats.

Chester licked his lips, and his eyes twinkled in anticipation because tonight it was Ginger. She was one of his favorite brown-eyed beauties: she was tall and lean, but well endowed in the areas that mattered most to him. Chester grew harder just watching her sashay toward him in four-inch heels.

His eyes roved over the barely there black lace bikini top and G-string. The color black nicely contrasted against Ginger's creamy, light-brown skin, soft enough to caress all night, he thought lasciviously.

For the moment, all thoughts of Palo Vista were out of his head. As soon as a few chinks were ironed out of his chain, business would be back to normal. He knew that he couldn't afford to slow down production in such a highly competitive marketplace for long.

Chester and his associates owned the drug trade in his part of Oakland, supplying some of the most influential citizens in town with their cocaine, heroine and prescription drugs of choice. Overhead costs were low with his prison connections, and demand was at an all time high. Life couldn't be much sweeter.

Ginger sat her well-apportioned, firm ass down on his crotch. Chester lifted her slightly in order to unzip his fly—this was the perfect way to end a hard day at work.

Stephanie dressed methodically in her uniform. She wasn't sure about the feasibility of her plan, but she would give it a chance. Most of the staff worked overtime, so she hoped that no one would think her return to the building was curious.

She made the drive to Palo Vista in silence. Her normal routine of listening to Suite 62, as she drove in, would have to wait until she was finished because right now she needed to concentrate. The paper with Mac's hastily scribbled note sat on the passenger seat.

GW/BS/GS/?OG/ 3 to 4 dels/per day. Low over/prfct op

How much?

Bro. This is a serious operation. They know I know. Need to get out of here now.

Stephanie swore under her breath. "Why didn't I listen?"

She didn't understand all of the initials, but she knew enough to be concerned about Neal and Winthrop. She'd replayed their conversation in her mind. Were they able to convince the coroner to alter his findings? Because she didn't believe that Mac Wilson would kill himself either. She felt as strongly about it as Bryant did. Mac was a survivor, a man used to doing what he pleased. Suicide would mean that he failed to find his own solution.

Stephanie considered who all of the other players might be. Palo Vista employed over five hundred people. This wasn't going to be any easy task, but she had to succeed for Bryant's sake.

One thing seemed clear though, considering the cryptic contents of the note and Mac's profession, it had to have something to do with drugs. But how? Certain words were obvious like dels for deliveries and prfct for perfect. But the big picture was still fuzzy to her.

She arrived at the facility and parked in the employee lot. She looked around to see which cars she recognized. Eason was in, but it looked as if Neal was out—his Jaguar wasn't in the lot anyway. She took a little comfort in that fact.

As she walked into the building, she noticed Green and Eason huddled together in a corner of the hall. Inter-office affairs were common in high stress professions like corrections, but these two were the last couple that she would have put together. Green was a short, stocky, African American woman who barely made the department weight requirement; Eason was one of the boniest, tall, white men that she'd ever seen. Together they looked like Fric and Frac.

Luckily, the warden was a creature of habit. Stephanie knew where he kept a spare key to his office, but prayed that they would ignore her as she went to retrieve it. She noticed that both looked extremely uncomfortable once they saw her, which indicated something wasn't right. She had to admit, seeing them pow-wow like that made her more than a little antsy. But Stephanie shrugged off the cold feeling of dread that sent chills up and down her spine so that she could finish the business at hand. She waved at them, and then kept moving towards the officer locker room where a master key was hidden in a drawer.

Once she was out of their view, she continued down the hall towards Neal's office. She didn't quite know what she was looking for, but she hoped once she found it she would recognize it.

She kept checking behind her, looking for signs that she was being watched or followed. By the time she reached the administrators office, sweat had dampened the armpit area of her shirt.

Few places in the world of modern technology still had old-fashioned keys, and the jail was no different. There were several places where a badge garnered you entrance, but in this area, you needed a key, too. She held the key to the administrator's office between her fingers, but she couldn't help thinking, *You are crazy for doing this.*

The door opened and Stephanie took a deep breath. She went to his desk first, and then used a hairpin on the center drawer. Remarkably, it opened. She found several more keys—a few of which looked like they might open the file cabinets. Adrenaline pumped through her, making her motions clumsy.

Inside the last drawer, she found quite a few invoices for laundry service deliveries. Some of the laundry was cleaned onsite, but because of the sheer volume, there was also a contract for the service. Stephanie was puzzled, the files didn't appear to be in any sort of order that she could discern. Some of the dates looked familiar, too—maybe they matched dates that Mac had written down.

She grabbed a pen and piece of paper off Neal's desk, intent on writing down as much information as she could. If she could tie together some of the information Mac had written down to the delivery records, it would all make sense.

She looked down at the signature box for each delivery. They were made at different times of the day, so she expected to see varying names; however, there seemed to be a pattern to whoever was available. The names Winthrop, Green, Eason, Baldwin and Samuels were over represented when it came to deliveries. Another disconcerting detail was seeing Neal's name. What would he be doing at the loading dock? A noise behind Stephanie made the fine hairs on back of her neck stand up. Stephanie turned around slowly.

"What are you doing here?"

"Finding out what a fraud you and your cohorts are. How could you do this?"

"Nice words, officer, but you need to save them for someone who cares. I'm afraid my moral compass isn't calibrated quite as high as yours. My actions are a little more motivated by the degree to which I'm compensated." Winthrop started toward her.

Stephanie took a step back, putting the desk in between her and Winthrop.

He sneered as he realized what she was doing. "Nice try, but futile. Let's not make this anymore difficult than we have to. You're coming with me."

He raised the two-way radio to his lips. "Eason, find Baldwin, and then get over here—I've found her. Prepare a room—someone else aside from Neal is going to have an *accident* today."

"Bryant, it's Laurie…I know that you don't know me, but please listen to me. I think Stephanie is in danger. She left for Palo Vista hours ago, and she isn't answering her cell phone."

"I'm on my way."

He'd said four simple words, but the concern in his voice told her that despite what Stephanie thought, he still cared very much. She just prayed that her friend was all right, and if not, that Bryant would make it there in time.

He gunned his Chrysler relentlessly until he reached Palo Vista. He didn't know what the plan was for after he arrived, but he prayed that the gate guard would cooperate with him.

Bryant headed straight for the visitor's gate and said, "One of the officers called me. There's a problem with the computer system." He flashed a business card. "I'm from the independent IT contractor's office, Wilson Communications. I think they're concerned about a facility wide crash, so you'd better let me in; I don't have much time."

"Let me see some ID sir," the harried guard said in his most disinterested tone.

Bryant reached over to the passenger seat to pull out his driver's license. He hoped the man was tired and bored enough not to give a damn at this late hour.

Bryant held his breath as the guard logged him in as visitor and then raised the gate to let him in. *You're going to get yourself killed,* he muttered as he dashed toward the door.

Bryant walked through the normal checkpoints, giving his spiel to each officer along the way. No one saw a call listed, but he was shown toward the administrative area nonetheless. He was almost there when Officer Green stopped him. "Mr. Wilson, what the hell are you doing here so late?"

Sweat formed pools under his arms. "Officer, this is an emergency. I know that I sound like a crazy person, but I have reason to believe that one of your officers, Stephanie Gunn is in trouble. You have to help me find her now."

Bryant raked his hands through his hair in frustration. He was running out of time. He heard commotion behind him; other officers were coming behind him now trying to figure out what he was really up to.

Panic prickled around the edges of his voice. "Officer, I'm begging you. She came here tonight because she wanted to learn about my brother's death, but I think she's in more danger than she knows. We have to help her."

Officer Green realized exactly who he was and changed her stance. "You'd better tell me what's going on and make it good."

Bryant knew he didn't have time to go into all the details, but right now he needed to convince this officer to help them, or they wouldn't make it out alive. "Officer Green. My brother, Macklin discovered something going on in this facility. I'm not sure what he intended to do about it, but he was afraid of someone. He gave Officer Gunn some information, and she came here tonight on her own to investigate. We have reason to believe that several high-level administrators are involved in illegal operations being run out this jail. If you don't believe me, help me find her, and she'll show you the proof.

Officer Green considered what he said for a moment. She sighed heavily. His words confirmed her suspicions of Eason and several other officers. Finally, she said, "Come with me."

She looked around nervously; they wouldn't have much time. This was the first time something like this had happened at the facility, it would take a few minutes for the other officers to become organized. If she was going to do anything, she had to do it now.

Green pointed down the hall. "You take those two rooms, and I'll take these. We've got to hurry, Eason left the front desk almost an hour ago. She may already be dead by now."

"She's not dead," Bryant snapped. "Just let me know if you find her first."

They separated in the dimly lit hallway. He tried to remain positive, but the truth was, his hope had started to wane. The prison was a huge facility; what if they were wrong? Stephanie may not even be down this corridor, and he could be wasting precious time looking in the wrong area.

He opened each door forcefully. He didn't care who he ran into, because stealth was not the goal. He knew that Winthrop's men could be around any corner, but he didn't care. All he wanted was to find Stephanie safe and sound. He would never forgive himself if something happened to her.

Winthrop marched Stephanie to a corner room that was rarely used by the staff that held a few odds and ends.

Stephanie looked around the room to see what they had planned for her. Then she saw him.

She shivered involuntarily once she realized who awaited her there. Baldwin tied her hands with wire handcuffs and gagged her mouth, leaving her helpless against her attacker.

"Enjoy yourself." He nodded toward Harris. Indicating that she was all his.

Harris shut the door behind Baldwin. Unfortunately, Stephanie knew too much about this inmate. His convictions for rape, torture and murder were still legendary in forensic circles. She could only guess at the plan. No one would ask why she was there after her shift, they would add more time to his six life sentences and in a few months, her murder wouldn't even raise an eyebrow. She would be lucky if she made the local headlines for longer than a week.

Gunns and Roses

Harris had a sadistic side and psychological make-up that only true serial killers possessed. There was no small wonder he was chosen to finish her off.

Maybe if she were lucky she would pass out before she felt too much. The knife he brandished gleamed in the semi darkness of the room.

He was close enough for her to smell dinner on his breath. The offensive smell nearly caused her to vomit. She fought back the panicked feeling that had begun to unfurl in her stomach.

Think, dammit. There has to be a way out of this.

Harris stroked himself to prepare for her. His hands made circular motions in his unzipped pants. He licked his thick lips as if she were a piece of meat to be savored.

Stephanie shuddered in disgust. Her heart pounded in her chest. She knew basic self-defense, but Winthrop had bound her hands too tight. She was barely able to move her fingers, let alone get a grip on anything to defend herself. She refused to look at him.

Stephanie looked toward the light in the hallway…if she saw someone walk by the door, maybe she could make enough noise to draw their attention.

There was a momentary flash across the doorway. When she looked up, incredibly, there was Bryant. He'd used the key to unlock the door. Stephanie had never been so happy to see anyone in her life.

Harris was so interested in having his way with her that he didn't pay much attention to the noise behind him. He wrongly assumed that it was Winthrop, Baldwin, or another prison official coming to watch or make sure that he had his way with her.

Bryant saw the inmate approaching Stephanie, and he didn't think, he just moved. He lunged at Harris from behind, knocking the knife out of his hands.

Stephanie threw every bit of force she could muster behind the kick that she landed on inmate Harris's groin. He landed face first on the ground, writhing in pain. The sound of his pitiful cries reverberated in the room.

Bryant rushed toward her after Harris had been knocked on the ground. He planted kisses along the sides of her face. "Oh God, I thought I'd lost you. Let me get you to safety. We'll have to find a way to make it back to my car without anyone seeing us. Do you know a back way out of this place?"

He removed the gag and handcuffs, checking her out to make sure she was okay. Other than her ripped shirt, she seemed to be in one piece.

Unshed tears shined bright in Stephanie's eyes. "How in the world did you know where to look? I thought it was over for me."

"I was running out of time and options, but then I saw your badge on the floor. I knew you had to be close. Green helped, too. She must have known something was going on, but was too afraid to say anything." He spoke quickly out of nervous energy. "Mac made things worse for himself. I know that now. Will you ever forgive me?"

Before she could answer, they heard, *clap, clap, clap*. Both turned to see Gus Winthrop. "That was so touching; too bad it won't help either one of you." He used his two-way radio to call Baldwin.

Baldwin reappeared almost instantly, disappointed that his earlier plan had failed and Stephanie was alive and well.

Baldwin looked toward Winthrop plaintively. "What do you want me to do now, boss?"

Bryant ignored the question as he looked directly at Winthrop. "You killed my brother."

"Not directly, but it was arranged. Big Mac made a lousy criminal. He kept getting in over his head. I think we did him a favor—with the governor's stance on crime, his next conviction would have sent him to prison for life. This way we saved the state money and you time. You would have been able to keep living the stellar life that you've chosen for yourself. However, now my partners and I can't allow you to disrupt our operation. We have a product to deliver and our customers are very demanding. As a matter of fact, we have a delivery scheduled for tonight."

Bryant noticed that the alarms had been turned off, indicating that no one else was looking for him. If they had a delivery, they probably wanted things to quiet down in order to return to normal as quickly as possible. No need to call unnecessary attention to the facility. Nosy cops would interfere with the schedule.

Bryant refused to be intimidated. "How do you think you're going to be able to get away with this? Your operation has already gone down the tubes."

Winthrop dismissed his comment with a wave of the hand.

"You can't make your problems disappear. How will you explain what happened? Too many people saw me come in. Hell, I'm surprised that I'm not in handcuffs now."

"Take them down to the dock," Winthrop instructed Eason. "They'll disappear on the way to the drop point. It will be months before they're found. Certainly well after the news and public lose interest in the story anyway."

Stephanie and Bryant were both handcuffed this time. Then they were led toward the door. Bryant stopped suddenly as if he was about to trip. He lunged toward Winthrop, knocking him directly into the cleaning supplies on the shelves. Winthrop's momentum carried him down with the bottles of cleanser, cracking several open. He screamed in pain as the toxic chemicals burned his skin and eyes. Before Baldwin could react appropriately, he met the same fate with Stephanie's help as she pushed him toward the bottles.

Their next move was to secure them. Bryant had no idea about taking down people or arrest measures, but what he lacked in academic knowledge, made up for in instinct.

After Baldwin, Winthrop and Harris had been tied up, they heard the sound of the police led by Officer Green bursting into the room.

"Damn, y'all made quite a mess in here." She stated as she motioned for the officers to take over. "You two, come with me." Stephanie and Bryant followed her safely out of the room back down to the administration offices, where they were met by chief of police instead of the Detention supervisor. He told to them that Neal's body had been found in the prison trash. His throat had been slit.

Stephanie grimaced. She didn't doubt it was by the same knife that glinted in the moonlight on the floor of the small room. The same knife Harris had intended to use to do her harm.

She looked toward Bryant who nodded in agreement and then she said, "Mac Wilson left information for his brother that I think will be helpful. I need to turn this over." Holding the paper from Mac in her hand, she said, "There's someone else's involvement that you should know about."

Smoot was in the strip bar when the police located him. They were trailed by ambulance-chasing journalists on the hunt for a good story. Both the police and the press interrupted his private party with Ginger and Venus in his office. He was caught with his pants down literally and figuratively. There was a nice photo of Smoot being straddled by Ginger who wore a strap-on, while Venus lay underneath him.

Gunns and Roses

The headline they would have loved to print would never make the local papers: **Councilman Gets It Where He's Been Sticking It**.

Nonetheless, Chester Smoot knew he was ruined. Even if the drug charges didn't stick, his life would never be the same. The conspiracy to commit murder charges would take care of that.

Stephanie and Bryant gave their statements to the detectives assigned to the case, and were finally released in the late hours of the evening. It was hard to recount the details of the drug operation and to know the reason Mac was killed wasn't because he wanted to expose them. They found out he wanted a piece of the action. Bryant had to come to terms with the fact that his brother was never going to change.

They were both exhausted, physically and emotionally. Bryant put his arms around Stephanie. As they walked, he covered her torn uniform shirt with his jacket. He held her face in his hands. "I'm very proud of what you did tonight. You made a difference to help take down a corrupt system."

He held her close. "Come home with me, Stephanie. We have so much to make up for, and frankly, I don't want to let you out of my sight."

Tension knotted her shoulders. The thought of being in her townhouse alone didn't appeal to her in the least after her experience with Harris. She thought about calling Laurie again, but decided against it. Honestly, she didn't want to leave Bryant either. She gladly accepted his offer.

"Let me drive you. I'll come back for your car in the morning," he added. "I don't want you to ever have to come back to this hell hole."

"Thank you. I don't think that I could bring myself to ever walk through these doors again anyway."

They exited the building under police escort. He thanked his lucky stars that Officer Green had been there to help him; otherwise tonight's outcome would have been very different.

Bryant helped Stephanie into the car and they headed toward Lake Merritt. Despite the circumstances, he looked forward to taking her to his home. He wanted nothing more than to take care of her. And he wanted to do it for a very long time.

They stopped by her place long enough for her to pack a bag. He waited in the kitchen while she grabbed a few essentials.

After they arrived at his place, the first thing she did was take a long hot shower in his black marble roman shower.

He waited patiently for her, even though he wanted to join her more than anything. He wasn't thinking sex now; he was thinking protection. Almost losing her had unsettled him. He wouldn't ever take that chance again. He hated the thought of someone causing her harm. The vision of Harris about to touch her in such a vile way invaded his thoughts. He made a silent vow that no man would ever threaten his woman again. Hmmm…his woman had a nice ring to it.

He heard Stephanie come out of the shower and then disappear into his dressing room. She emerged a few minutes later dressed in a short cotton sundress.

He had poured wine, which had been chilling while he waited for her. He took her by the hand and led her to the living room. His loft felt twice the size of her townhouse, though she had living space on two floors, and he on just one.

While he'd waited for her to come out of the shower, Bryant had turned on music, lit several candles around the room and put flowers on the table. Roses, which she had told him were her favorite.

Stephanie took it all in, allowing herself to experience the beauty after such a horrifying ordeal. Bryant let her wander around, checking out his place until her nerves settled down and she felt more comfortable.

The view outside had a way of drawing you in. It was breathtaking. Stephanie found herself, despite her desire to look around, captivated by the sights outside. She stood rooted to the spot where she had the best vantage point.

Bryant held her from behind as they watched the stars outside his bay window twinkle in the night sky. In the distance, she was able to watch the lights shimmer off the water of Lake Merritt.

She felt safer in his arms than she ever had before. "Ummm, this feels good."

He whispered into her hair, "Yes, it does. Don't feel the need to ever leave."

She giggled. "Are you making some sort of proposal?"

"Yes, I am. Are you accepting?"

He turned her around, kissing her soundly as motivation for the answer he sought.

Stephanie leaned into Bryant's embrace. His strong arms encircled her body, before he leaned down to kiss her gently. He took his time, languidly filling her mouth with his tongue, exploring her...tasting her...loving her.

Stephanie broke the kiss after several minutes. "I think we're a bit overdressed, Mr. Wilson."

He answered her by slipping the sundress over her head, revealing her red bra and lacy thong. His body's reaction to his favorite color was exactly as she'd hoped. Stephanie smiled wickedly. "See something you like?"

His searing kiss was her answer. Bryant increased the pressure of his kiss and the grip he had on her exposed ass. He brought her closer, nudging her legs upward. She wrapped them around him, gyrating her body against his length.

Stephanie felt her body pulsate in response. This was the man she knew she would love forever.

Bryant wanted to be patient, but she drove him to near madness. He stopped the kiss long enough to begin to undress himself. "Do you think we should head to the bedroom," he asked.

Stephanie glanced around the room, which seemed fine to her. She was in no hurry to leave their present location. Not as long as she was in his arms. "Maybe in a minute."

With Will Downing's "Emotional" CD playing in the background and the backdrop of the stars, the night and the mood were just right.

Bryant lay her down on the plush sofa that sat in front of his large entertainment center. He finished undressing himself and teased her as he removed her bra. He teased her ripe nipples to tight buds with his fingers.

The fragrance of the burning sandalwood candles scented the air. She loved the musky masculine aroma that emanated from them—everything was perfect, she thought. Feeling good, safe and sexy, she teased him right back as she stood up to slowly remove the thong.

Completely naked now and kissing passionately, they fell back onto the plush oversized sofa. Bryant protected them, then positioned himself over her, but he didn't enter her just yet. He wanted to prolong the sweet agony of being close, but not in her.

Stephanie kept her impatience at bay, but just barely. His sensual kisses and teasing had her body on fire. She waited as long as her body would allow; then Stephanie rolled him on his back, taking charge.

His surprised smile made her bolder. Stephanie tucked her hair behind her ears, and then leaned down to kiss him, but instead of kissing, she nipped his lips with her teeth. She came at him first hard, and then soft.

He played her game...for a while. Then decided to turn the tables again. He slightly lifted her body. He needed to taste her. He admired her firm breasts, caressing each before taking her nipples one at a time into his mouth.

Stephanie positioned herself over him so that she could enter her wet, slick space. Their coming together was fierce, feral and above all, perfect.

Gunns and Roses

Bryant held her in place with a tight grip on her ass. Stephanie threw her head back as Bryant plunged deeper into her haven, pushing her down to meet him stroke for stroke.

His position was just right to stroke her clit at the most pleasurable angle. She felt herself approaching her peak. The world began to shatter into pieces. There was nothing but light and sensation and most of all Bryant. Each thrust brought them to higher heights of fulfillment.

Guttural moans from Stephanie and Bryant filled the room, bouncing off the walls of his loft space. Will's singing had nothing on the harmony they created together. Their explosive climax had them both keen in ecstasy.

Once his head cleared, he said, "Stay with me."

"I am."

"Not just tonight, forever."

She sighed happily. "I am."

Handcuffs Mean Never Having to Say You're Sorry

by

Gwyneth Bolton

Acknowledgements

The first thank you goes to the Happy Hundreds of the Central New York Chapter of Romance Writers of America. I really don't think I can thank them enough for adding me late to the challenge. I know that I wouldn't have made time to write without it and the daily encouraging e-mails. Second, I have to thank Lil' Kim for making hot music and having such a sick flow. If *Naked Truth* is any indication, we have yet to see just how much fire this emcee can bring. Third, thanks to my husband for providing inspiration and understanding when I just *have* to write. Thanks to the Parker Publishing, LLC family for giving me a chance to be in this wonderful anthology with fabulous authors such as Beverly Jenkins and Katherine D. Jones. And last, but certainly not least, thanks to my editor, Deatri King-Bey. As always, it was wonderful working with you. Thanks for helping me make this novella the best it could be.

1. Schemin'

P ull out ya nine, while I cock on mine—!" Tamara Downing left
the four-story brick building that housed Murder Row records
rapping Lil' Kim lyrics and aiming her imaginary gun. Her real
Newark PD issued piece was in the car.

Yes, things were going her way. Tommy Coles had finally noticed
she was alive, and it would only be a matter of time before she could
put his behind up under the jail. NPD believed that he ran a prostitution ring out of Murder Row, luring girls in with dreams of stardom.
Several of his former "video models" had gone missing, and one was
badly beaten but wouldn't talk.

The ringing of her cell phone snapped her out of her momentary
revelry, and she quickly pulled it out of her handbag as she made her
way from the building to her car. She'd just turned the dang thing on
again since she always turned it off when she was working.

Giving the dark parking lot a quick once over, she mentally
prepared herself for any trouble. Murder Row Records was known for
unsavory characters, and she had no desire to get caught out there by
someone who saw her as an easy mark. And, even though she'd been
born in Newark and raised in East Orange, New Jersey, she knew that
dark parking lots in Brick City—Newark's unofficial nickname—
didn't mix with petite young women in super-tight lycra mini dresses.
She could more than handle herself if pressed to do so, but it
wouldn't exactly bode well with her undercover assignment if she
started going all *Alias* and *Xena: Warrior Princess* in the parking lot.

Letting her feet move a little faster when she spotted two strange-
looking men in the shadows, Kara answered her phone softly. "Yeah."
She tried to answer it as quickly as possible. The Lil' Kim ring tone

she'd downloaded that played "Shut Up, Bitch" just might have given the jerks in the parking lot the wrong idea.

"It's about time you answered the phone, baby. I've been so worried about you. You didn't stop by the past two Saturdays like you normally do."

Mama Paula. Tamara loved the woman who'd saved her life by taking her in after her mother died. But Mama Paula brought worrying to new height.

"I'm fine, Mama Paula. Honest. But I can't talk now." Holding her cell phone to her ear with her shoulder, she started to unlock the door to her red poor-girl's version of a sports car.

Mama Paula hesitated slightly, and Tamara knew instinctively that couldn't be good. Mama Paula only went silent when she felt a little bit guilty or ill at ease about something she'd done. When it came to Tamara's life or business that could only mean one thing. "Oh. Okay. I was just worried. That's why I asked Lance to—"

Several curse words ran through her head, but she had way too much respect for Mama Paula to utter any of them. "Oh, Mama Paula, tell me you didn't ask Lance to check up on me. You know I don't like the way he steps in and tries to—"

Before Tamara could finish her sentence, a gun and a badge were in her face. The shadowed men that she'd thought were thugs turned out to be something worse.

"Unh, Mama Paula, I have to go now." Tamara hung up the phone without waiting for a response. One of the men had already started cuffing her, and he clearly needed her other hand free to finish the job.

"She's going to be mad as hell at you for this."

Lance King glanced at his childhood friend, Mark Smith, with disdain. Mark had chosen the Newark Police Department, and Lance had chosen the DEA, but both men fought crime and injustice wherever they found it. They were usually on the same page. But ever since Tamara had made detective and had been placed in Mark's division, Lance and his best buddy seemed to agree on less and less.

Lance glanced at the irritated and angry Tamara through the interrogation room window. She couldn't see him. But he could see and hear her, could almost see the steam rising from her head and hear the razor sharpness of her tone as she chewed his men out.

Tamara couldn't be more than five feet, but one would never know it listening to her when she was angry. The brown-skinned beauty with baby-doll looks could out-cuss a sailor sailor if she thought someone was trying to disrespect her or she felt someone she loved was in jeopardy. Having been on the receiving end of some of her more well-known verbal blasts during the past ten years, he didn't particularly look forward to entering the interrogation room to face her.

"You could have done it my way and just pulled her off the case. Or better yet, you could have listened to me and never put her on the case."

Tommy Coles was bad news, period.

Lance had run into him in previous operations, and he was happy to finally be in a position to take the man down.

Lance pulled his gaze away from the fuming Tamara and shrugged. "Nah, you had to make me pull rank. Now the DEA will be taking over the case, and it'll be wrapped up so quickly, trust me. Lil' Bit will have all new reasons to hate my guts before long."

Not that she needed more reasons to hate him. He was pretty sure the woman had a longstanding list she added to on the regular. At least, when he was able to get within ten feet of her. Most of the time she avoided him, which made it a little difficult to plead his case.

If he ever got her alone for a day or two, with nothing or no one around to interrupt, he was sure he could work his magic. And maybe, just maybe, he wouldn't even need to apologize. She'd just be able to see how much he cared and would forgive him.

Handcuffs Mean Never Having to Say You're Sorry

Yeah. Right.

Maybe having his DEA team pose as NPD blue and pull her into her own precinct wasn't the best of ideas. But hey, the woman left him no choice. She wouldn't return any of his phone calls. He'd been trying to call her for the past two months to let her know there was a possibility that their cases might overlap. Then his mother called all worried because she hadn't seen Tamara in a couple of weeks. He had Tamara pulled in because he wanted to let her know he was on the case, and he'd be arresting Tommy soon. A simple phone call could have sufficed if she returned his.

Mark shook his head and leaned with his back against the surveillance glass. "She was getting close to breaking the prostitution case herself. She's not going to appreciate you honing in." Chewing on a toothpick and smirking as he spoke, Mark seemed to be taking an enormous amount of pleasure in Lance's predicament.

"She never does." Lance sighed. It went with the territory as far as he was concerned. "We're closer to busting his ass on the drugs. The sooner we get Tam outta there the better. I wish we could pull her out now without drawing too much attention. This wouldn't be a problem if she hadn't been on the case in the first place. Plus, I've heard some things hanging around those fools that I don't like. Mama's worried, and she'd kill me if something happened to Lil' Bit that I could have prevented."

"*Lil' Bit* is a big girl now. She can take care of herself. Trust me, she is not going to take too kindly to the DEA hauling her in from the Murder Row parking lot. She's going to claw your throat out when she gets a chance. Me? I'm just going to watch it go down. That's why I decided it would be better for you to pull rank than for me to pull her from this case. I don't want that little spitfire mad at me."

"I can't believe you're scared of Lil' Bit." Lance would have added a laugh to the incredulous tone he used, but he wasn't so cocky as to think that the woman couldn't put the fear of God into someone, especially when she got mad enough.

168

It amazed him that a woman with such a petite and curvaceous frame had a mouth that could do more damage in fewer words than anyone he'd ever met. When she got angry, those big, bright brown eyes flashed and danced. They were almost as vibrant and passionate when she was mad, as they were when she was making love and in the moments of hot, steamy desire. *Almost.*

He noticed that she'd cut her shoulder-length hair into one of those little pixie cuts, and the style made her look even more innocent and doll-like than any grown woman should look. How could she blame him for wanting to protect her and take care of her?

"She's not the same little kid." Mark pushed away from his leaning spot and took a seat at the small wooden table in the center of the room. "And she doesn't want you in her business. She made that clear when she came to work for me. And I quote, 'don't be telling that wack-ass DEA friend of yours any of my business. If he asks anything about me, don't tell him a damn thing. I don't want him in my life.'" Mark imitated her timbre and twisted his head back and forth in perfect sista-girl style.

Lance winced. Hearing Tamara's words from his best friend's mouth cut him deep. It let him know for a fact that really nothing short of being stranded on a deserted island with Tamara would make her listen to him and hopefully forgive him. So, he'd have to come up with a solid Plan B. Tamara's words and her attitude toward him meant it would be hard as hell to get her to see reason.

But reason she would see, or his name wasn't Lance King.

Letting out a sharp hiss of breath, Tamara vowed that if she ever saw Lance King again, she'd skin him alive. How dare he send his DEA goons to harass her while she was working a case? And how dare he have them haul her into her own precinct like a common criminal? Okay, so maybe she hadn't returned any of his phone calls, even the ones marked urgent. But that didn't give him the right to haul her in. It was hard enough being a woman with those sexist cavemen she worked with reminding her of her gender time after time. They would never let her live the arrest down.

The inane questions Lance's men asked her proved they were just holding her until Lance showed his stupid face. She was willing to bet the jerk was in back of the surveillance window watching her along with his buddy Mark.

Mark knew better than to let Lance know her business. And if he didn't before, she would make sure he never forgot again. Mark Smith might have been her boss, but she fully intended to give him a piece of her mind for teaming up with Lance against her.

When Lance finally did walk into the room, she thanked God that she was too angry with him to be swayed by his muscular frame and smooth demeanor. It wasn't as if walking clichés didn't still make her salivate and his Tall-dark-and-handsome, tall-drink-of-water vibe wasn't still in full effect. She just wasn't biting.

Her eyes roamed his body, noting the confident assured swagger that marked each of his steps, and she swallowed. Okay, maybe she was biting, a little. But she wasn't swallowing.

Holla. Back. His shoulders appeared broader. Thighs firmer. Arms stronger. Eyes dreamier. The man just plain got finer. Where was the justice in that?

Pulling up a chair and straddling it backwards, Lance parked himself right in front of her. Tamara knew there was a God, and he obviously smiled on Lance because handcuffed to her own chair she couldn't scratch his eyes out the way she desperately wanted to. *Hauling me in. Humiliating me in front of my colleagues. Putting my case in jeopardy. Oh hell no!*

"So Lil' Bit, I don't need to tell you why you're here. The Murder Row case is ours now."

Lance made sure he looked her in the eyes when he spoke, and she made sure she stared him right back in the eye.

"Mark should have never put you on the case, and they don't want to just pull you off it. They think it will look too suspicious. But I'm thinking you can be so distraught that you were hauled in for questioning that you can tell Tommy Coles you no longer feel comfortable working there. That way, I can just wrap this up and you'll be safely outta there. I plan to have this wrapped up within the next day or so."

"Forget you, Lance. How you just gonna waltz in here and take over a case I've been working on for the past two months?" Tamara all but hissed the words and even tugged at her handcuffs. If she could get out, he would be sorry. The Murder Row case had been her first major undercover operation since making Detective. She really wanted to bust Tommy Coles on the prostitution, especially after the way her mother died.

Rubbing his chin in a slow, easy, appraising manner; he offered casually, "I did some digging, and this is not the case for you."

"You can't just pull rank and stop me from doing my job. It's not fair." Appealing to the reason he clearly didn't use probably wasn't the best option, but she did so anyway.

Shrugging, Lance pushed the chair back as if closing off all conversation. "Life isn't fair, Lil' Bit. Now will you cooperate and tell Mark you're fine with stepping down and letting me and my team handle this?"

Jerk. "No."

"Figured that much." He got up from the chair.

"Then why'd you bother?"

"Because I care and because I can." Lance pushed the chair back underneath the metal table.

Tamara watched as he walked out of the room. Soon after he left, they released her. She didn't even bother responding to her colleagues in blue as they heckled her leaving the building. It would probably take her years to live this experience down. *I can't stand Lance King! Urggghhh!*

Handcuffs Mean Never Having to Say You're Sorry

Stepping out into the crisp Newark night air, she quickly saw that she didn't have to worry about how she would get home.

The Murder Row limo waited for her outside the precinct.

"Get in, Darling." A smooth voice attached to an even smoother head demanded.

Great. Tommy Coles. That idiot Lance probably ruined everything. Tamara slid into the limo and decided to play it brazen. She'd come too close, and she wasn't about to let the DEA, in the form of Lance King, throw salt in her game.

When she got into the limo, the record label mogul and suspected criminal, gave her a once over and told the driver to take off.

They rode in silence, and Tamara started to get a little nervous. The only thing worse than being nervous was not being able to show it. Fidgeting around in her seat wouldn't do. Neither would stammering or compulsive swallowing to get rid of her sudden dry mouth. No, playing it cool was the only way to go.

Biting the inside of her jaw slightly, she sat back as if she didn't have a care in the world. After looking out the window and taking in the passing tenements and high-rise buildings that made up downtown Newark, she turned toward Tommy. He seemed to be studying her every move. *Not good.*

She didn't want to end up among the many missing people that crossed Tommy or thugs like him, so she decided it was time to do something. When in doubt, pull out the Jersey Girl charm that some people mistook for attitude.

"When I took this job as your receptionist, I didn't think I'd be hauled in for questioning." Deciding full on indignant girl in the hood montage was the only way to go, Tamara rolled her eyes, swayed her neck, and twisted her lips to the side for good measure. "I didn't say anything 'cause I don't know anything. But, I'm saying though, even if I did, I wouldn't have said nothing. I don't roll like that. Darling Downing ain't no snitch."

172

Tommy must have stared at her for a full two minutes before he even gave the indication that he might respond.

Her heart pounded in her chest, and she tried to keep her blasé cool-girl demeanor up as he seemed to be deciding what to do with her.

Leaning back and brushing imaginary dirt off his shoulders, he paused for a moment before speaking. "What did they ask you, Darling?"

Shrugging as if she could care less, while, meanwhile, her entire life flashed before her eyes, Tamara sighed. "They wanted to know about drugs and prostitution. I told them far as I knew the only thing coming out of Murder Row was dope music. And the last time I checked, they couldn't arrest anyone for making people dance. You know what I mean?" She slurred her last question together into one word the way all the rappers and hip-hop heads she'd been around the past two months did.

Tommy smiled, but she kept her twisted I-got-an-attitude expression on her face.

"You sure you didn't tell them anything?" Eyes slanted slightly, Tommy didn't seem to be buying her act at all.

Blowing out an exaggerated breath, she looked him right in the eye. "I don't know nothing. What was I supposed to do, make shit up?"

Tommy laughed. "I like you, Darling. You got a sexy little body and a hardcore attitude, and I was thinking of promoting you and getting you from behind that receptionist's desk." Tommy watched her carefully. "I'm going to hold off on my plans for you for a minute. See what happens with all this. If your story pans out and you didn't tell the cops anything, then we'll be cool. And I'll show you ways to use all that body and attitude to get paid. If not, then you're going to have a whole lot more problems than this."

Tommy slid over and leaned way too close for her liking. Pausing for only a moment, he lowered his head and covered her lips with his.

Now, on an average day, Tamara would be the first to admit that Tommy Coles had the fine, whip appeal action going on full blast. The tall, suave, cocoa-complexioned brother had it going on. Muscles like whoa and a smile like damn. And, if she didn't know for a fact that he was a smooth criminal and shadier than the majority of his so-called record deals, she might have welcomed his kiss. Knowing all of the above, the best she could do was fake it.

Since she didn't want to blow her cover, she opened her mouth and purred slightly, allowed him to suck her tongue just a bit before pulling away as shyly and demurely as she could, all the while wanting to claw his eyes out with her acrylics.

"Mr. Coles...wow...I—" Affecting a soft stammer and diverting her gaze just enough to let him think that his kiss had knocked her off her feet, Tamara tried to figure out her next course of action; just in case Mr. Smooth Operator had a hard time taking no for an answer.

"I've wanted to taste those luscious lips of yours for a minute now. I sure hope you're telling the truth and didn't blab your mouth to the cops. 'Cause I really want to taste other parts of you." He gave what she figured he thought was a seductive wink as she tried not to puke.

Tamara lowered her eyes and let out a soft sigh. *Play it up for all it's worth*, she told herself. "I didn't, Mr. Coles. Honest." Glancing up and looking him dead in the eyes, she offered for the closer, "I would never play you or Murder Row like that. I'm a down-ass-chick, and I believe in riding, and even dying for the crew I'm rollin' with. That's real. That's how I do."

Tommy nodded. "We'll see, shorty. I'll catch you at the office tomorrow."

"Thanks." Tamara got out of the limo and tried to keep herself from cursing. She'd been so close to getting in and bringing Coles down.

As soon as Tamara got into her apartment, she picked up the phone and called Mama Paula. It was late, but she knew the woman would be up and worried since their last call ended so abruptly.

"Mama Paula, it's me. I'm at my place and I'm safe. Your son just had his men pick me up and take me down to my own precinct like I'm a criminal. I'll be the laughing stock of the whole department now. I can't believe him. The DEA posing as Newark PD hauled me in." Rubbing her head, she paused before continuing. "I'm a detective now, Mama Paula. I can't have the DEA coming in and taking over every case Lance thinks is too *whatever* for me. Call him off please."

Several times when she'd been a beat cop, Lance, in one of his undercover personas, would show up, surveying her scene, checking up, and sometimes getting way too involved. His heroics might have had some women swooning at having their own personal knight in shining armor. And if Lance had wanted anything to do with her besides saving her neck and looking out for her, she might have been one of them. But her motto was simple, *if you don't want me, you can't save my ass, sorry.*

"Oh, Lil' Bit, he just worries about you." Mama Paula chuckled a little before offering in her usual calm and soothing voice, "We all do. You're like a one woman mission, and sometimes it don't hurt to have a little help."

Oh brother. Mama Paula was about to get on her wouldn't-hurt-to-have-a-little-help kicks. That could only be followed by meet-a-nice-man-settle-down-give-her-some-grandbabies speech. Tamara certainly wasn't going to tell her that the only man she'd ever considered settling down with had rejected her and turned into a one man protection team. Besides, she reasoned, *Mama Paula wouldn't want someone like me for a daughter-in-law anyway, even if dreams came true.*

"I don't need help." *Especially not from your always-in-my-business son.* "Mama Paula, I'll try and see you this weekend. Tomorrow is Friday. I'll either come by after work, or I'll stop by on Saturday. Okay?"

"Why not come by for Sunday dinner?"

The only time she made it back home to East Orange and Mama Paula's was when she was sure Lance wouldn't be there. "Sundays don't work for me. But I will see you on Friday or Saturday. I love you, okay. Bye now. Get some rest. And don't forget to call off Lance." Tamara hung up the phone.

"It's not going to work you know."

Startled, Tamara screamed and nearly jumped off of the bed. Turning to see Lance leaning against her bedroom door, she cursed. "Breaking and entering is a crime. And I would be well within my rights to shoot your ass right now."

Nonchalant and way too cool for her taste, Lance shrugged. "I just wanted to give you one more chance to back down. I suggest you don't go in tomorrow." He walked over to her bed. Standing there in slacks that fell just right on his muscular thighs, he used his sexy dark brown eyes to shoot his warning.

Deciding she wouldn't let his mocha-complexioned, sexy-dimpled self get under her skin any more than he already had, Tamara pursed her lips. "I suggest you stay out of my business."

Lance sat down on the bed. "Is this about us? Because you don't need to go out and get yourself killed to prove I messed up." He leaned forward, and it seemed as if all the air in the room disappeared.

It was all she could do to breathe, let alone speak.

What is it with dudes tonight? Do I have a sign on my forehead that reads it is all-about-you-stud-kiss-me-invade-my-personal-space? "Your ego is mad big! Everything I do doesn't revolve around you. Now, if you could show yourself out of my apartment. I have to work in the morning."

Lance leaned over just slightly and brushed his lips across hers. "Sleep tight, Lil' Bit. I guess I'll see you tomorrow."

"Oh, don't feel obligated to do so. You could always just—oh, I don't know—mind your business." She shot him a warning glare of her own, one she hoped he would see fit to take.

He let his hand rest on her thigh for a moment as he pretended to think about it. "Yeah, that doesn't really work for me. But thanks for the advice."

His gaze held hers for a few minutes that literally felt like hours. If she could have thought of one snappy thing to say or had the state of mind to formulate a sentence, she would have been fine. Swallowing several times, it was all she could do to keep her eyes focused on him. She wasn't about to let him see how he unnerved her.

Lance opened his mouth as if he was about to say something, and she twisted her lips to the side and hit him with her most *diva-fied* stare. He closed his lips and squinted like he had something to figure out. Whatever it was, she hoped he would do it out of her presence. There was only so much a girl could take and still keep her clothes on. Lance needed to vacate the premises with a quickness.

Getting up from the bed, he turned. He again opened his mouth like he was going to say something, and then he stopped. Turning back around, he left and only then did Tamara's breathing return to normal.

2. Do What You Like

A man on a mission, Lance walked into the shady after-hours spot in search of Tommy Coles. The seedy, hole-in-the-wall club had the thick smell of sweat and just a hint of illegal substances. The latest Murder Row rap tune blasted from the speakers, and it was apparent, just from the general vibe, that they depended on not just the music Tommy put out to set the mood. Lance knew he had to make it his business to make sure Tommy's entire operation was shut down for good.

Tamara didn't want to listen. *Fine*. She didn't want his help. *Too bad*. Enough was enough, and Lance knew things between them would get worse before they got better.

Tamara never forgave him for what she saw as his rejection of her. He only recently forgave himself for what he saw as his taking advantage of her. The thing was, even if he could go back in time and change things, he wouldn't change a thing.

Sex with Tamara, the one night they had spent together, blew his mind. He wouldn't change that experience, even if it meant she would never find it in her heart to forgive him. The memories of her sweet, lush body got him through many a lonely night while undercover. He had to watch and carefully monitor the connections he made. Becoming intimate while in deep cover was always more trouble than it was worth.

Pausing against a wall in the club, Lance felt the memories of that night begin to waft their way across his mind. He'd been home after his first year training with the DEA, and Tamara had come home from her first semester at college. She and Kia had gone to different schools, so the girls were spending the majority of their winter break partying and having fun. His mother was just happy to have them all home at the same time.

Up until that moment, he'd always thought of Tamara as another little sister, someone to look out for. She'd changed after being away from home those few short months, and his twenty-five-year-old libido responded unusually strong to the eighteen-year-old.

She'd started seeing a little punk that Lance had known was no good. And he had finally proved once and for all that the creep was indeed a thug drug dealer and had him and his up-and-coming crew arrested. Tamara politely cursed Lance out instead of thanking him.

She'd never gotten upset when he'd looked out for her before, not the way his sister Kia usually did. So, her sudden change stunned him.

He'd sat silently while she told him all about himself. Before he knew it, he was kissing her and she had kissed him back. Her mouth had tasted like candy rain, quenching every thirst he'd ever felt and even some he had no idea he had.

His hands had literally ripped off her clothing, and he had her pinned against the wall. The moment it had taken to unbuckle and pull down his trousers went by in a blur. He was inside of her sweet, warm sticky heat in seconds and broke through her hymen seconds after that.

The sharp cry that had come through her lips at that moment startled him. He'd wrapped his arms around her and held her. The both of them had been still until she slowly arched her back against the wall and started to rotate her hips.

He'd taken that as her adjustment and covered her mouth with his. Kissing her, he slowly took Tamara and himself closer to satisfaction with each thrust of his hips.

Just remembering the way she felt wrapping his sex with her own made him shudder. He should have stopped then and there when they had both reached fulfillment. But instead, he'd spent the entire night loving every inch of her sexy little body.

Then, in the light of day, realizing he had betrayed the vow he made to look after her when she lost her mom, he told her that what happened between them could never happen again. *Well, who's sorry now?*

He moved from the wall he was leaning on and walked over to Tommy Coles's table. Tommy's bodyguards moved to block him and were immediately called off by Tommy.

Tommy stood and gave Lance a pound. "Well if it isn't Stan the Ruler! Long time no see man. I haven't seen you around these parts in a minute. What's crackin'?"

"Nothing, man. Everything is everything. I had to lay low after that DEA busted up the operation. I was out of town when it all went down, but you know I'm holdin' it down for Pat until he gets out of prison." Lance had crossed paths with Tommy in his under-cover persona of Stan "The Ruler" King. Although he had long since taken out most of the crooks whom he'd connected with as "The Ruler," some, like Tommy, still had their day coming.

"Shit, from what I heard that's gonna be a minute. So, do you still have access to those contacts? Those Colombian cats I'm fuckin' with trying to break a brotha. I might be interested in hooking up with a new supplier."

Greed and always looking for a cheaper way to make a bigger buck had been the ruin of many crooks. Tommy Coles wasn't any different.

Lance nodded slowly. "Word. You know I got you, man. I always say it's better when we keep this shit in the family. Shit, support Black businesses. You know what I'm saying? I'm with that. I can have you some stuff soon. Let me know what you want."

"I need as much as you can get me as soon as you can get it. I'm expanding my turf. I even got some new little dime pieces I'm about to put on the stroll." Tommy chuckled and an evil leer came across his face as he appeared to be thinking about the new victims he hoped to exploit. "This one little hot piece who's a receptionist for me right now looks like she was born to fuck. She got a smartass mouth though. I'd have to get her open and hooked first to control her. You know how it goes, man. It's hard out here on a pimp." Tommy held up his hand, waiting for Lance to give him a pound in agreement.

It was all Lance could do not to bend the fool's hand back, breaking it along with his smug face. Lance slapped him five. "I'll tell you what. I'm going to get at my people and get you as much supply as I can. You want me to call you—"

"Nah, man. Just bring it on by Murder Row. I do all my business there. That way, I keep control, you understand?"

"Sure, man. You'll make sure I can get right in to see you so I can get right out when we're done, right?"

"I'm putting you on VIP, man. You just let my sexy little receptionist know who you are, and she'll bring you right back to me."

"Well, all right then. I'll holla. Stay up, man." Lance gave Tommy a pound and walked off steaming. Tommy Coles was going down. And Lil' Bit was going to finally be made to see that it was time for them to stop running. He didn't care if he had to lock her in a room until he got her to listen to him.

3. The Jump-Off

Rose from the ghetto it was hard from the get-go, then I showed the hood the world ain't just made for rich folk…Tamara sung along with Lil' Kim's "Whoa" in her mind as she listened to her iPod and pretended to work. As the receptionist at Murder Row records, she pretended on multiple levels. She faked working when anyone was looking because she truly hated filing and answering the phone. And then there was the fact that she wasn't really a receptionist.

Tamara pulled the earphones from her ears and almost spit out her vanilla latte when she looked up. Turning off Lil' Kim, she took a deep breath. The jerk had followed through on his threats. Lance King waltzed into Murder Row Records like he owned the place. Her first undercover gig, and he had to pull this. Well, she wasn't going down without a fight.

"Welcome to Murder Row Records. Can I help you?" She rolled her eyes and used the home-girl-with-an-attitude tone she'd been using ever since she went undercover as a receptionist with the gangster rap label.

"The name's Stan, baby. I'm here to see the big man, Tommy Coles." Lance spoke his words in the cool blasé manner of a drug dealer, pimp or common street hustler.

The skin on the back of Tamara's neck prickled. She knew that Stan "The Ruler" King was one of his many undercover aliases. He'd been working for the DEA for years. She gritted her teeth.

Narrowing her eyes and twisting her lip to the side, Tamara leaned back in her chair, pulled out a nail file and started fiddling with her nails. "Do you have an appointment?"

"Why don't you check your book, Lil' Bit?" Lance winked and nodded toward the open appointment book on her desk.

No he didn't go there and call me by my childhood nickname up in here! Bristling, Tamara stared at the book. There was no appointment for Stan King. However, in big, bold, red letters on the top of the page for the day it said, *Stan "The Ruler" King is expected to stop by. Just let him in whenever he does.*

Though the last thing she wanted to do was let the egotistical, arrogant man back there. Short of blowing her own cover, she had no choice. She had been playing Darling Downing, ghetto princess receptionist, for almost two months, and she would be damned if she would let Lance ruin it for her. She also wouldn't idly sit by while he bogarted his way in and took over her operation.

Standing, she put on her fakest smile and tried to pull down the ultra-tight, super-short skirt she was wearing, which always managed to rise up while she sat. "If you'll follow me, Mr. King, I'll take you right to Mr. Coles. He's in a meeting, but he requested that you be let in the moment you arrived."

"Thanks, Lil' Bit." Lance said as his eyes roamed her body.

"Darling."

"Pardon me?"

"The name is Darling Downing, not Lil' Bit. I'd appreciate it if you used my name."

"Darling." Lance let the word roll off his tongue with such suave intonation, she almost felt her legs give out. He shook his head and frowned. "If it's all the same to you, I'll just call you Lil' Bit. I like that much better."

Gritting her teeth, she led him to Tommy's office.

Besides bad record deals, Murder Row records was known for beat-downs, shootings, possible killings, drug running, money laundering and prostitution. The prostitution was the reason Tamara had been there two months. So far she hadn't made it too far past the reception area of Murder Row. But she had been close to being invited into the inner circle. If Lance hadn't sent his goons after her…if he hadn't pushed his way in as usual…

"Mr. *Stan* King is here to see you Mr. Coles. The appointment book says to bring him back as soon as he gets here." Tamara couldn't help glancing at Lance and cutting her eyes. As soon as she did it, she regretted it. Tommy Coles caught her and frowned.

She hurried out before she did anything else to jeopardize her mission. She went back to her desk and wanted to sulk, but put on Lil' Kim instead.

The hard-core sexy lyrics usually had a way of taking her to a space where she could calmly face any crap life tried to throw at her. She identified with the Brooklyn girl on a basic level, even though Tamara hailed from the East Orange, New Jersey and currently resided in the Bricks of Newark herself. Everything from Kim's fierce loyalty, to her quest for love and ultimately—albeit never admittedly—approval reminded Tamara so much of herself it was scary.

And she wasn't even going to touch the similarity between she and Kim both falling for the older men who had mentored them and not having that love reciprocated. Heck, there was only so much inward analysis a girl could take, and she wasn't touching that one. Suffice it to say, finding a sense of outright and damn near outrageous sexual freedom in the lyrics was just the added bonus that kept her buying the sexy rap diva's music and singing along.

Listening to Lil' Kim couldn't work its magic with Lance King so close by. Tamara would have given anything to know what was going on in Tommy Coles's office. She knew for a fact that she was going to kill Lance *aka* Stan *aka* "The Ruler" when she got a chance. Envisioning all of the cruel and unusual ways she could torture him, she barely noticed when the front door came flying in and the office became suddenly swamped with DEA agents. *What the hell?*

With guns pointed in her face and DEA yelling for her to get her hands up, Tamara did the only thing she could do. Stand with her hands in the air and plan for the quick and utter demise of Lance "the case stealer" King.

4. No Time (For Fake Ones)

Lance walked into the DEA's Newark interrogation room ready to hear complaints and outright anger from Tamara. Maybe she had a right to be pissed, but he couldn't see it from where he stood. Okay, maybe he could see it, but he couldn't really let it concern him. It was time to put things in motion and get Tamara to see that they belonged together. He could see it now. They needed to be on the same page. If he had to keep her in the interrogation room all night, then so be it.

She might not like the lengths he'd gone to make sure she was safe. But that didn't mean he wasn't going to keep doing it. He cared. A lot.

Lance had heard from one of his sources that Tommy had a new girl he wanted to pimp. Tommy Coles had some big plans for his hot little receptionist, none of which Lance could *ever* let happen. He was already working on shutting down Cole's little drug operation. He saw an opening to do that a little quicker and took it. Case closed. Lil' Bit would just have to deal with it. It sounded strong and good playing the argument out in his head.

The glare she gave him when she glanced up and saw him walking in the room would have made a lesser man run in the other direction.

"You're such a jerk, Lance. I can't believe you pulled this stunt. And take these damn handcuffs off me!" Tamara wiggled in the metal chair and pulled at the cuffs, halting her movement. Her big, bright brown eyes flashed in anger, and she was far removed from the sweet baby-doll appearance she normally wore. So much anger pulsed from her the only doll she could be compared to at that moment would have been the chocolate bride of Chuckie, fangs and all.

Surveying her carefully and noting the intent to do serious harm that flowed from her every pore, Lance decided it would be best to keep her cuffed for a minute. Besides, seeing her handcuffed to the chair was actually sexy. It gave him all kinds of other ideas about what he could do with some more time, a little creativity, and not little Tamara Downing. Maybe there was a way to get her to listen to him that didn't involve the two of them on a stranded island after all. It was something to think about. Meanwhile, he needed to find a way to calm her down a bit.

"I know you think I honed in on your bust but—"

"Think you honed in! Negro, please! You straight jacked my bust and you know it. Why is it that you can't stay the hell out of my life? You've been sticking your nose in my business ever since I was a teenager. I'm sick of it. Back off."

Lance let that slide because she was upset. The truth was, he had been saving her neck from the time she was the snaggle-toothed little kid who used to play with his sister Kia.

The two girls had been best friends. And even though he was seven years older than them, he'd always had a soft spot in his heart for Lil' Bit. He always would. When her heroine-addict mother would leave Tamara in the house alone for days on end, he had been the one to go and get her once Kia told him about it. He'd been the one to make sure Kia never kept that information a secret and let him know whenever Janet went out on one of her binges.

The brave little kid who had been willing to sit home alone because she didn't want to get her mommy in trouble snagged a special place in his heart as an unofficial kid sister. The smart, spunky woman she became stole his heart with what started as one night of passion. If he ever wanted to get the piece of his heart she held back, he was going to have to make her see the light.

"Why are you tripping, Lil' Bit? I was just doing my job. Serving my country. Taking riff-raff off the street. Protecting the innocent and not so innocent. Standard fare for the DEA. I'm sorry if it made your little undercover operation unnecessary. But once you talk with your superiors, you'll see that all the proper channels were followed. Our cases just crossed, and I don't have to tell you who holds more weight. We were just closer to getting him on the drugs. And for the record, I have been on this case a lot longer than you."

Those big beautiful eyes narrowed into slits, and her teeth clenched. "Uncuff me, Lance. I want to go home."

Studying her carefully, Lance took a couple of steps forward and stopped. "I'll uncuff you if you promise not to do anything crazy once I'm in arm's reach."

As she stared at him in contemplation, Lance knew she was seriously considering doing him harm.

Hesitantly, he walked over and unlocked the cuffs. She sat still, and he rubbed her wrist were the metal had pressed into her skin. Touching the soft silkiness of her wrist sent a jolt through him. How did he manage to get excited just rubbing her wrist? That seemed to be one for the record books. Right up there with people who got turned on by weird body parts like ankles.

"I'm really sorry it went down the way it did, Lil' Bit. But you could've just listened to me last night and just left the case alone." If she had listened to him, she would have only been arrested once. He'd given her the perfect way out of the case. All she had to do was tell Coles she didn't appreciate being arrested, and she couldn't work somewhere where the police could haul her in at any given moment. It would have been the perfect cover and wouldn't have drawn any suspicion.

Touching her skin and being so close to her that he was able to get a good strong dose of her scent probably wasn't the wisest move in the world. Being in proximity only made him yearn for her more. It was time to put both of them out of their misery. Since he couldn't arrange a trip to the Bahamas or Hawaii, he'd have to think of another way to get her alone long enough to listen.

Moving away slowly, he eyed her with slight trepidation. "I'll ake you home once everything is processed with Tommy and the thers."

A soft hiss escaped her lips, and she cut him a nasty look. "I can ake a cab."

"I'm taking you home, Lil' Bit." He had a lot of things he anted to say to her, things that couldn't and shouldn't be said in he DEA interrogation room.

"Would you please stop calling me that?" The way she sucked er teeth and slashed him to pieces with her eyes and tone, you ould have thought he'd called her a hooker or something, nything but the sweet childhood nickname folks around the way ad been calling her all her life. What else did you call a short little irl with a big mouth? The nickname just stuck.

He shrugged. "Why? It's your name."

"My name is Tamara, not Lil' Bit. I'm a grown woman, not a id. Call me by my name, please."

Not able to argue with that, Lance paused. She was certainly a rown woman. Grown didn't even begin to describe her.

Softening his voice in a manner that he hoped showed her that e cared about her and what she thought, he ran his hand across his ead. "I can't help it. We have history, Tamara, and that history ncludes me calling you Lil' Bit."

"You didn't call me Lil' Bit the night you took my virginity, ance." A small smirk quickly came across her face, and then just s quickly went away. "So I know you have it in you to call me by y name."

Oh, so she just gonna take us right there, full speed ahead. Fine. es, he had called her a lot of things that night, passion filled ames, sweet seductive names, even loving names he had kept to imself but called her all the same.

Their discussion about that night had been a long time coming. f she wanted to go there he was willing. He just hoped she was able.

Because once he got her alone, they were going to put the past behind them once and for all.

Lance took the handcuffs he still held in his hands and locked her left arm to the back of the chair. "I'll be back in a few to take you home, Lil' Bit. We have some things to settle."

Jerk! That's right. Run. Tamara jerked her hand and silently swore when the cuff bit into her skin. She couldn't believe she had actually sat there and let Lance cuff her again.

With him standing there massaging her wrist, she could barely think straight. His refusal to call her anything but Lil' Bit hadn't helped either. It was because he'd refused to see her as anything other than a kid that he hauled ass after they had sex the first time, her first time.

She still remembered vividly what it felt like to have him fill her. At first, she'd been shocked. But once the shock wore off, she couldn't get enough. He spent the night loving her in ways she'd only dreamed of only to turn tail and run when the daylight came. *Chicken*!

Tamara wanted to be seen as a woman. If Lance couldn't appreciate her for the woman she was, then she vowed to forget all about him. He wanted a little girl, a kid sister he could protect. She needed a man who understood that she was a grown-ass woman.

Giving the handcuff one more yank, she huffed and narrowed her eyes on the door. The next time Lance brought his behind in the holding room, she would make sure he let her go.

When he finally came back into the room, she almost laughed at how he circled her cautiously. He should have been scared. All the crap he'd recently pulled went way past all the years of him getting in her business and coming to her rescue when she had neither asked for nor wanted his input or guidance.

Whenever it even looked like she was going to get in trouble, here he was to save the day. But when it came to facing her grown-up feelings for him, Superman turned into Mighty Mouse. Fine. She could deal with that. But if she had to deal with that, then he needed to do her the favor of keeping his distance.

"So, is everything settled? Can I go home now?" When cuffed to a chair, it paid to be a little cordial. How else was she supposed to get the fool to unlock the handcuffs?

"Yeah. They've processed Tommy. They've moved them all to another building for questioning." Lance shrugged. "Hopefully, we have enough on them to get him off the streets and shut down that den of crime he calls a record label."

It was all she could do not to leap from her chair, handcuffs and all. "What do you mean, you hope? If you can't hold him on what you have, why the hell did you screw up my investigation? I was close to being brought in to his inner circle."

Shaking his head defiantly, Lance sneered. "Yeah, as one of his whores. Tommy had plans to put you on stroll." One look at his face told her that he had no intention of letting that happen.

"So what? We could have handled that. We had other officers in place to act as clients."

"There was no guarantee your division would have been able to control that." Waving his hand in a mixture of dismissal and disgust, Lance continued, "Plus, Tommy tries the merchandise first, and he usually likes to get them real open, getting them hooked on drugs."

Her mother had been a strung-out junkie whore, and because of that he must have thought she wouldn't have been able to handle herself when faced with drugs. Even more because of where she came from she would never be good enough for Lance to give his heart too.

Pushing her insecurities as far away as she could, she tried to focus on the part that would have the least likelihood of making her burst out in tears. "Oh, so that's it. You didn't trust that I'd be able to do what I was trained to do because my mom died as a junkie?"

"That has nothing to do with it, Tamara." Even though his appearance suggested vehement denial, she could hardly believe him with the facts so blatantly staring her in the face.

"Oh so it's Tamara now? Interesting. Take these cuffs off me. I'm outta here." A sharp pain throbbed across her chest, as stuff she'd been sure she'd forgotten ten years ago, started to swell up.

For so long she'd wondered why. Why after the mind blowing, atmosphere-altering lovemaking they had shared that night, Lance ran like his life depended on it. The only conclusion she came up with at the time was her past, at least her mother's past. What man would want the daughter of a junkie who didn't even know who her father was as a girlfriend, let alone wife?

She decided back then that she was fine with Lance's decision. Even though she would never forgive him for not feeling she was good enough, she still had Mama Paula, Kia and now Kia's daughter Jenny. She still had family, even though her real mother was dead and she had lost the man who she'd always seen as a hero and would always be the love of her life. It hurt. But as long as she didn't have to see him, it didn't sting as bad.

"I said I'd take you—"

She took several calming breaths and tried to push all the thoughts of rejection and not being good enough to the back of her head. "Take these cuffs off!" She had to get out of there before she lost it and started crying like a punk. She refused to go out like that. She cried that morning when she begged him to see her as an adult and give them a chance. She'd be damned if she would let him see her cry again.

Lance walked over and unlocked the cuffs. He took a swift step back as she stood. She didn't bother turning to look at him as she left the room.

Damn it! Lance rushed out behind Tamara and grabbed her arm when he caught up with her. "I said I was taking you home."

"I can get myself home. I don't need you, Lance. For anything!" Her eyes had a slight gloss, and he knew from experience she was barely holding it together.

"After I take you home, you can go on about your merry little way, and you don't have to worry about me getting involved or trying to help you out anymore." Even as he said the words, he knew he couldn't ever really keep the promise. He would always look out for Lil' Bit.

"Yeah. Right. You wouldn't be able to stay out of my business if your life depended on it."

Letting out a sigh, he pulled her down the hall. Enough time had gone by. They needed to have it out once and for all. *Time for Plan B.*

"Put your seatbelt on," he suggested once he got her out of the building and into his SUV.

The expression on her face said "go to hell." He figured she probably meant it and would have gladly sent him there personally if she could. However, he wasn't letting any of that hinder his mission.

"Buckle up, Tam."

Cutting her eyes quickly, she grabbed the seat belt and fastened it. He started the car and pulled off.

"So exactly what is it you hope to gain by taking me home? I'll still be pissed at you. I won't like you any more or less than I do right now." She closed her eyes and turned her head toward the window before offering snidely, "In fact, you have nothing to worry about. I don't think I could possibly have a lower opinion of you. It's physically impossible."

"Ha, ha, ha, Lil' Bit. I'd forgotten how hilarious you could be. Maybe you should give up being a cop and take this act on the road. You could be the next queen of comedy."

She didn't miss a beat with her comeback. "Hey, you and your savior complex gives a girl a lot of material to work with. I might even have enough for a one-woman show."

"Do you think I like having to constantly look out for your behind?" Okay, so maybe he did. Sue him. "I was trying to do you a favor. It's not like I wanted to just bust in on your operation, but I heard some things on the street, and I was already moving in on him for his drug operation. The DEA had jurisdiction on this one. And if he's in jail for drugs, he can't run his prostitution ring."

"And I'm supposed to believe you just happened to hear something involving me and Murder Row? That's bull. You were sticking your nose in where it didn't belong."

"So what if I was? Just because you've done an excellent job of pushing everybody away, as if we don't mean anything to you, doesn't mean we have to stop caring about what happens to you." He cared about her and he had no intention of allowing her to make him feel guilty or feel like he should apologize for it.

"I haven't pushed everyone away. I see Mama Paula, Kia and Jenny all the time."

"You don't come to Sunday dinner, and Mama said she hadn't seen you as often as she used to. She was getting worried." Lance knew that the only reason Tamara missed the longstanding Sunday dinners at the East Orange house where they'd all grown up was because she was avoiding him. He couldn't allow it to go on any longer.

"I was on a case. You know the demands of the job, Lance. You could have simply soothed her worries and went on about your business. But instead, you chose to put your nose knee-deep in mine."

"Okay, fine. So maybe I did get a little out of line."

She sucked her teeth and let out a harsh "ha," before she spoke. "A little? You are so out of line you are almost out of the universe. This is my job. I'm not a kid anymore. And I don't think it's *cute* or *heroic* when you stick you nose in where it doesn't belong."

Lance sighed, wishing the sexy, angry woman sitting in his car was a kid again.

The sad fact was the older Lil' Bit got the less enthralled she became with his looking out for her, and those feelings of adoration somehow intensified into a teenage crush that tested every bit of endurance he had.

The one night, after saving her from what could have been an ugly situation with her small-brained-big-dreamed-Scarface-wanna-be boyfriend, things came to a head. And Lance ended up making love to Tamara.

Guilt didn't even begin to describe how he felt about having sex with the eighteen-year-old woman he had protected since she came to live with his family as a scared eleven year old. Lance let out a sigh as he remembered how he had left town as quickly as his feet could carry him and stayed away until he was sure Lil' Bit had given up any hope of repeating what happened.

"Tam, we need to move beyond the past and put this all behind us."

More teeth sucking followed by an attitude laced "mmm mmmm" was the only response she gave him.

As he turned into the driveway of his townhouse in West Orange, he tried to think of a way to get Tamara to listen, forgive and move on. Judging by the way her eyes widened when she realized that he wasn't taking her to her home but instead to his place, it wasn't going to be as easy as he hoped it would be. Good thing he didn't give up easy and had a nice supply of handcuffs handy to make sure Lil' Bit couldn't bolt before he had his say.

"This isn't my home, Lance. I've had enough of you to last me ten lifetimes. I want to go home."

"I'll take you home after we talk. This has been a long time coming, Lil' Bit."

Folding her arms defiantly across her chest, she took on an I-shall-not-be-moved stance. "Too many years have gone by, and frankly, I don't think we have anything to discuss."

Handcuffs Mean Never Having to Say You're Sorry

He watched the sparkling fire in her eyes and almost went into a daze. The big, bright boldness of her stare always made him want to bend over backwards to give her anything her heart desired. That had been the case even before he realized the woman he always thought of as a kid sister could very well be the love of his life.

Sure, he'd run scared when he slipped up and taken her virginity. That was because even then, he wasn't sure she was ready for the intensity of his emotions. Hell, he wasn't even ready. But he was ready now. He glanced at her and took in her spitfire sexiness. Yeah, he was more than ready.

"I'm not going to sit here and argue with you, Lil' Bit. The sooner we hash this out. The sooner I can take you home. Let's go inside."

5. Crush on You

Lance might have lacked his typical stellar sense of awareness where Lil' Bit was concerned, but after about a half hour of her flouncing around his townhouse like some kind of sex kitten talking about letting bygones be bygones. He knew the little minx was up to something.

She apparently thought that by feigning interest and attraction she'd get him to take her home sooner. Poor thing didn't know she was playing with fire.

Lance watched as she pulled her sexy legs up under her and lounged on his couch not bothering to pull down that too tight and way too sexy mini skirt. He reasoned that as usual he'd have to help Lil' Bit. Someone had to teach the woman that sometimes when you play with fire, you get burned. That sometimes a slow, smoldering, somewhat contained heat can flare up into a hot, sizzling, out-of-control flame.

Lance took a seat right next to her on the sofa. Wrapping his arm behind her head, he let his hand briefly caress the back of her neck. "I'm glad you and I are on the same page here, Tam."

The startled expression that came across her face was priceless. But she bounced back with the speed of a cheetah, not missing a beat. Leaning forward so that her ample cleavage almost spilled from her tight little shirt she offered, "Yeah, you know, you and I have history. And some of that history...." She pursed her lips into a seductive half-smile half-flirty pout. "Some of that history might be worth repeating." She batted her eyes and let out a soft Marilyn Monroe lilting sigh.

Smiling, because her pouring it on thick was turning him on, Lance leaned into her space even more than he already was. "That's exactly what I'm hoping. In fact, I'm counting on it."

"Huh?" She sputtered before narrowing her eyes and continuing her game. "I mean, wow, this is a bit of a shock. You seemed so scared of changing the dynamic between us. I just assumed you'd still be overwhelmingly, almost paranoid, psychotically adverse to us *hooking up*." She smirked before slowly licking her lips, saying hooking up like she halfway expected him to bolt from the room.

"That was ten years ago, Lil' Bit. I've had ten years to kick myself for not taking full advantage of our chemistry. Ten years to ponder just how good we would be together. Ten years to remember just how perfect and right you felt in my arms." Deciding that showing was better than telling, Lance leaned forward and covered her lips with his own.

What the heck is going on? Tamara mused as her mouth instantly opened to Lance's demanding kiss. She'd started teasing him and behaving in a sexually suggestive manner because she figured it would make him run for the hills. Instead he seemed totally ready and willing to get it on. And apparently—given the way her tongue forged ahead and her mouth widened to accept his probes—so was she.

His hand started to meander and roam her body as if he was refamiliarizing himself with every single one of her pleasure points. *Ah hah, nipples. Bing, bing. He found two.*

She reacted the same way she did the first time she realized the slightest twist and pull on the tight aroused nubs could make her head spin and her panties wet.

The circular motions of his tongue in her mouth and his hands on her breasts had her panting. Closing her eyes, she reasoned it had been a minute since her last boyfriend. And "Sweet Stick," her battery-operated buddy, just hadn't been making it as hot as she craved. Why shouldn't she take advantage of what Lance the case stealing DEA agent was clearly ready, willing, and *oh so* able to give.

He'd get a case of oh-no-we-crossed-the-imaginary-line-in-my-head-that-keeps-you-safe-in-never-never-land-as-in-never-to-be-touched as soon as they were done anyway. Then he'd hightail it to take her home as fast as he could. In the meantime, she could get a little loving to tide her over. It didn't seem like a bad idea at all.

This time she wouldn't even try to reason with him. She'd get her some maintenance and press on with her business. She was over him anyway. *Ahhhhhh, yeah,* she mused as his hand found its way under her skirt, tearing a hole in the pantyhose and pushing aside the panties. *Bing.* He'd found another pleasure spot.

Were his fingers magic? They had to be. Were they always so dang on point? She didn't know the answer to any of the random questions roaming around in her head. But she did know Lance King was rocking her world, and she would let him.

She stretched open her legs and gave him more access. Judging by the methodic probe of his fingers, he knew exactly what to do with the extra wiggle room. In a matter of minutes, she writhed uncontrollably, and her back arched in an angle that she didn't even know was physically possible.

Lance stopped kissing her to watch her, and she kept her eyes open—albeit slightly wide and awestruck—and totally on him.

Once the last vestige of the orgasm left her, she felt her eyes shrink back down to their normal size. Swallowing slowly, she let her head fall back on the armrest of the sofa. Her breathing finally came back to normal, and she leaned forward.

"This is—"

"Perfect," Lance ended with his own proclamation and covered her mouth again.

Holla. Back.

Handcuffs Mean Never Having to Say You're Sorry

Before she could force her mind to voice another protest, Lance was pulling her off the sofa and draping her on her knees in front of it. With him behind her and the sounds of zippers, ripping foil and sighs of relief converging into one, she knew what was coming even before her skirt was hiked up and her panties came sliding down.

Lance entered her in one swift move, causing her to lunge forward briefly into the cushion. The sofa cushions stifled her moans of pleasure, as Lance moved his hips back and forth. The slap of his pelvis on her behind sounded like music, a smooth clap that only needed a kick and snare to bring in the funk. She didn't need any help bringing in the noise as she screamed out satisfaction when he hit the right spot over and over again.

"You like that don't you, Tam. Tell me you like it Lil' Bit"

"Ahhhhhh! Yesssss. I like it. You know I like it."

"It's mine. Isn't it Lil' Bit? This is mine. It's always been mine. Say it."

A moment of clarity in the mist of orgasmic pleasure struck her and she realized that while it certainly was his, Lance King had rejected it and her. Even if he was now plowing into her like he'd never left and bringing her to the brink of heaven repeatedly with his glorious hands and sweet magic stick, he was the one who'd walked away when she would have gladly given him every part of her.

"It could have been yours but you didn't want it. So you can just enjoy this little romp while it lasts, 'cause it ain't gonna happen again."

Clearly, Lance didn't like the response because his hips picked up a more vigorous pace, and his skilled hands found their way to her left nipple and clit. Working her into a sexual frenzy, making her cum out of her mind, these seemed to be his new missions.

The orgasm that swiftly shook her entire body gave fruit to his labor. "Oh. My. God."

"Come, on Lil' Bit. I know I messed up. But I also know as sure as I know my own name that this is mine. You are mine. So why don't you be a good girl and tell me what we both know. Whose is this? Who do you belong to? Say my name baby."

Arrogant egomaniac. No way would she admit she was his. Especially not when she knew he would have some crisis of conscious as soon as they were done. He would freak out because he fucked Lil' Bit and he was supposed to protect Lil' Bit. *Blah. Blah. Blah.* She'd been there, done that, and didn't want the funky T-shirt to prove it.

She turned and smirked at him before answering. "This is all mine, Lance. But if you're slinging it like that, I might just let you hit it again. You know...if my schedule allows...Ohhhhhhh! Ohhhh, myyyyy!"

Lance rubbed on her clit and hit her spot in tandem with a nibble on her neck added. He leaned into his stroke. All of this caused another orgasm to shake her body beyond all reason.

"I love you, Tam. I have always loved you, and I want us to be together. Now tell me you're mine. I'm about to blow." His sexy grunt in her ear caused her orgasm to ricochet and repeat over and over.

"Ummmmmmmm. Ahhhhhhhh. Ohhhhhh." She couldn't form words with that kind of intensity making its way through her. And she wouldn't even if she could. Admitting that Lance King owned her heart, body and soul, was never going to happen.

Luckily for her, she didn't have to worry about another orgasm causing her to go back on her vow. Lance came in a long, keening grunt. His body shook and he grasped her tightly as he released. The moans and vibrations from him caused her to have one more mini explosion.

Multiple orgasms had a new name, and it was Lance.

She didn't know how long they stayed in that position. Her leaning into the sofa cushion. Him leaning into her. But soon she was being lifted off the floor and carried away.

Lance gently placed her on the bed before walking away.

Here it comes, she thought. *He's going to come back all distraught like, Tam, baby, we made a mistake. We can't go there. We can't do this again.*

This time she would be cool. No sobbing. No pleading. She was a woman of the world. The Queen B like Lil' Kim, and hey, there was plenty of good sex to be found out there, somewhere.

Yeah, but none like Lance, she thought ruefully. And if she was honest with herself, it was about way more than the sex and getting some routine maintenance done with Lance. He had her open, heart and soul.

Lance came back into the room totally nude with the condom removed and a long row of gold foil packets hanging from his hand to the floor.

Before she could even ask what he planned to do with that many Magnum XLs, he tossed the condoms on the nightstand and sat on the bed.

He started undressing her, and her mouth fell open. "See, Tam, if you had simply admitted what we both know, I could have taken you home. Let you get some rest before we go over to Mama's house and fill her in on the good news. But you always were hardheaded. Now I have to keep you here and make love to you, make you cum until you acknowledge you are indeed all mine." His nonchalant matter-of-fact tone along with the straightforward expression and diligent removal of her clothing had her momentarily stunned.

What happened to the we-made-a-mistake speech she'd been expecting?

Her clothes were quickly tossed to the floor. Once she was naked, he got up.

"Okay, Lance, I don't know what kind of joke this is, but I think we've both had enough for one night." Time for one of them to bring things back to normal. Clearly, that wasn't going to be Lance.

He walked back over to the bed, and before she could say a word, his lips crushed her mouth. Instinctively, she leaned back and no sooner than she did, she regretted it. Lance caressed her, lifting her arms above her head as he plundered her mouth. She didn't even notice until it was too late that he had handcuffed her to the freaking bed.

"Darn it, Lance! What are you doing? Take these things off me!" She shook the cuffs and found herself almost snarling.

"I can't, Lil' Bit. I'm not letting you go, until you admit where you belong." Lance's chocolate brown eyes had so much expression in them that she had to look away.

"You're an DEA agent. I don't have to tell you the sentence for kidnapping." Not that she would have ever pressed charges on him or anything. But he still had to know his little "cuff-Tam" game wasn't cool.

"No, you don't have to tell me that," he responded before kissing her deeply. "But you do have to tell me who has your heart. Who has always had your heart? And who you belong to?" He kissed her again. "Don't worry you don't have to tell me now. We have all night."

That was exactly what she was afraid of. An entire night of his mind-blowing orgasms, and she'd admit to anything, even her heart's one true desire. That couldn't happen.

6. Magic Stick

L ANCE!"

Watching as Tamara wiggled the handcuffs, screamed his name and a barrage of obscenities all as she glared at him, Lance fought back a chuckle.

"See, Lil' Bit, if you could have only managed to scream that out a little while ago when I asked you who you belonged to, you wouldn't be handcuffed to the bed. Now you have to wait until I get up the nerve to ask you again, and that might take a minute, because my feelings are kinda hurt."

Faking a pout, he climbed onto the bed, careful to avoid her kicking feet. "I have something for these too if you need help keeping them still," he offered as he caressed her leg. The image of her spread eagle on the four-poster had some appeal.

Her sexy lips formed a snarl, but she stopped trying to kick him.

"Okay, Lance, this isn't funny. What's up with you? Have times been that hard? You're resorting to kidnapping now?"

Taking in the naked, curvy package on his bed, Lance could barely restrain his desire. "Desperate times call for desperate measures."

Sucking her teeth in disbelief, Tamara just glared at him. "And just why are you all of the sudden so desperate? Why now?"

He could have answered her any number of ways, and each would have been a version of the truth. The truth was, seeing her again had made him realize he missed her more than words could express. The truth was, her sexy body and the way it felt to make love to her had haunted him for years. He no longer wanted to live without her in his life.

He decided that he would lay it all on the line and come clean. Lil' Bit needed to know exactly what she was dealing with. "Because I have been waiting for you to get over your little attitude and forgive me, and you're too stubborn to do that on your own. Since neither one of us are getting any younger and I'd like to be married—preferably to you, the woman of my dreams—before thirty-five, I'm really hopping a weekend of mind-blowing love-making will get you to see the light."

He hadn't thought that his declaration would be met with sarcastic laughter, but that is exactly what came as a response from Tamara's mouth. The slow, seductive cackle that fell out of her mouth made him realize it would take a lot more than handcuffs and "I'm sorry" to win her over. He hoped that he would be able to pull it off.

"You have got to be kidding me! Now I'm the woman of your dreams? You hightailed it away from me as fast as your feet could run when we had sex ten years ago. Why should I believe that you all of the sudden want forever and a day?" She shook her head incredulously and let out a hissing breath for good measure.

"Because it's the truth. Look, I handled things poorly back then. But, to be fair, you were barely eighteen and I was twenty-five. In a matter of seconds, I went from being your pseudo big brother to your lover, and hell yeah, that freaked me out."

Coming clean had its drawbacks, and admitting his fear was one of them. His personality hadn't exactly been built for the baby-I'm-sorry routine. "But there was also the fact that I had just started working for the DEA. I was going to be away a lot. And I didn't want you missing out on your college experience because you were pining for me."

"That's a bunch of crap, and you know it. And, anyway, that was then and this is now. Okay, I forgive you for being a punk and running away from me back then. But I don't want to be in a relationship with you or anyone else right now. I have my career to think about. A career that you and your idiot friend Mark are trying to stifle!" She shot him a harsh stare and tugged at the cuffs. "I can't believe you busted in on my case, had no shame about it, and then handcuffed me to a bed. You are a piece of work, Lance King. You are really something else."

"I'm not sorry for busting Tommy Coles. The drug trafficking charges will get him off the streets. And I'm confident that some of his people will crack, and we'll get him for the other stuff." Lance's anger flared up when he thought of how Tommy had gloated about his plans to put Tamara on the ho-stroll.

"There was no way in hell I was going to let him shoot you up with smack and try to turn you out. That just wasn't going to happen. Did you miss the part where I said you are the woman of my dreams, the woman I want to marry?" He gazed at her, willing her to understand.

Her eyes met his gaze, and, for a moment, it seemed as if she would see reason. Then, just like that, she turned away from him and shrugged.

"Then you ought to know that muscling in on my case is not the way to my heart. The great mind-blowing sex might get you speed-dial status on the cellie, but it ain't gonna get you my heart. So you can just unlock these and let a sista go now."

Lance almost considered just letting Tamara go. Maybe it was too late for them. Then he saw those huge brown eyes, the eyes he could get lost in, and he knew without a doubt he had to try.

"I'll tell you what, Tam. You give me the weekend to change your mind. To prove to you that we we're meant to be together. If I haven't gotten you to say that you love me by the end of the weekend, then we can part ways on whatever terms you decide. If you want me out of your life for good, as much as it would hurt, I'd respect that."

He shrugged and offered something he knew he would have a hard time giving, but he hoped would show how much he meant the words he spoke. "I'll even try to stop protecting you. But you'd have to be patient with me on that one, cause for so many years that's all I've ever wanted to do, Lil' Bit. So do we have a deal?"

"If that's all, you can uncuff me, and let me go home now. Because I do love you, Lance." She smiled sweetly at him, and his heart almost pulsed right out of his chest. The sweet smile quickly changed to a smirk, and she snapped, "Love ya like a play cousin. Now take these things off me!" She jiggled the cuffs for emphasis.

Ever the comedian, Lance had to admit she was funny, even when her little jokes were on him. "Play cousin doesn't work for me anymore. I want more. We deserve more. So do we have a deal? I'll unlock these. You'll hang out with me this weekend, and if by Sunday you haven't said you love me, then, I give up and take you home."

"So let me get this straight." She pursed her lips in mock consideration. "That's a weekend full of—ummm, great sex and all I have to do is *consider* the possibility of a future with you, and admit I love you or *not?*"

"That's right. But we'd spend the weekend doing more than just having sex. We would have to talk and get past everything that has been in the way of us being cool over the past ten years, Tam." He knew if he had enough time, he could get her to see the light, and they would have a whole bunch of fun getting to that point. Who needed to be stranded on a deserted island when they had hand-cuffs?

Nodding and smiling, she finally responded. "Right. Okay. Unlock the cuffs. I'm game. Let's do this."

"For real?" He squinted his eyes and watched her carefully. He was sure that if he unlocked the cuffs, she would find a way to leave him without even trying to work things out.

She nodded again. "Yeah."

"Honest?" Lance tilted his head.

She sucked her teeth and huffed. "Yeah!"

"Word?"

Handcuffs Mean Never Having to Say You're Sorry

"Boy, if you don't take these cuffs off of me now, I'm changing my mind."

"Okay," Lance said as he unlocked the cuffs.

As soon as she was free, she smiled. He figured they might just be all right. That is until her hand shot up and smacked him upside the head.

"Woooooo," was the only sound he could make as he tumbled backwards on the bed. Shorty packed a wallop for sure.

"You're gonna get enough of putting those dang handcuffs on me! What's your problem?" She picked up the cuffs and studied them. "And these things aren't standard issue. What kind of kinky sex are you into?"

Sitting up and rubbing his head, Lance grinned. "You've got all weekend to find out, Lil' Bit."

To his surprise, Tamara smiled her own little grin that had always signaled trouble when she was a kid. "Well, I guess I do. And I think it's high time we flipped the script in here."

Agile couldn't even begin to describe how quickly the woman moved. Stunned went nowhere near Lance's expression when he found himself on his back with Tamara straddling him and one of his arms cuffed to the head board.

"I think it's your turn to spend some time in cuffs. But don't worry. If you're a *really* good boy, I might unlock them...eventually."

The woman he'd loved since he was twenty-five, and if he was honest long before that, was naked and on top of him. Even cuffed to the bed, he couldn't see anything wrong with that. And neither could his penis. "Take your time, Tam. Like I said, we have all weekend."

Her head came down and her lips connected with his in a searing kiss. Letting his tongue explore her luscious mouth in ways he'd longed to ever since he made the mistake of walking away from her, wasn't a difficult thing to do. He even managed to use the arm that wasn't cuffed to the bed to caress her curvy little body.

She lifted her head and left his mouth, trailing kisses from his neck to his chest.

The soft teasing flicks of her tongue were followed by the delicate pinch of her teeth. The seductive combination would have been more than enough. Tamara taking his penis in her mouth was the act that sent him over the edge. The fact that she periodically focused those big, bright baby-doll eyes on him while she sucked him out of his mind was what had him calling out her name with more fervor than he ever could have imagined.

He thought he saw a hint of a smirk or a smile or maybe it was just her devilish little grin. He didn't know; and heck, he didn't care. The only thing he knew for sure was that if Tamara didn't stop soon, he would blow.

"Tam, baby, that's enough. I can't last much longer."

She kept working her mouth, suctioning him with gentle pulls and tugs that made his penis feel as if it were in a warm embrace.

"Tam! Tam! Baby, uhhhhhhh…ohhhhhhhhh…Tam, come on. Stop now. Tam!" The first force of his orgasm refused to be contained and Tamara pulled up using her skilled hands to jerk the rest of his cum as he twisted and writhed on the bed from the impact.

When the last pieces of his orgasm finally left him, he opened his eyes to find her still caressing him and still watching with those beautiful eyes.

"I see someone has picked up a skill or two over the years." They hadn't exactly covered the act of fellatio ten years ago.

"Did you like that?"

"Oh, I think like is maybe too mild a word." Lance was surprised to find his penis already responding to her ministrations. "Haven't you shamed me enough," he teased. "Having me scream out your name and jumping around on the bed out of control? You want more?"

"That was just a warm up. We've only just begun. By the time I'm through with you, you're going to really know what it means to *say my name...*" She reached over and grabbed a condom off the nightstand.

Watching her open it, place the condom in her mouth and lean over his now rock hard erection didn't have anything on actually feeling her work those lips and mouth on him again as she slid the protection over him. He could have sworn he felt her tongue lick every ridge and vein going down.

Once the protection was on, he had to take a deep breath to prepare himself for what was going to happen next. "Shorty, wanna ride?" he joked.

"Yeah," she said in a throaty whisper that almost made him come undone right then and there. "I wanna ride on the magic stick."

As Tamara straddled Lance and lowered herself onto him, she tried to remind herself that she was only doing it to teach him a lesson. She wouldn't take anymore of his crap, and she wanted him to know it. Playtime was over.

But a funny thing happened as her pelvis merged with his. It wasn't just the overwhelmingly intense pleasure that hit her as soon as her sex wrapped around him. And it wasn't the erotic fire that licked her thighs like lightening with each arch of her back and swivel of her hips. No, it was the uneven thump in her heart and the thoughts of forever circling her mind, which had her all of the sudden tripping and second guessing herself. She had to find a way to back pedal. *Quickly.* If things kept up at the rate they were going, she would be leaving herself open for a world of hurt.

Lance must have sensed that she was mentally retreating even as she continued to work her hips and ride him, because he wrapped his free arm around her and pulled her down, crushing his lips to hers as he grasped her hips and grinded. He held her still and pumped upwards with deep penetrating thrusts.

Since she was supposed to be in control of the ride, she should have been upset. But she was too busy trying to stave off the impending orgasm that threatened to rock her body. Instead of getting mad that Lance co-opted the romp, the same way he co-opted her case, she sucked on his tongue vigorously and tried to stop the tightening of her sex that refused to let go of his pulsing flesh.

"Ahhhhhhhh. Ummmmmmmmmmmmm." The orgasm shattered through, and her body started to buck on top of his.

Lance simply held her and continued his steady, long, penetrating thrusts. His hips lifted from the bed, and he continued to find refuge in her now quivering sex.

She had to take control again. But first, she had to catch her breath.

Lance ended the kiss, but he still held her. "I love you, Tam." His words were soft and sweet, and if she hadn't been there before, she might have believed them.

Breaking his hold, she sat up with a spring, and bounced back down. She continued the swift action moves as she let her hands trail the well-defined muscles on his chest.

A sheen of sweet highlighted each ridge and ripple. Bending her head, she let her tongue taste and savor the saltiness of his skin, the evidence of how hard he'd been working to bring her repeated orgasms. She licked him as she rode him and tried to block out his words of love and his caressing hand.

I should have put both of those hands in cuffs, she thought as she felt him gently and reassuringly rub the small of her back.

"Tam, I love you so much. Please give us a chance."

"Would you shut up?"

"No, I want you to listen to me. I'm tired of things the way they were."

Tamara covered his mouth with hers and moved her hips vigorously. *Enough is enough.*

Handcuffs Mean Never Having to Say You're Sorry

She heard Lance let out a sigh as he let his free hand work its way down her back and over her behind. He cupped her and navigated her up and down, moving her to his rhythm. That he worked so diligently with just one hand made her wish she'd unlocked his other hand.

His tongue tasted like sweet, rich, deep brown sugar. She found herself wanting to savor his mouth.

When she pulled her tongue away, she sat up and continued to work it. "Shut up, you're ruining my concentration."

Lance opened his mouth like he was about to say something, but didn't. Instead, he just met her thrusts with his own, and took her on the ride of her life.

The pulsing penetration caused her to lose any form of reason. And soon, all she could think about was the next orgasm threatening to rip through her.

It seemed as if that was the only thing Lance could think about as well, because he moved his hips in determination. Clearly, she was no longer in control of the ride. The phrase "bucking bronco" came to mind, followed by "raging bull." The only thing she could do at that point was hold on and hope she didn't fall off. Although, the way her sex tightened around his, there was no way she was leaving until satisfied. And that wouldn't be long off.

Tamara grabbed onto his shoulders and held them just as the scream of satisfaction left her lips. Lance kept stroking, as her orgasm rippled through her like shock waves.

Holding her in place as he moved swiftly in and out, Lance came with a ringing shout of his own. Once he did, he let her go and just stared at her.

She prayed he wouldn't start that I-love-you-what-about-us crap again. She really didn't have the energy to deal with it and the hot sex, too. Really, how much could a girl take?

"So, why don't you unlock a brother from these cuffs so we can hit the shower for round three," Lance whispered seductively.

Holla. Back.

7. How Many Licks?

Lance stared at Tamara's beautiful body in awe. Sure, he remembered exactly when she'd turned into such a knockout, but damn if seeing her glistening wet in the shower didn't bring that awareness to new heights.

The woman worked his last nerve with her stubbornness. She seemed determined to deny her feelings for him, even when he could tell she wanted him, that she loved him. However, he never lacked in determination either. And he wondered just how much it would take to get to the center of Tamara's heart. He knew he would enjoy finding out.

The water cascaded off her body as she soaped herself and seemed to be trying her best to ignore him. He knew she would be a tough one. What he hadn't known was that she would literally not listen to anything he had to say. How was he supposed to apologize if she wouldn't hear him out? His Plan B needed some altering quick or he really would go the rest of the weekend without getting her to admit she loved him. That wouldn't do at all.

Kneeling in front of her in the spacious shower, he gently spread her legs and allowed for some tongue exploration as he contemplated his next move.

Jumping slightly when his tongue touched her, Lance noticed that she calmed swiftly and tilted her head back. With no resistance or rejection, he continued to probe her core with his tongue, searching for answers and suddenly loving every minute of it.

Tamara placed her hands on his head as her body began to shake. Lance loved what his slightest touch seemed to do to her.

"What are you doing? Why are you doing this?" Her questions were strained as her knees gave way.

Holding her up, Lance continued to stick his tongue as far as it would go, lapping up all of her juices, swallowing and demanding more. No need to answer her. She wouldn't believe him anyway.

She tasted divine. The sticky nectar had to be addictive. The memory of her had stayed with him all those years, and he'd *never* tasted anyone like her. No one ever made him feel the way that soft seductive young woman had made him feel. Even though he knew then no one ever would make him feel that way again, he'd thought he could live with it. He'd never been more wrong.

Reaching behind him to grab one of the condoms he left on the edge of the tub, Lance stood. Tamara seemed able to stand on her own two feet now, so he left her leaning against the shower wall for a second to protect them.

Her beautiful eyes widened slightly as she watched him come toward her fully erect and totally sheathed.

"Haven't you had enough?" Tamara asked in a breathless pant.

"Never that." Smiling, he lifted her slightly and held her against the wall. Entering her with one swift thrust upward, he knew he'd found his home in her arms. It was time for her to admit it.

After their numerous romps that afternoon, he couldn't believe that neither one of them seemed satisfied. That must be what ten years of being deprived did; it had made them insatiable.

Each move of his hips met a firm push of hers. The pull and push of their lovemaking set an easy, even pace. She wrapped her legs and arms around him and rocked. Her gentle sway, combined with the warm trickle of water took him to a place of sweet serenity.

Covering her mouth with his, Lance relished in how right it felt to be making love to Tamara. He felt her arch and then shake softly as she tilted her head back against the shower wall. Nothing would ever compare to the feel of her coming around him.

By all rights, the feeling should have sent him over the edge. It amazed him that he was able to last after her multiple penis-milking orgasms. He could only surmise that pleasuring her helped him to gain control. At the end of the day, giving her pleasure was far more important then his own release.

Her tongue twirled in his mouth, and he almost lost his concentration. It was all about her, about getting her to see the light. Lance tried to steel himself to her counter-seduction. Skilled and strong-willed didn't even begin to describe Tamara.

He closed his eyes tightly as she clenched her sex in rapid succession and maneuvered her tongue around his mouth as if she were on a hunt. Her determination would have been admirable if he hadn't been so dang close to cuming.

Breaking away from the kiss, Lance tried to ignore the throbbing feeling threatening to overtake him. The newly minted little police detective gave new meaning to the phrase 'sex as a weapon'. That he had been the first to show her how to use it wasn't lost on him. And, nothing sucked worst than having someone use your own weapon against you. He had to regain control.

"So, Lil' Bit, you ready to tell me the words I want to hear? You ready to tell me who you belong to? Who has your heart, girl?" Thrusting upwards into her warm and welcoming sex, he figured he really only had a few more minutes before he blew.

"No, but you can go ahead on and admit ten years away from *all this* was too long for you. And you messed up big time turning me away." Smiling, she let her tongue slowly trail the side of his face before stopping at his ear with a seductive nip. "You can tell me how much you've missed this and how much you're going to miss it when this weekend romp is all over. Because we're going to be over."

"Not if I can help it." Steeling himself to the boiling explosion that threatened to overtake him, he continued his thrusts with determination.

"There's nothing you can do to stop it."

"If that's true, why don't you just let me try? Why don't you just give me a few hours where we can just talk and get everything out in the open? Let me try and explain—" Begging probably wasn't going to help, but he was running out of ideas.

"Unhhhhhhhh. Ahhhhhh." Her eyes shut tightly and her legs squeezed him almost breathless as the orgasm ripped through her.

Lance's words got stuck in his throat as they both rode out her release. It would only be a matter of time before he came also. So, he needed to get her to agree to at least hear him.

After a series of pants and a soft shudder, she opened her eyes. "There's nothing to explain. You just weren't feeling me back then. It's no big deal. Why kill the mood with a bunch of shoulda, woulda, couldas? Why not just enjoy the moment?"

"Because I love you, that's why." He kissed her, and the taste of her lips sent a fire through his veins. "I love you. Just listen to me."

Her next orgasm had the both of them climbing the shower wall. She let out a scream as her sex tightened on around him, and he couldn't contain his release any longer. Clenching his penis like a vice, she took everything he had.

When they both found completion, she buried her head in his shoulder. "Okay, Lance. I'll listen to what ever you have to say, in the morning. But it's not going to change anything."

"All I'm asking for is a chance."

8. Single Black Female

O*kay, Tam, how did you manage to let Mr. Smooth Talker talk you into listening to him? Not smart!* She'd managed to find other ways to distract him from conversation all day Saturday. But come Sunday morning, Lance seemed unshakable. That's why instead of going home successful after dodging the onslaught barrage of his love declarations, Tamara fiddled with her fork and pushed the egg, ham and cheese omelet Lance made for her around on her plate. Goodness knows she certainly had worked up an appetite after their weekend of bedroom recreation, but she couldn't seem to eat as she sat across from him in his kitchen breakfast nook.

Besides the closeness of the small space, she kept wondering what Lance was going to pull out of his sleeve next. What was he going to say to try to convince her to put her heart on the line? And how the heck was she going to be able to resist it when he had just rocked her world and proclaimed his love?

She'd known she'd be playing with fire by taking Lance up on his offer for an afternoon of sex. She just didn't know how much their sizzling attraction would burn her.

"What's wrong? Don't you like the omelet? I can make you something else if you'd like." Lance polished off the last of his food and eyed hers.

Figures he'd be able to eat while I'm sitting here in antsy antici- pation. Steeling herself to her nervous, jittery stomach, Tamara finished off the majority of her omelet without saying a word. She thought she might just be able to quench her hunger and be satis- fied, until Lance opened his mouth.

Handcuffs Mean Never Having to Say You're Sorry

"Ten years ago, when I first made love to you, it took me by surprise." He paused, as if with an opening like that he needed to be sure he had her attention. "I always knew that you were special, and I tried to keep my feelings for you as pure as possible. But there was something about that day that made it impossible for me to resist you. I spent the next two years kicking myself for taking advantage of you. The two years after that, kicking myself for being an idiot and pushing you away when I should have held you close. And every year after that, trying to get close enough to you to make you see I was a fool and to give us another chance." He tilted his head and a lopsided but oh so sexy smile crossed his face before he continued.

"This is as close as I have gotten. And, Tamara, even though it is against the law, I'm willing to keep you here until you stop fighting it. I have handcuffs and I *will* use them."

Looking up from her plate, she sighed. She had almost finished her food, and now she wouldn't be able to eat another bite no matter how hungry she was. Her stomach fluttered, and her heart skipped as she pushed the plate away.

Sweet sixteen and never been kissed was an understatement for her high school years. She focused on her studies and didn't worry about men at all. Kia did that enough for the two of them. And Tamara didn't want to give Mama Paula another reason to worry. She just wanted to be good so that Mama Paula would never regret taking her into her home.

On her sixteenth birthday, just after Lance had graduated from college and joined the DEA, she got her first kiss and her first boyfriend all in the same day. It would have been nice if they'd come in the same package. Lance gave her a peck on the lips that literally sent firecrackers off in her soul, and Sean Harris asked her to be his girl.

Lance never approved of Sean, and he proved to be right. It was the first of many times that Lance would either come to her rescue or interfere in her love life. It wouldn't be the last. When she was eighteen, Sean ended up being Lance's first big drug bust, and Lance ended up being Tamara's first everything.

Toughen up, chick. No need to take the trip down memory lane. We know where that road leads, and we can't afford it. "We don't need to rehash the past, Lance. What's done is done. We can't go back and change it."

"I'm not saying we can change the past, but we can change the future. I want us to be together." Lance slammed his hand on the table, and she jumped.

He really had the persistent thing down. If it had been any other couple, anyone besides her and Lance, she would have been rooting for the big get back together scene. Heck, she liked a good love story as much as anyone else. But that was before she had time to really think about what a Lance/Tamara combo would mean.

She'd come to think that Lance might have actually done her a favor by rejecting her all those years ago. If they didn't try to be together, then she only lost him. If they got together and things didn't work out between them, then she could stand to lose the only family she'd ever had. No matter how good the loving was, she couldn't lose that. Blood was thicker than mud, and if Mama Paula and Kia had to decide between Tamara and Lance, they would pick Lance no doubt.

Shrugging, she tried to feign nonchalance. "Like Mama Paula always says, the people in hell want ice water, but they ain't getting any."

"Why are you afraid? I've never known you to exhibit this much fear. You never let people see you sweat." Lance considered her carefully, a little too carefully for her taste. "Oh, I know you've been scared, and I know you have the same fears as any normal human being. But what always intrigued me about you is the way you put on your bravest front and faced any of your fears head-on. All except for *me*—except for *us*. So, that has me thinking that you must be plenty scared. What are you afraid of?"

"Please, Lance, get real. I ain't neva scurred!" She affected the timbre of a southern rapper before cutting her eyes and sighing.

"If you think I'm afraid of you, you must be out of your mind. Your ego has grown over the years. Why does this have to be about me being afraid of you—of us? Why can't it just be that a sista just isn't ready to settle down with an *older* man? Maybe I'm enjoying my youth and love being single and open to all possibilities."

Leaning forward, he placed his head in the palm of his hands. "Why don't you come to the family dinner at Mama's on Sundays? Why don't you come by Mama's on holidays? Why haven't you done any of that since you left for college?"

"Because, I'm busy. I don't neglect Mama Paula. I stop by and see her often when I'm not working on a case. She knows that."

"Yeah, and you visit Kia and Jenny, too. The only thing you don't do is come around when you know I'm going to be there. That has been happening for ten years, and it stops today." He slammed his hand on the table again. "If you are going to keep turning me away, then be woman enough to do it in my face. Stop all this running and hiding."

Okay too close to home for sure. When did this happen? "You've got a lot of nerve, Lance."

"If you can keep turning me away while I'm right here," he got up and walked in front of her chair, his hand slowly caressed her cheek as his thumb trailed her lips, "right in front of you, then I'll know that I messed up too badly ten years ago. And I'll leave you alone. But I'm asking that you do us both a favor and end our misery."

"I'm not miserable," she lied.

"Yes you are. I know you love me, Tam. I can see it in your eyes just like you can see it in mine. I see it, Lil' Bit. Look at me. Tell me you don't see how much I love you and how sorry I am right in my eyes, baby."

Gazing in his eyes, she saw it, and the power almost made her lose her breath. He didn't have to say anything else. It was all in his face. If she'd been looking for it, she would have seen it a long time ago. But she had too much to lose. "It doesn't matter. It's too late."

Lance leaned forward and covered her lips with his. The kiss set fire to her soul. She felt every hair on her body come to attention, and her heart pounded heavily in her chest.

Even though his tongue lazily explored her mouth as if it hadn't a care in the world, she could feel the desire at stake in the kiss, the possession occurring with the claim of his lips. If she were honest with herself and not still buying into the self-delusion that made her foolishly agree to a weekend of passion with Lance in the first place, then she would admit that each time he'd kissed her and made love to her since he bulldozed his way into her case and her life had been about making that claim.

Stupid, stupid girl. Allowing her tongue to tangle with his, she knew ignoring her passion and straight up need—to say nothing of her love—for the man was no longer an option. But where did that leave her?

Wasn't he still the man who screwed her and said oops my bad? Didn't he still have that annoying tendency to butt his head into her life and try to protect her from everything and anything?

Halting the kiss, she pulled away. Time to make one more attempt to get things under her control. She could do it. Maybe she could find a way to have Lance for a little while and not lose her family in the process. "Stop."

"Why?"

"Because, we need to set up some ground rules if we are going to carry on with this affair." She'd thought of the perfect idea. Sure, it wasn't his idea for them to get married. But it was better because she stood to lose less when things ended up not working out. They could have an affair. A *secret affair*. A *hot, steamy, sultry, secret affair*.

"Affair?"

"Yeah, that's what you want right? For us to continue to have sex until it's out of our systems for good?" Okay, she knew it wasn't what he wanted. It wasn't what she wanted either, but it was all she was willing to risk.

Lance leaned back in his chair. Perplexed seemed like a good word to describe his expression, and it became almost contagious as he kept her under his gaze. She almost started to rethink the words she'd just said.

"What?" She let out a nervous laugh. "Why are you looking at me like that? You want this to continue don't you?"

Lance shook his head. "We need to go get ready. It's Sunday, and it's almost time to head over to Mama's house."

"Oh, I don't do Sunday dinner at Mama Paula's. I—"

Lance covered her mouth with his and effectively shut her up. "You're going. That's one of our ground rules we can make up the rest later. But for now you have to stop doing all the things that kept you from acting like you are a part of our family. You're no longer running away from me, so you can come to Sunday dinner again."

Telling him she hadn't been running from him seemed pointless, so she decided to go and get dressed for Sunday dinner at Mama Paula's.

9. No Matter What People Say (We Got Jt Going On)

Lance couldn't understand why Tamara seemed so nervous about having Sunday dinner with the family. She'd been with them ever since she was eleven years old. She and Kia had been best friends since Tamara beat up one of their little classmates who tried to bully Kia. Kia had always been bigger and taller than Tamara. But Tamara seemed to be able to scare people in ways that his softer, somewhat sheltered little sister never had been able to. Even though the two women were total opposites, they remained the best of friends.

Tamara became a daughter to his mother the moment she moved in with them. He knew for a fact that Tamara spent most of her Saturdays shopping and hanging out with his mom. So why was she tripping now?

He watched her sitting at the table fiddling with her fingers and watching her plate with too much interest. Conversations were going on, and she hadn't offered her two cents once. *Opinionated Tamara not jumping in on the issues? That's just plan unnatural.* Oh, something was up with Lil' Bit. He only wished he knew what.

"Auntie Tam, are you coming to my play on Wednesday night?" Jenny's class would be doing a first-grade interpretation of *The Lion King*. The little girl peered at Tamara with the biggest, brightest eyes, and he suddenly became glad that he'd already said he'd be there. The little girl had ways of getting what she wanted.

Kia cleared her throat and reached over to pat Jenny's hand, the not-so-smooth move obviously meant to try and stop Jenny from bothering Tamara. "Jenny, I told you that Auntie Tam is busy with work and can't come to the play."

"Nah unh." Jenny's eyes widened and her mouth flew open as if she had caught her mother telling the biggest fib. "You said she wasn't going to go any place near where Uncle Lance would be. But she's here now and Uncle Lance is here. So, she might come to the play now, too."

Lance didn't know who looked more embarrassed, Tamara or Kia.

Tamara shot Kia an annoyed glare, and then smiled at Jenny. "I'll see about the play, Jenny. I may have to work. But if I don't, I'll be there."

"Yay!" Jennifer squealed, and then a concerned expression came across her face. "You're still coming right, Uncle Lance?"

"Yes, I'll be there."

"It's so good to have all of you here on a Sunday just like the old days." Mama took a sip of her ice tea and beamed.

He knew she worried about Tamara a lot, probably more than necessary.

"I know. This is great." Kia let out a chuckle before turning and glaring at Lance. "I never thought I'd see the day. I don't know what you did to piss Tam off, Lance, but I'm glad you finally worked things out, and we can get back to being a family again."

"Well, if he would stop minding her business, and stop being so overprotective, then maybe Tam wouldn't stay so mad at him." Mama shot him one of her annoyed looks.

Lance raised his eyebrows at his mother. Sure, he usually made it his business to check up on Tamara, but his mother was either in on it or behind most of it. She was the one who begged him to go check up on Tamara because she hadn't heard from her in a couple of weeks.

You would have thought his expression would have stopped Paula from talking, or at least get her to acknowledge the role she'd

ᅟ

 ᅠ

played over the years in getting him to watch out for Tamara. But no, she kept right on talking.

"And you know it's so silly, Lance. Tamara's got a good head on her shoulders; she doesn't need you sticking your nose in where it doesn't belong. Especially when it comes to her personal life." Paula gave him a pointed glare. "If you keep that up, she'll never meet someone and get married. I need me some more grandbabies. I've given up on you ever meeting someone."

Tamara kept her eyes on her plate and chewed on her lower lip. Lance turned to his mother and decided it was as good a time as any to show Tamara that he was very serious about the two of them getting together.

"Well, Mama, you don't have to worry about any of that anymore. I totally approve of Lil' Bit's new man, and I suspect you'll be getting those grandkids along with a nice big wedding sometime soon. In fact—"

The loud sound of a fork hitting the plate with a sharp clang halted his speech, and Tamara broke in with her two cents.

"Lance, this is the problem with you. You're always pushing. I'll tell my business when I'm ready." Tamara finally took her eyes off her plate and glared at him.

"Well, what if I'm ready to tell my business?" What was the big deal? He loved her. She loved him. His mother would get her grandbabies. Case closed. Mystery solved. Everything would be perfect.

The angry expression she wore quickly became one of panic. Lance tried to figure out why she didn't want his mother and sister to know that they were developing a relationship.

"Can I speak with you for a moment? Alone!" Tamara got up from the table. "Excuse us, Mama Paula," she said as she walked out of the room.

Throwing his napkin down on the table, Lance went along to see where she was headed. Sparing a glance at his mother and Kia beforehand, he noted that they seemed just as confused and perplexed as he was.

"What the hell do you think you're doing?" Tamara spun around as soon as he entered the living room where she waited for him, eyes flashing and lips curled in an angry attitude-laced twist.

Taking a seat on the armrest of the plastic-covered sofa, he shrugged. "I was about to tell my family that I've found the woman I love and plan to have a family with."

"Well, I think we should just keep things under wraps until we are sure." Tamara rolled her eyes and bit out her words in an angry, stilted whisper.

"I am sure." He had never been more sure about anything in his life.

"Well, I'm not sure. I need some time." She paced the floor like a caged jungle cat. "And if things don't work out between us, I don't want things to be strained between me and Mama Paula or Kia."

"I don't want to have a secret affair with you, Tam." He wanted everything, all or nothing.

"Why is it always what you want? You didn't think it was wise for us to be together ten years ago, so I had to put all my feelings aside and go with your flow. Now you're ready to be with me. And I'm supposed to risk my relationship with the only family I have, the only real family I've ever had, because you decide you want me now?" She sucked her teeth and let out a disgusted hiss.

"Well, I won't do it," she bit out. "It was hard enough going through the last ten years without you. I couldn't go back to having you as a brother and protector. I couldn't have you as a lover. But at least I still had Mama Paula, Kia and later Jenny. If you make me lose that, I will *never* forgive you." Tears started coming down her eyes, and he actually felt his heart breaking. She wiped them away angrily and took deep halting breaths.

"You're not going to lose anything, Tam. Mama, Kia and Jenny love you. I love you." Getting up from the sofa arm, he walked over and tried to put his arm around her.

Shrugging him off, she continued to wipe her face. "If you do, then you will give me the time I need. Mama Paula might not approve anyway. She knows my history, knows about my mom. She probably wouldn't want her son with somebody like me."

"You're talking crazy now, Lil' Bit." Enough was enough. He pulled her into his arms and held her.

"Anything that isn't exactly what you would say or do is crazy, right?" Tamara shook her head in disgust. She used her hands to push him away. "My mother was a drug addict, Lance. Mama Paula didn't even like me hanging around Kia when we were kids. I was young, but I remember she never used to let Kia come over. I know she really didn't want me to live with y'all when my mother died. But I think she has come to like me. And I *love* her. She's the only mama I have. I know I was pissed at you when you rejected me, but I had come to think that you were right. I can't lose them, too, Lance. I'm sorry." Tamara jetted from the room, leaving him stunned.

By the time he came back out, she was leaving with Kia and Jennifer.

Grabbing his jacket, he started after them.

"Unh unh, Lance. Leave her be," said Paula. "This is the first time she's been to Sunday dinner in a long time. I know you came together. What I don't know is how you got her to forgive you for whatever it was you did to her. And why she hightailed it out of here when you were about to tell her business. Is her new boyfriend a bad person that we should be worried about? Because if not, you need to just butt out and let the girl live her life." She pointed to the empty space at the dining room table that he had just left. Her eye slanted slightly, causing him to recall all the subtle ways she had at threatening kids and placing the fear of God in them. If anyone could stop somebody with just a look, his mother was the one.

Lance heaved a sigh and slung his jacket across the chair. Figuring he might as well tell his mother everything, he sat her down and spilled his guts. Starting from the first time he made love to Tamara, to the estranged ten years that he tried to deny what he felt, and his realization that he could no longer live without her, Lance gave his mother an ear full.

227

He couldn't get a read on her once he got to the part about Tamara being afraid that their seeing each other would cause her to lose them as a family. It hadn't made any sense to him when she said it, but his mother's silence caused him some concern.

He knew without a doubt that Tamara would be his woman, his wife. If his mother had problems with that, then she needed to start figuring out how she was going to deal with it. Because she would have to deal with it.

"Tamara is a sweet girl. Any mother would be lucky to have her as a daughter-in-law. And I'm not just saying that because I raised her." Paula smiled as if pleased with the news, and then her eyes narrowed slightly. "You have to be careful with her, Lance. She lost so much at such a young age. If you aren't really serious about her this time, you need to leave her alone."

"Of course I'm serious about her, Mama. That's why I really need to go and try and get her to see reason. I think once she realizes that you're cool with it that should help. I can't believe she is so unsure about how much we love her." He couldn't believe he was actually having this conversation with his mother.

"Do you remember when her mother died, how frightened she was and how I had to let her sleep in my bed for months when she first moved in with us? Or how she went out of her way to protect Kia from anyone that might have done her harm? Or the way she used to look up to you with wonder and awe? She was always the most well behaved child in this house. I think she really thought if she wasn't good we'd send her away." Paula paused and shivered at the memories.

Lance knew what made her shiver. He remembered those days. Tamara used to have some pretty frightening nightmares. Sometimes he could still hear her screams and the heaving sobs. He'd decided back then that he would make sure no one ever hurt her again. That he had ended up hurting her himself, caused him several years of deep soul searching.

"How many times did her mother reject her in favor of drugs, getting high and sleeping with men? Of course she's unsure." Paula's voice went up a few octaves as she spoke, and then she glared at him. "I can't believe you of all people took my baby's innocence, and then rejected her! I'm not surprised she's been avoiding you like the plague for the last ten years."

Lance winced. It wasn't as if he didn't already feel like a jerk. But Mama was right. He had to find a way to make things right. He just didn't know if he really had it in him to go in for another round with Tamara so soon after having her walk out on him. "I guess I better go and apologize to her. I've got to get her to see reason, if you're ever going to get those grandbabies you want."

Standing and then bending over to give his mother a hug, Lance smiled.

Paula sucked her teeth playfully and cut her eyes. "Truth be told, I don't know if you're good enough for my Lil' Bit. But, I suppose that if she loves you as much as I think she does, you'll have to do. I guess I couldn't really get my son the DEA agent to check-up on himself. So I'm taking you at your word that you love our girl and you're going to do right by her."

"That's cold, Mama. That's just cold. But yes, you have my word. I will." Lance laughed because he knew his mother meant it in only the best of ways. She loved the woman he loved. Life was good and would get better as soon as he got to Tam. He figured he would give her some time to calm down. Besides, he didn't think his ego could take it if she slammed the door in his face. In the morning, she would be able to see reason. He hoped.

"Go and get your woman boy. And make sure she's here next Sunday for dinner."

His mother had faith in him. That was as good a sign as any.

Handcuffs Mean Never Having to Say You're Sorry

"Okay, so what was that about, Tam?" Kia asked as she lounged back on the sofa and kicked her feet up on the coffee table.

Since Jenny was busy playing with Tamara's old stuffed doll collection in Tamara's bedroom, they didn't have to worry about the kid listening. But Tamara still felt telling Kia what was really going on between herself and Lance was *not* an option.

Waving her hand dismissively and sighing in the process, Tamara shrugged before responding. "Girl, you know Lance is always tripping. I don't know what is wrong with that man. He is always trying to worm his way into my business."

"Yeah, whatever." Kia leaned back and smirked. "When did you start dating my brother?"

"Wha—dating, your brother? I'm not...what would make you say such a thing?"

"Don't play. I could tell something was up when you showed up together. And I also noticed the way my brother looked at you." Kia started laughing. "Talk about sprung!"

"Girl, you're tripping. It's not even like that." Tamara ran her hands through her short spiky hair, and glanced at everything in the room but Kia. Looking at her best friend at that moment would have been the equivalent of admitting guilt. "You know he's always been like a brother to me."

"Yeah, I know he *used* to be like a brother to you. But you haven't even let him be anything close to that in ten years." Twisting her lips to the side and narrowing her eyes like she was the detective, Kia leaned forward. "Up until today, you haven't been willing to be in the same room with him. So what's up?"

"Nothing!"

"Yeah, whatever. I'm not stupid, Tam. I'm your best friend." Kia crossed her arms in defiant indignation. "You really gonna keep something this big from me?"

Guilt weighed heavily on Tamara's chest, but she still tried to think of a way to get over it without confessing. Coming up with nothing, she decided to spill her guts. She didn't want to lose her best friend, but she didn't want to lie to her anymore either.

Kia's face took on a bright and blazing smile that grew wider and wider the more Tamara told her. By the time Tamara finished telling her best friend all about her dealings with Lance, Kia beamed with seeming delight.

"Wow, girl, he was your first?" Kia wrapped her legs under herself, leaned forward and spoke in a whisper that only hinted at how excited she was. "Y'all got down like that and you held out. You didn't tell me? I'm hurt! And you were actually going to keep this from me? Tam, that's so wack! I tell you everything."

Kia was right. There was very little Tamara didn't know about Kia's sexcapades. Even her on-again-off-again relationship with Jenny's father had been the topic of many a conversation over margaritas between the two. And for the most part it had been reciprocal. Kia knew where all the skeletons were in Tamara's love affair closet, all except for one. *The one.*

"I didn't want to risk losing you and Mama Paula. You're all the family I have." Tamara sighed and bit her lip. "Do you think Mama Paula would be okay with it?"

"Tam, she loves you! Of course she'd be cool with it." Kia shook her head as if it shouldn't have even been a question in Tamara's mind.

"But I just figured that, you know, given what happened with my mom and all and how she never really approved of—well you know she had some hesitation about taking me in back then." Taking a deep breath, Tamara almost regretted coming clean to Kia. "I didn't want to do anything that would make her think—"

"Oh, Tam, Mama only hesitated about taking you in because she didn't want to get in the way of you ending up with your own family. And she thought that as a single mom herself, she might not be the best parent for you if a two-parent family wanted you. She wanted to do what was best for you. And once she saw our family was the best situation, she went in all the way. You became her child. She loves you." Kia got up from her seat and walked over to Tamara. Sitting next to her, she gave her a hug.

"I know that. I just get nervous." Letting out a breath she didn't know she'd been holding, she thought it might just work after all. "And the past ten years feeling like I lost Lance—it was just hard you know?"

"But he realizes what a jerk he was. Are you going to give him a chance?"

Tamara nodded her head affirmatively. "I want to so bad. But your brother has to learn that he can't keep butting into my business. He has got to learn that he can't protect me from everything. I don't need the constant protection. You know? Hello! I'm a cop."

"Good luck with that, girlfriend!" Throwing her head back in laughter, Kia sat up with tears in her eyes.

Tamara simply pursed her lips and glared at her best friend. "All right, Kia. You don't have to laugh that hard. It ain't that dang funny. Your brother is a pest!"

"Yeah, and he's apparently your pest. Come to think about it, Lance must have loved you a long time. Remember how he used to triple and double screen any dude that showed any interest in you?" Cackling now, Kia had to hold her stomach.

The bubbling laughter from her best friend would have normally had her joining in and laughing herself to tears. Even when the joke had been on her, Tamara usually couldn't resist cracking up with her friend. However, she saw quickly that when the topic was her and Lance, she couldn't find it in her to laugh it up.

"Well, girl, I know you have to head on out and get Jenny ready for school tomorrow. So, I don't want to hold you up." Tamara got up and stretched. "And I'm *so-oo* tired." Yawning, Tamara started walking towards the bedroom where Jenny played with Tamara's stuffed animal collection, many of which Lance had actually won for her back when she was a kid and he used to take them to fairs and theme parks in the summer. She didn't have to guess at the reason why she'd kept them all over the years, even though they clashed with just about everything in her apartment.

Kia followed her with her hands on her ample hips. "All right then, Lil' Bit. I can take a hint. I'll take my nosey self and my child home. But I just want you to know I expect to be fully informed on every step of your relationship with my brother. Come on, Jenny. We're going to go home now. Tam, call me later once you figure out how you're going to work it out with—"

"All right, Kia, dang. Not in front of the kid. We don't know how things will end up." Tamara had to interrupt Kia. Sometimes she swore the woman didn't think before she opened her mouth.

"Fine. Call me," Kia snapped.

"Yeah, I'll do that." *Not.* At that moment, Tamara realized that the only person she really needed to be talking to was Lance. Too bad she wasn't quite ready to do that yet.

10. Came Back for You

Rolling over, Lance reached for his cell phone to check the time. Instead of going to Tamara's place like he'd promised his mother he would, he went back to his place to sulk.

Apparently, even he had a limit for the amount of rejection he could withstand before taking a break. Ten years of Tamara telling him to basically go away and leave her alone was clearly the magic number. Also, he had promised her that if he didn't get her to admit she loved him by the end of the weekend, he would let her go. He hadn't been able to do that. So by all rights, he should give up. Too bad he couldn't see himself ever really doing that.

His cell phone read that he'd missed four calls. He hoped against hope that at least one, if not all four, were from Tamara saying she realized she was wrong and begging him to forgive her for giving him a hard time. Even as he thought it, he had to laugh. That would be the day.

After dialing his voice mail and listening to the messages, three from his superior at the DEA and one from Mark, his blood went cold and a feeling of eerie apprehension overcame him. Tommy Coles had been released on bail, and Lance had a feeling that the first person Tommy would go looking for was Tam. Lance tried calling Tamara to warn her and didn't get an answer. Leaping from his bed and throwing on the first piece of clothing in his reach, he made his way to Tamara's place. Even though he knew she would probably have a fit about his checking up on her, he had to make sure she was okay.

When Tamara woke up the next morning the only thing that ould save her was a good strong cup of coffee. She'd tossed, turned nd yearned for Lance the entire night. She'd turned off her ringer ecause she didn't feel ready to talk to him. In the light of day, she lt only a little ready, but she needed a dose of caffeine first. Yeah, ie needed to call him. But first, she needed to figure out what she anted to say.

Reaching for the French Roast, Tamara hummed the hot Latin eat to Lil' Kim's "No Matter What People Say."

"You know, you really had me fooled, Darling."

Startled, the bag of coffee fell from her hands and spilled onto ie floor as Tamara turned and found Tommy Coles standing in her tchen.

Isn't he supposed to be in jail? And how did he get into my house! he one thing she knew for sure was that she would get a good arm system if she lived through this. Lance popping up in her crib as one thing. Tommy Coles was a whole different story.

"Mr. Coles! Oh my goodness." She let her eyes grow wide and er mouth hang open. "I was so-oo worried about you. Those DEA 1ys kept me down there forever." She patted her hand on her chest r effect and offered a dramatic pause. "What happened? Why did iey bust in and arrest everyone?"

"Why don't you tell me, Darling?" Tommy's eyes narrowed, and e kept the slants pinned on her.

"I don't know. They wouldn't tell me anything at all. They kept king me the same questions that the cops asked. And I didn't say iything because like I said, I don't know nothing." She shrugged id leaned back against the cabinet.

Great. Tommy Coles thinks I ratted him out to the cops. If I live see Lance again, I'm going to smack him upside his head. This is actly why he needs to mind his own business.

Tommy walked over and stood right in front of her. Tamara took deep breath and tried not to appear as if she was on guard. If he'd come all the way over to her place, clearly he had a reason, and he must have his suspicions.

"You see I really find that hard to believe since you were pulled in for questioning the day before my shit got wrecked." Placing his hand behind her neck, he caressed it softly for a moment, and then clenched his hand pulling her roughly forward.

"Look, Mr. Coles, I was your receptionist. What could I have possibly said to the cops that would have made the DEA come busting in there like that?" Blinking rapidly in a way which she hoped showed just the right mix of fear and honestly. Tamara decided to lean into his harsh pull instead of trying to break away. "I'm really sorry that happened to you, but I didn't have nothing to do with it."

"You're lying. But that's okay. Thanks to you, we have all day to figure out the real truth." He yanked her close and brought his lips down harshly on hers.

Tamara cursed her flimsy nightgown as she tried to pull away. When she finally managed to wiggle out of his grip, he backhanded her across the face.

Placing her hand over her mouth, she backed away in an effort to give herself room to maneuver. Sure Tommy Coles had about a foot on her in height, and he also had her by about 150 pounds, but the man was about to go down. No one slapped her across the face and got away with it.

She let her eyes get wide with innocence and offered in her most pleading please don't-hurt-me voice, "I swear, I didn't do or say anything. I really like you, Mr. Coles, and I was hoping we could, you know, but I guess—" Tamara broke off her words as she kneed him in the groin and used the palm of her hand to push his nose back into his head.

Tommy hit the floor, grabbing his privates with one hand and his nose with the other. "I'm going to snap your fucking neck, you little bitch."

Tamara grabbed the closest thing to her, her glass coffee pot and, with some hesitation because it meant she would have to forgo her cup of java for the moment, she bashed Tommy's head as hard as she could.

Wiping her hands together in a pleased motion after letting what was left of the coffee pot fall to the ground, she snapped, 'Well, first you'd have to get a few stitches and oh yeah, wake up, Mr. Coles." Taking in his lounging bloody face, she let out a sigh.

As she leaned against the counter, Tamara cursed to herself. She really had to look into getting better locks.

Just then, the front door to her apartment came crashing in and Lance entered with gun cocked and ready. He took one look at her and Tommy on the floor and placed his gun in the holster.

Day late and a dollar short. But what else should I expect from a guy who wants to develop a relationship ten years after making love to me for the first time. "You're going to pay to fix that door, Lance. How are you just going to bust my door down like that?"

Lance touched her cheek and wiped the blood from the corner of her mouth. "He hit you?" The angry glare that came across his face showed Lance was ready to kill.

"He's out. Just look at him and look at me. Just—just cuff his behind." Tamara stepped over Tommy and cut her eyes at Lance before leaving the room to get dressed. Her heart all of the sudden started pounding in her chest, and the reality of what could have happened to her made her feel the sudden need to go breathe in a paper bag or something.

After taking care of Tommy and making sure that he was put away for good this time, Lance went back to Tamara's place. He couldn't stop thinking about the fact that he could've very well lost her. He knew that he couldn't let another minute pass without making her his own. *For good.*

She had remained at her apartment to make sure her front door was repaired. She handed the bill to him as soon as she let him in.

Glancing at the three-hundred-dollar tab, he shook his head. Leave it to his Lil' Bit to keep it real. "You know, most women would be ecstatic to have a man who's crazy in love with them come busting through the door to rescue them."

"Well, I'm not most women. I don't need rescuing. Never did. And if we are going to be together, then you betta recognize. I'm a cop, an undercover cop. My job can be dangerous. So can yours. You don't see me busting in on your job. So I would appreciate it if you stopped doing that to mine." Tamara stopped long enough to glare at him and take a breath. "And just because we're going to be seeing each other to see how this thing—"

"Lil' Bit," he interrupted. "We are going to be doing more than seeing each other. We need to go on and set the date, and you and Mama and Kia can start planning the wedding now. I want us married as soon as possible."

She sighed, rolled her eyes, and placed her hand on her hip before she spoke. "Now see, that's the kind of controlling stuff I'm talking about. It's all about what you want, right? What about what I want. What about—"

"You want me. Stop fighting it." He ran his hand across his head and exhaled. "You're wasting time. Marry me, Tam. Marry me. Have my babies. Make me the happiest man in the world." It was rude to cut people off and not let them finish what they were saying, but Lance couldn't help it. He could have lost her today. Playtime was over. He pulled her into his arms and kissed her.

Her mouth opened, and she fell right into him. Her tongue lit a fire to him, and for a moment he almost forgot the reason he kissed her in the first place. The only thing he could think was how right it felt. How at home he felt and how dang perfect Lil' Bit was for him.

238

Breaking away from him, she took two paces back. "Suppose I on't want to get married right now? Suppose, I don't ever want to et married?"

"That's—not—an—option." Pulling her into his arms, he issed her again.

Walking her backwards as he kissed her and led her to the edroom, Lance realized that last night truly was the *last* night he anted to spend without her in his arms. The time had come for 1em both to face the future together.

Glad she'd only put on some sweat shorts and a T-shirt, he uickly set about removing the cotton garments.

"Unh, Lance, we still need—"

"Shh…less talking. Let's just listen for a minute to what our earts are saying." Lance gently laid her on the bed and began to isrobe himself.

She opened her mouth to say something, and he noticed that 1e stopped and her mouth hung open as he took off his shirt. amara desired him as much as he desired her. And he believed ith all his heart that she loved him. She had to.

Joining her on the bed, he covered her mouth again quickly efore she could start her fifty-million-reasons-why-we-can't-be->gether diatribe.

Touching her and kissing her sent fire through his blood. Hot, idn't even begin to describe his feelings. How the hell did he 1anage to walk away from her ten years ago? How did he go all that me without tasting her?

He let his kisses travel down her belly and into the sweet valley ≥tween her legs. Not bothering to try and halt his need to devour much of her as he could, he knew it would never be enough.

"AAAHHHHH! LANCE! LANCE!" It didn't take long for her › reach her peak.

Lance lapped up every drop of her exquisite release and stopped easuring her long enough to tease her, "I love it when you call out y name, baby. I think I need to hear that again." He proceeded to

239

tease her folds, torture her clit and massage her sex until she clasped her thighs tightly around his head and screamed out his name three more times, back to back to back.

Once she came down off her orgasmic high enough to loosen her tightened hold, he got their protection and moved his full body between her legs. Covered, he entered her in one full thrust.

Tamara didn't think she could stand much more of Lance's loving. And she knew that she would never be able to go back to her normal Lance-free life after knowing what he could do to her, and feeling how much he loved her. She wondered if their love could last. She also knew she had to come clean with him about her feelings once and for all.

Each thrust sent her spiraling. Every touch made her quake. She made the mistake of looking into his eyes and saw all of his love and the nature of his determination.

He wasn't going to give up. *Ever.* She never had a chance.

With short, seductive, movements of his hips, Lance kept his eyes pinned on her. She couldn't look away. She could see all of his desire, all of his need. She knew that it mirrored exactly what she felt inside.

"I love you." Lance put his back into it as if on a mission. "I love you, Tam. I don't want to spend another day without you."

She felt her sex tightening around him and knew she was about to come yet again. The man must have had some kind of ever-ready battery hooked up to him because she knew for certain he had more energy than humanly possible.

"I know you love me. And I know I messed up years go. I'm begging you to give us another chance." He bent his head to her ear, took it in his mouth, and started to nibble softly. "We've got to work it out. I love you."

"AAAAAAAHHHHHHH! Oh, Lance, what are you doing to me?" Just as she was about to respond an orgasm more powerful than she'd ever had rocked her to the core.

He stared her in the eye and wouldn't let up. "I love you. I love you, Tam. Please."

She didn't know if it was the intense pleasure he gave her or the fact that his words had finally broken past her barrier, but the tears started to fall down her eyes. She couldn't stop them.

His lips kissed away each one, and he kept right on thrusting and taking her there. She didn't think she could take it if he said he loved her again. It would be way too much to bear.

He must have sensed that she had reached some sort of emotional overload because he just continued to make love to her until they each peaked.

Afterward, he held her and gently wiped away her tears one by one. Tamara gazed in his eyes, and even though her vision was lightly blurred, she saw the love. She saw it and she knew it was time for some reciprocity.

"I love you, too, Lance. I always have, always will. I'll marry you. But you have to promise me you will at least try to ease up on the protective-get-all-in-my-business deal." Even as she added that last part, she knew it would take a long time to get him to a point where he even made a half-hearted attempt to do that.

At least he pretended to consider it, and she guessed that she would have to work on getting him all the way there. "I promise to try. It's just…baby, I couldn't take it if something were to happen to you. You're my world." He laughed. "But judging by the way you put a hurting on Tommy Coles, I might just have to let you have my back instead. Dang, Lil' Bit, you took the boy out!"

"Yeah, you betta recognize! I can handle mine. So, what do you say? Can you try and hold off on the knight in shining armor routine? You know, let me ask for help if I need it?" Tamara gave him a pointed glare. It wasn't a deal breaker. She figured she had the rest of their lives to train Lance King in the art of letting a sista handle her business.

Lance kissed her deeply before responding. "I will try my best, Tam. All I know is that I love you, and I don't want to live without you. So, let's go tell Mama, Kia and Jenny about the wedding."

Smiling and feeling like her life was finally on track, she just kissed him. Yeah, it took them ten years, but they finally got it together. Everything would be all right. *And, if he ever gets out of hand, there's always handcuffs...*

About the Authors

Beverly Jenkins is the premier African American historical romance writer in the country. Her first novel, Night Song, was published in 1994 by Avon. She has received numerous awards for her works and has been featured in many national publications, including the *Wall Street Journal, People Magazine, Dallas Morning News* and *Vibe Magazine*. She has lectured at such prestigious universities as Oberlin University, the University of Illinois, and the University of Michigan. She speaks widely on both romance and 19th century African American history. In February of 2004, Ms. Jenkins' first contemporary novel of romantic suspense, *The Edge of Midnight*, was released.

Born in Detroit, she and her family live in southeastern Michigan. Beverly graduated from Cass Technical High School, and majored in Journalism and English Literature at the Michigan State University. She is active in both her church and community, and in November 2001, was named a YWCA Woman of Achievement. Please visit Beverly at www.BeverlyJenkins.net.

Katherine D. Jones, author of the Special Corruption Unit series, is a multi-published author with several magazine articles, short stories and books in print. Katherine regularly writes for nationally distributed magazines, *Black Romance, Bronze Thrills* and *True Confessions*. Her SCU series consists of the novels, *Love Worth Fighting For, Worth the Wait*, both published by BET Arabesque Books; *Undercover Lover* and the final book in the SCU series, *Deep Down*, published by Kensington Dafina romance. Her third novel, *Undercover Lover* was recognized in Essence Magazine as suggested reading for Valentine's Day 2006. Katherine describes her writing as contemporary romance fiction with a twist, because she likes to give her readers an unexpected ride. You can visit her website at www.katherinedjones.com.

Gwyneth Bolton was born and raised in Paterson, New Jersey. She currently lives in Syracuse, New York with her husband, Cedric Bolton. When she was twelve years old, she became an avid reader of romance by sneaking her mother's stash of novels. In the nineties, she was introduced to African American and multicultural romance novels, and her life hasn't been the same since. While she had always been a reader of romance, she didn't feel inspired to write them until the genre opened up to include other voices. And even then, it took finishing graduate school, several non-fiction publications, and a six-week course at the Loft Literary Center titled "Writing the Romance Novel" before she gathered the courage to start writing her first romance novel. She has a BA and an MA in creative writing and a Ph.D. in English. She teaches classes in writing and women's studies at the college level. When she is not working on her own African American romance novels, she is curled up with a cup of herbal tea, a warm quilt and a good book. She welcomes response from readers. Please feel free to write her at P.O. Box 9388 Carousel CTR, Syracuse, New York 13290-9381. You can also e-mail her at gwynethbolton@prodigy.net or feel free to visit her website at http://www.gwynethbolton.com.